P9-DNR-438

The Intruders

A BUCK TRAMMEL WESTERN

THE INTRUDERS

WILLIAM W. JOHNSTONE
AND J. A. JOHNSTONE

THORNDIKE PRESS
A part of Gale, a Cengage Company

Thorndike Press, a part of Gale, a Cengage Company.

Following the death of William W. Johnstone, the Johnstone family is working with a carefully selected writer to organize and complete Mr. Johnstone's outlines and many unfinished manuscripts to create additional novels in all of his series like The Last Gunfighter, Mountain Man, and Eagles, among others. This novel was inspired by Mr. Johnstone's superb storytelling.
Thorndike Press® Large Print Hardcover Western.
The text of this Large Print edition is unabridged.
Other aspects of the book may vary from the original edition.
Set in 16 pt. Plantin.

**LIBRARY OF CONGRESS CIP DATA ON FILE.
CATALOGUING IN PUBLICATION FOR THIS BOOK
IS AVAILABLE FROM THE LIBRARY OF CONGRESS.**

ISBN-13: 978-1-4328-9118-3 (hardcover alk. paper)

Published in 2021 by arrangement with Pinnacle Books, an imprint of Kensington Publishing Corp.

Printed in Mexico
Print Number: 01 Print Year: 2022

The Intruders

Chapter 1

"Clean up Blackstone! Clean up Blackstone!"

So yelled the thirty or so marchers from the Citizens' Committee of Blackstone. Their number was enough to fill the width of Main Street in front of the Pot of Gold Saloon.

Sheriff Steven "Buck" Trammel stood guard in front of the saloon to prevent the crowd from storming the place. He might only have been one man, but at several inches over six feet tall and two hundred and thirty solid pounds, he loomed large over the crowd. He looked larger still from the boardwalk.

The piano player from the Pot of Gold mocked the marchers by banging out "The Battle Hymn of the Republic." The patrons joined in, slurring the words loudly.

"Blasphemy!" Mike Albertson exclaimed. Trammel had heard the man with the crooked back was a retired freight driver who had given up the life of a long hauler to do the work of the Lord. He was the leader of the marchers and raised his voice louder than his followers as he said, "How dare they mention the Lord in a den of such iniquity! Let us go amongst them and defend His holy name from the mockery of drunken rabble."

The marchers, who were mostly older men and women, took several steps toward the boardwalk.

Trammel took a single step forward and said, "That's enough. You've had your say. Now go home. All of you."

The crowd's chants of "Clean Up Blackstone" died down and their banners sagged. Some of the marchers at the back of the crowd took a couple of steps backward.

Because everyone knew Buck Trammel did not say much, so when he spoke, it was best to listen.

But Albertson held his ground. Instead, he limped forward and pointed his finger up at Trammel. "Last time I checked, Marshal, this here territory was still part of the United States of America, and that means we can march anywhere whenever we're of a mind to do so. Says it right in the Constitution." He glared up at Trammel.

"Or are you one of those types who never got around to learning to read?"

Trammel stepped down from the boardwalk without using the steps. He still towered over all of the marchers. Most of them moved back a couple of steps as the big lawman approached.

Only Albertson held his ground. "You don't scare me, big fella. I've gone through tougher and bigger than you."

"No, you haven't." Trammel pointed at the star pinned to his vest. "Says 'Sheriff,' not 'Marshal.' Or are you one of those types who never got around to learning how to read?"

Albertson did not look at the star. He stood with a stoop, probably from all his years spent hauling freight all around the territory and beyond. "I don't care what you call yourself, Trammel. You've got no right to order us to leave."

His followers cheered as Albertson pointed past Trammel toward the Pot of Gold Saloon. "But you do have every right to tell them to leave. To tell them to obey the law. Them and their kind. It's getting so it ain't safe to walk around town, be it morning, noon, or night. Drunken cowhands from the Blackstone Ranch and miners roaming the streets in a laudanum stupor."

Albertson pointed to a shrunken old woman clutching a bag. "Why, Mrs. Higgins here found one of them passed out on her porch the other morning. Gave this poor, God-fearing woman the fright of her life."

"I know all about it." Trammel looked at Mrs. Higgins and said, "I came right over and got him out of there, didn't I, Helen?"

The old lady's scowl turned into something of a smile. "Yes, you did, Sheriff. You came in and dragged him away in no time flat."

Trammel looked back at Albertson. "I kept that drunk in a cell until he sobered up. Then I fined him and threw him out of town. I know you're new around here, Albertson, but this town is used to drunks and knows how to handle them."

The old freighter pointed to the new buildings that had more than doubled the length of Main Street. The locals had taken to calling that section of town New Main Street. "And just how do you expect to handle all of them new places once they're open, Trammel? How many of them are going to be saloons? Your friend Hagen sure ain't telling us."

Trammel said, "Adam Hagen's not my friend, but he does own those properties. Why don't you ask him what he has planned? Or ask Mayor Welch."

But Albertson and his followers had come to Main Street to shout and argue, not for answers. "Asking either of them is pointless," Albertson said. "Hagen is crafty enough to keep his true plans hidden, and Welch is gullible enough to believe him. And King Charles Hagen is content to look down on us from his ranch house and watch this town crumble without so much as lifting a finger."

The crowd offered a full-throated cheer, and Albertson raised his voice so he could be heard over them. "We will not be deterred by lies and placation. We will not be fooled into thinking Hagen's plans are for the benefit of anyone but himself."

The old freighter's eyes narrowed in defiance as he glared up at Trammel. "And we will not allow a Judas goat with a star on his chest to tell us to be calm and go home."

Trammel snatched Albertson by the collar and pulled him toward himself before he realized he had done it. He easily lifted the man just enough so that Albertson was standing on his toes.

The marchers gasped and now took several steps back.

"You listen to me, Albertson, and listen well," Trammel said. "I'm nobody's Judas goat, got it? I don't belong to either of the Hagens. I don't belong to Montague down at the bank. I don't belong to anyone or anything but the law and the town of Blackstone. If you ever doubt it, come see me at the jail and I'll be more than happy to convince you."

He released Albertson with a shove that sent him stumbling back toward the marchers he led. Several of them rushed to keep him from falling down. He knew he would regret manhandling the rabble-rouser later on, but now was not the time.

He faced the crowd. "You've all made your point. You've had your march. You've spoken your mind and you've been heard. Now it's over. If I see any of you clustered together within the next five minutes, I'll lock you up for disorderly conduct."

Trammel did not have to ask if he had made himself clear. Judging by the looks on their faces, they knew.

And from how they had just seen him take on Albertson, none of them wanted to risk the same treatment.

Trammel stood his ground alone as he watched the marchers reluctantly fold their banners and head back to their homes.

As the crowd thinned out, only one man was left in the middle of Main Street. A thin man in his late twenties, his black hair and spectacles gave him a studious look. This man was not Albertson, but Richard Rhoades of the town's newspaper, *Blackstone Bugle.*

Trammel shut his eyes and hung his head. He had not seen the reporter during the march. If he had, he would have tried to keep a better handle on his temper. Grabbing Albertson would be the bright bow his story needed for the paper's next edition. And he couldn't blame Rhoades for printing it. He could only blame himself for giving the newsman something to print.

"How long have you been there?" Trammel called out to him over the heads of departing marchers.

"From the beginning." The reporter finished jotting something down in his notebook as he walked toward Trammel. "I was with them when they began gathering at Bainbridge Avenue and followed them the whole way here. They had about thirty marchers by the time you broke it up. An impressive number for a town this size if you ask me."

Throughout his career as a policeman in Manhattan, and then as a Pinkerton, Trammel always had a healthy distrust of newspapermen. They tended to distort the truth to fit whatever message they were trying to convey. But Rhoades was a different sort. Since he had come to town a year before, Trammel found his reporting honest and had even grown to like the man.

"Guess you're happy I grabbed Albertson like I did. That ought to make a nice addition to your story."

"Maybe," Rhoades agreed, "but I'm not going to use it."

Trammel hadn't been expecting that. "Why not? Your readers will love it."

The reporter shook his head. "Albertson said he wouldn't be manipulated by anyone, and neither will I. He goaded you into grabbing him because he knew I was there. When he gathered everyone together, he told me to keep an eye on him because he was going to give me 'one hell of a story' for my article. I won't give him the satisfaction of printing it."

Trammel's mood improved some. "I'll make it a point of keeping a better handle on my temper when he's around. He won't rile me so easily next time."

Rhoades leaned in closer so no one could hear him say, "Personally, I think you should've slugged him for stirring up all this trouble."

Trammel had thought about that a lot

since Albertson had first come to town six weeks before. The crippled freighter had started grousing about conditions in the town almost from the start. People were always looking for a reason to complain, and men like Albertson had a knack for getting the worst out of them. "What do you think his aim is? About starting up all this trouble, I mean. I've known a lot of freighters in my day, and every one of them would prefer whiskey and women over marches and such. It doesn't make any sense to me."

"Me neither," Rhoades agreed. "He claims he was a freighter, but if he was, he's the most eloquent mule skinner I've ever heard."

The small question that had been rattling around in Trammel's mind now loomed large. "That's been bothering me, too. You think he's a phony?"

"He seems sincere in his complaints," Rhoades said. "There's no denying that. Now, as for his motivation, I'm still trying to figure that out." Trammel watched an idea dawn on the reporter's face. "He says he's worked freighter outfits in Texas and Missouri and Kansas. I have colleagues in those areas. I'm going to write them to see if they've heard of him. I doubt we'll learn much, but I'll feel better having tried it."

Trammel watched Albertson walk back toward Bainbridge with two old ladies on his arms. He was gesturing wildly, probably carrying on with the same rhetoric he had used in front of the saloon.

"Think you could wire your friends instead?" Trammel asked. "The town will pay for it."

"In that case, of course." Rhoades looked curious. "But why the urgency?"

"Because I think Albertson is working up to something big," Trammel said. "Today's march proves it. His attempt to barge into the saloon tells me he's looking to escalate things. The sooner we know who and what he is, the quicker we'll know what he's really up to. Might be able to stop him before he does it."

"Let's hope so." Rhoades pushed his hat farther back and scratched his forehead. "I've got to tell you, Sheriff, for a small town, Blackstone's sure got a lot of intrigue going on."

Trammel could not argue with him there. "Too much for my taste. When do you think you could get down to Laramie and send out those telegrams?"

He pulled his watch from his waistcoat and frowned. "It'll be well on dark if I leave now and I have tomorrow's edition to get out. I'll do it first thing in the morning. That soon enough for you?"

It wasn't, but it sounded like it would have to be. "I appreciate it, Rich. And I appreciate you leaving my grabbing of Albertson out of your article."

"Don't give it a second thought." Rhoades grinned. "Besides, no one wants to read anything that casts 'the Hero of Stone Gate' in a bad light."

"Knock it off." Trammel had hated that moniker since the day Rhoades had hung it on him after he kept a group of Pinkertons from taking over King Charles Hagen's Blackstone Ranch the previous year. "I told you not to call me that."

"That's the problem with you, Buck. You're too modest. I spelled your name right and gave you a legend. You should be pleased. The people of this territory have put you on a pedestal."

Trammel knew he was right. And he also knew what people did with things on pedestals.

They pulled them down after they were sick of looking at them.

Chapter 2

Adam Hagen had watched the entire spectacle unfold from the second-floor balcony of the Clifford Hotel. His hotel.

From there, he could watch the whole town. He could see the carpenters working on the structures he had ordered to be built on lots he had purchased along Main Street. He could see the new houses he was building on the new Buffalo Street, too, in anticipation of the people who would flock to Blackstone when his plans took shape. He had even seen the marchers assemble on Bainbridge, then head toward his Pot of Gold on Main Street. He had watched them pick up more followers along the way until they reached his saloon and hurled insults and prayers at the place.

He almost felt sorry for the poor fools. They were so ardent in their righteousness. Strident in their belief that they could change the future of Blackstone.

But Adam Hagen knew there was only one man who could do that, and it was not King Charles Hagen. Soon, it would be King Adam Hagen.

He had ordered the porch to be added to his room to aid in his convalescence after having been shot in the right arm by renegade Pinkerton men several months before.

He squeezed the small bag of sand in his right hand again for the countless time that day. He ignored the sharp pain that webbed through his body following each squeeze. His convalescence had taken a toll on him, particularly his looks. His fair hair had begun to turn white in places, though he was just past thirty. His smooth skin, which the ladies loved, now had lines brought about by pain that had not been there before.

A doctor down in Laramie had told him the exercise was his best chance of regaining some use of his right arm. The doctor had been cautious enough to tell him that he was unlikely to ever have full use of the arm again, but with diligent exercise, he might be able to hold a fork again. Perhaps even write his name without much difficulty.

But as for gambling and gunfighting, those activities were out. The doctor advised him to learn how to make do with his left hand for now.

But Adam Hagen had no intention of making do with anything. He had made do long enough as the banished son of King Charles Hagen. And now that he knew the man he had called "Father" all those years was actually his uncle, he planned on going far beyond making do.

He intended on making revenge.

Hagen had almost cheered when Trammel snatched Albertson by the neck. The old man had been baiting him and almost got what he deserved. But Buck was a smart man, quick to anger and even quicker to calm down and listen to reason.

It was why the people of Blackstone loved him. It was the quality Hagen had admired most in his former friend.

And it also happened to be the only weakness in his considerable armor. A weakness he intended to exploit when the time came.

He knew Trammel would rebel at first. After all, Hagen hadn't nicknamed him Buck without a reason. But eventually he would see that his old friend was right and had given him an embarrassment of riches. Hagen hoped Trammel would be prudent enough to focus on the message and not the messenger. Hagen still owed him for saving his life by getting him out of Wichita the year before.

If he did not, Hagen just might have to kill him, and that would cast a shadow over all he had dreamed these past months in convalescence.

Hagen watched Trammel finish his conversation with that weasel reporter from the *Bugle.* His first order of business upon taking over the town would be to buy that damned paper and shut it down. But for the moment it served its purpose.

He watched Trammel lumber back toward the jail, which was right next door to the Clifford Hotel. Hagen did not have many regrets in life, but he regretted that he and the big man were no longer friends. Trammel abhorred his selling of laudanum at his saloon and the laudanum he allowed the Chinese to sell in a canvas tent next door.

But he had not regretted it enough to stop selling laudanum. In fact, laudanum played a key role in his plans for revenge.

He saw Trammel cast a quick glance up to his balcony and, upon seeing him, quickly look away.

Hagen got out of his chair and went to the side railing as he called out, "Behold the return of the conquering hero! That was a mighty impressive sight to see, Buck. They complain about the new saloons on Main Street, but say nothing of the houses I'm building. They're a fickle bunch indeed. At least you turned them before they got themselves hurt. They wouldn't have received a warm reception in my saloon."

Trammel stopped walking and glowered up at him. Hagen had to admit the sheriff was a frightening sight when he was angry.

"I've told you not to call me that," Trammel said. "We're not friends anymore, Hagen, so quit acting like we are."

"I'm still your friend," Hagen said, "even if you're not mine."

"If you mean that, then quit selling dope," Trammel said. "You've got half the men on your father's ranch using the stuff, and most of the coal miners. Quit rotting their brains and you and me can be friends again."

Adam appeared to think it over, though he had absolutely no intention of stopping the flow of laudanum into Blackstone. If anything, it was just the opposite. He decided to have a little fun with the sheriff. "A wise proposition. Why don't you come up here so we can talk about it instead of shouting at each other like this?"

"And look like I'm up there to kiss your ring?" Trammel shook his head. "No chance."

Hagen laughed. "You always see me in the worst light. Even after all we've been through together. I'm not your enemy, Buck. You saved my life, and I'll never be able to repay you for it."

"Don't thank me," Trammel said. "If I'd known what you'd turn into, I wouldn't have bothered."

"Yes, you would," Hagen told him. "You're a natural hero, Sheriff Trammel, and this world needs heroes. It always has and always will."

Trammel looked like he was going to say something more but didn't. Instead, something in the distance captured his attention.

And when Hagen looked in the same direction, he understood why. Dr. Emily Downs was getting into her wagon.

Hagen imagined some might call her pretty. He had always thought of her as elegant, with an agile mind that made for pleasant company.

She had captured Trammel's heart from the moment they had arrived in Blackstone and, for a time, they had been a very happy couple.

But their relationship had soured after Trammel's troubles with the Pinkertons at Stone Gate. She had been a widow once and had no intention of becoming one again. She'd shut her heart to Trammel, and Hagen knew it had wounded the big man deeply. It had hardened him in a way that had made Hagen angry. She had given up Trammel because he could no sooner change who and what he was than Hagen could grow a new right arm. He had expected more from a woman of science, but as a widow, he could not fault her reasons.

Hagen watched Trammel forget the world around him as Emily released the brake and snapped the reins, bringing her horse to a quick trot. He saw Trammel stand a little straighter and something of a smile appear on his face as she steered the wagon toward Main Street. Even the sight of her was enough to make him happy, and Hagen's heart ached for him.

She would pay for hurting him, and soon. But not that day.

She sat ramrod straight and made a point of keeping her eyes forward as she approached the Clifford Hotel. Hagen knew she could hear him as he called out, "And a blessed day to you, our fair Dr. Downs. Our humble town is grateful for you gracing us with your presence."

"Mr. Hagen," she said as she rode by, then added, "Sheriff Trammel."

Buck tipped his hat, entranced as she rode

by without the slightest glance his way. "Nice to see you, Emily."

She said nothing more as she continued on her way.

Hagen pitied his former friend. He waited until she had passed out of earshot before saying, "Quite the peacock our Dr. Downs has become since throwing you over. I wonder how she'd fair if she lost her plumage."

Trammel slowly raised his head and looked at Hagen. "If you touch her, I'll kill you."

Hagen had no doubt he would and forced a laugh. "Why would I touch a hair on her head? I happen to like Emily. Besides, she has the virtue of being the only doctor in town. But cheer up, my friend. Fate is a great equalizer and, sooner or later, she'll regret having treated you so poorly."

Hagen watched Trammel's anger fade away before he turned to enter the jail. "Just leave her alone. And quit calling me 'friend.' "

Hagen decided he had given the sheriff a tough enough time already and let him go without another word. He went back to his chair and resumed squeezing the small bag of sand.

He cast an eye up the long hill to where

King Charles Hagen's ranch house sat. It was a mighty place that lorded over all beneath it like a behemoth. It looked indestructible from here, but Adam knew nothing built by man would last forever. He looked forward to the day when he watched that house burn to the ground. No, he would not attack the house from the front. He would attack his father's empire at its foundation and watch it fall in on itself.

Yes, King Charles Hagen's end would come soon. But first, Buck Trammel would receive his reward, and sooner than he thought. And Emily Downs would learn what happened to those who displeased him.

He winced as he squeezed the bag of sand tighter as he looked at the Hagen ranch house on the hill and remembered a verse from the Bible. "Your glory, O Israel, lies slain on your heights. How the mighty have fallen!"

CHAPTER 3

Lucien Clay decided he hated chess and probably always would.

The black and white boxes and the odd figures that sat upon them gave him nightmares. The way the pieces moved made no sense to him. His teacher had explained the rules to him countless times, but only a few of them stuck. Not even the names made sense. Pawns and knights and kings and queens. The whole game sounded foreign and fancy to him, and the strategy it took to play it served to make him dislike it even more.

The chiding of his teacher did not help matters.

"You're not concentrating," Albert Micklewhite scolded him. "Chess requires your full attention or you're bound to lose. How many times must I tell you that?"

Lucien shrugged. "As many times as it takes, I guess. Might help if there weren't so many damned rules."

"Ah, now I see the problem," Micklewhite said. "A man like you doesn't like the idea of rules. That's fine. Think of the game in a way that you can appreciate."

Lucien looked at Micklewhite from across the chessboard. "You calling me stupid, Al?"

"God, no," Micklewhite said. "Instead of thinking of the rules of chess, think of each piece as having its own nature. Its own vices, if you will."

This was getting more confusing by the minute. "What the hell are you talking about?"

Micklewhite selected a pawn. "For example, in the opening move, a pawn can be moved two squares ahead. But after that, it can only move one square at a time. Physically, can I move it sideways? Of course, but that's not what pawns are for. There are other pieces on the board that can do that."

Lucien had understood the pawns from the beginning, but remembering what the rest of the pieces did was a jumble to him. "Can't we play something American? Like cards or craps?"

Micklewhite slowly shook his head. "Those are games of chance, Lucien. What I'm trying to teach you is the importance of planning ahead, and chess is a wonderful way to teach you how to do that. You're a cunning businessman. A man of great will. It's gotten you far in life. But if you choose to expand beyond the limits of Laramie, which you told me you wanted to do when you brought me here, you must train your mind to think ahead. Every move you make, be it in chess or in life, has a consequence. A vulnerability. As Charles Buxton once said, 'In life, as in chess, forethought wins.' "

Micklewhite sat back in his chair, though he was still crooked. "Now do you understand what I'm trying to teach you? It's not about chess. It's about life."

Lucien looked at the board and its pieces again. He willed himself to want to learn the game. He knew it would help him in the long run. But Lucien Clay had never been one for long runs.

"I see what you're trying to teach me here, Al. I really do, except there's only one problem with it."

Micklewhite sighed heavily. "Which is?"

"That for your idea to work, everyone has to agree to the same rules," Lucien said. "They have to obey the rules. They can't distract you and take a piece off the board or change one of their moves when you're not looking. Pawns don't always act like pawns, especially if they think they're really kings."

Micklewhite threw up his hands in frustration. "This is hopeless. Yes, those things can happen, but it's not the way the game is played."

Lucien recalled something Micklewhite had just said to him. "Take what you said about each piece having its own nature. That it can only do what the rules say it can do."

Micklewhite smiled. "Precisely."

Lucien drew the derringer he kept in his sleeve and aimed it at Micklewhite's forehead.

Micklewhite did not move.

"Now," Lucien continued, "let's say the pawn comes up against one of these things that can hurt him. Say another pawn, or a bishop. Say my pawn pulls a gun on the other pawn and blows him down. Bang. No more threat. And that bishop, if he's smart, will jump the hell out of his way if he knows what's good for him. Maybe he even changes color and starts working for the other side."

Knowing he had made his point, Lucien put the derringer back in his sleeve. "See, Al. That's the way life really works. Not everyone plays by the same set of rules. And your whole strategy idea ain't worth much unless everyone plays by the same set of rules." Lucien sat back in his chair and smiled. "Do I look like a man who likes rules, Al?"

Micklewhite cleared his throat and ran his finger under his collar. "No, Lucien. No, you don't. It's why you brought me here in the first place."

Lucien slapped the arm of his chair. "That's it! It all goes back to what I just said. You're that bishop I just talked about. The one who changes his colors and works for the other side." He pushed himself away from the table and went to pour himself a whiskey from the bottle on his desk. "Now that's a game I know how to play. I could enjoy playing by those rules. So, tell me, how's this Mike Albertson act of yours playing up north?"

"It's promising," Micklewhite told him. "I think I've got the locals pretty well worked up by now. I've rented a room with this kindly old gal named Mrs. Higgins."

Lucien finished pouring his glass and looked at Micklewhite. "Rich widow? Is she pretty?"

"Not all that rich, and she's eighty."

"Since when have you allowed a few wrinkles and creaky bones get in your way?"

He poured another whiskey for them. "An old con man like you should keep his options open." He gestured toward the chess board. "You know, strategy and all that stuff."

"There's nothing to be gained by bedding Mrs. Higgins," Micklewhite said, "though her friendship has helped me enlist the help of some of the other people in town, especially after today."

Lucien put the cork back in the bottle and opened his humidor to select a cigar. "Meaning?"

"Meaning I worked on Trammel like you told me to. It's taken a while, but I finally got under his skin today. I even got the big dope angry enough to grab me."

Lucien's eyes rose as he cut off the end of a cigar. "That is good news."

"I thought he might hit me at first," Micklewhite said, "but no such luck. He cooled off and just ordered us off the street."

Lucien brought a flame to his cigar and brought the two glasses back to the table. "Good thing he didn't belt you. He might've killed you, and you're no good to me dead."

"Hardly," Micklewhite scoffed. He pointed a thumb to his crooked back. "I didn't get this at a tea party."

"No," Lucien said as he sat down and

puffed on his cigar. "You got it when you fell off a horse while running out of town with a posse on your heels. Or was it the farmers who wanted to skin you alive for selling them that snake oil you were peddling?"

Micklewhite forced a smile. "Some things are better left in the past, Lucien. Just like your forced allegiance to Madam Peachtree for all those years."

Lucien did not like to remember the time when he was under the old hag's thumb. He liked Micklewhite throwing it in his face even less. He removed his cigar from his mouth and pointed it at Micklewhite. "You ever mention that again, I'll put this out in your eye."

The con man raised his hands in surrender. "Looks like we've both got things in our past we'd sooner forget."

Lucien decided to focus on the present. "How soon before those houses that Hagen is building are finished?"

Micklewhite shrugged. "A month or so, from what I've heard, but that's only gossip that the Higgins woman tells me. You're Hagen's partner. You would know better than me."

Yes, Lucien thought. *I'm his partner. For now.* But his time at Madam Peachtree's beck and call had taught him a vital lesson. No one ever got rich by working for someone else. He split the laudanum and gambling trade in the territory down the middle with Hagen. It had made him even richer than he had been before.

But any man who was as hell-bent on destroying his own father as Hagen was could not be trusted. And he did not need to be a chess player to know that 100 percent of everything was a lot better than 50 percent of something.

"A month sounds about right," Lucien said, "but keep an eye on them. Hagen's anxious to start making money by renting them out. As soon as the paint is dry on the last one of them, we burn them down. That ruckus you're kicking up will make people think your bunch is behind it somehow. Trammel and Hagen will be chasing their tails trying to find out who did it, which is very good for us."

Micklewhite sipped his whiskey and set it back on the table. "You see, that's the part I don't get. You'll lose just as much money as he does when those houses burn. And it's not just your money, Lucien. You promised me twenty percent of the town when you take over."

He had at that, and Micklewhite never let

him forget it. "I can afford to lose the money more than Hagen can. Sure, the two of us split everything fifty-fifty, but when I pull out of our arrangement, he'll be left hurting for money. His fight against his old man will be in full swing by then, based on what he told me, and that's when he'll be vulnerable. I'll let those two tear at each other until both sides are exhausted. Then I'll move in and push them aside. I'll own the whole town and the Hagens will be a distant memory."

Micklewhite slowly turned his glass on the table. "I don't think it'll be that easy, Lucien. The Pinkertons thought the same as you and look how Trammel handled them. He might look like a big oaf, but he's smarter than he ought to be. He's tougher than he looks and he's mighty tough."

Lucien waved him off. "I'm not worried about him. It's just him and that simple-minded ranch hand he has as a deputy. If he survives the battle with the Hagens, he'll be ripe for plucking when I come in. It'll be easy, and I'll have them all boxed in, just like one of your . . . whatever you call these things on the board here."

"The queen," Micklewhite said. "Trapping her is how you get checkmate and win the game."

Lucien laughed and waggled his cigar at him. "See? That's what I said before. In my game, it's the king who loses. And wins." He popped the cigar in his mouth and sat back in his chair. "King Lucien Clay." He winked at Micklewhite. "I like the sound of that."

"And his bishop, Albert Micklewhite, with twenty percent."

If things played out the way Lucien wanted them to, Micklewhite would be long dead before that happened. "Yeah. You would like the sound of that, wouldn't you?"

Chapter 4

The den in Charles Hagen's ranch house was more befitting a king than a rancher. This had always been his intention.

He became aware that he had acquired the title of King Hagen among the locals when he procured the last ranch next to his, making him the largest cattleman in Wyoming.

As a child, Charles had despised nicknames, particularly the diminutive familiarity of "Charlie," which his father used to call him. No one had called him Charlie in more than fifty years. He was King Charles Hagen now and did his best to live up to the name.

The den in which he now sat was made of dark wood and heavy stones pried from the very land upon which his great house now stood.

The bookcases of the den were lined with tomes of poets and philosophers from antiquity. He had made a point of reading all of them, many more than once. Forgetting the past was a dangerous enterprise in his opinion, and Charles Hagen had always considered himself a cautious man.

The heavy desk behind which he now sat was also made from the timber that had once filled this land. His leather chair was from the hides of the cattle he had brought here to graze on it. The coal oil in his lamps came from the mines he owned close by. Everything about this house stood as a testament to the Hagen family's will to take hold of the land and make it their own. It was a trophy of his mastery of mineral and men.

He sat impatiently while one of the many men over whom he lorded his power thanked him for saving his life.

"I can't thank you enough for getting me out of that jam down in Laramie, Mr. Hagen," John Bookman said. "It meant a lot."

"Yes," Hagen agreed. "It made the difference between you spending the next ten years swinging a pick and breaking rocks as opposed to being here and working for me. Attempted murder is a difficult charge to have swept under the rug, John. You're lucky the judge was an old friend of mine."

"I know that, sir," Bookman said, "and

I'm forever grateful. You had my loyalty before, but now —"

Charles Hagen raised a hand to stop him. Supplication had its limits, even for him. Bookman was dark-haired and range lean. He was as tough as the land he rode, maybe even tougher. Seeing him grovel like this did Charles Hagen no good. "You can thank me by resuming your duties and running this ranch. You can start by telling me how many of our men are hooked on that poison my nephew is peddling in town."

"I'd say more than half of them have a problem with the smoke, sir," Bookman reported.

Charles looked at him. "How many more than half?"

"I'd say about sixty percent of them, sir."

The number almost floored him. He had never partaken of laudanum himself but had seen it ruin many a man. "How did so many get infected so soon?"

"I'd say the problem has been building up for a while now," Bookman told him, "and it seems to have gotten worse while I was in jail."

"But your replacement assured me the problem was well in hand."

"Simon used to be a good hand, sir, but it looks like he's got a problem with the dragon, too. He spends a fair share of his time at your nephew's laudanum den."

"My nephew," Charles spat. It felt good to finally be able to speak the truth about Adam Hagen again after so many decades of lies about his lineage.

Adam Hagen was not his son and never had been. He had raised the boy, true, but he had never felt any more affection for him than he would feeding a stray dog that had wandered on to his property. Adam had been his sister's boy, and he supposed he had some Hagen blood in him, not that it showed. Charles's sister had paid for her indiscretion by dying in childbirth. The boy's father had paid for corrupting her by having his bones scattered by the coyotes who had fed on him.

"That would explain how they've all been acting as of late," Hagen said. "They're sluggish and half asleep most times."

"The pipe isn't as bad as whiskey hangovers, but it's making them slow-moving as hell. Some of the men who've been smoking longer are the worst. They're sick a lot and they're forgetting things. One of them left the corral open a couple of nights ago. We almost lost those fifty horses we were going to sell to the army."

"Fifty!" Hagen proclaimed. Such a loss

would have not only affected the ranch's finances. It would damage his reputation with the army. He had worked too hard to secure those contracts to allow anything or anyone to damage them.

And there was only one man to blame.

"This is Adam's plan to ruin me, isn't it? He has plotted against me since the cursed day he crawled back into Blackstone. Now that he knows he's not my son, his anger has only gotten worse."

"It's not just the cowhands, sir," Bookman explained. "A fair number of the miners have started to visit the den, too. A lot of those boys have plenty of aches and pains, and the laudanum helps them feel better."

"At the cost of their souls." Hagen had become a king and remained a king because he knew exactly what to do at exactly the right time. "I know you've just gotten out of a great difficulty with the law, but I'm going to need you to do something for me."

Bookman sat even straighter in his chair. "Of course, sir. Anything."

"I need you to take a couple of the good men we have remaining and burn down the Pot of Gold Saloon as well as the laudanum den behind it. I need you to do it tonight. We must cauterize the wound before this gangrene spreads to the rest of our operation. It's already gone too far for too long as it is."

Bookman surprised him by saying, "I hate to disagree with you, sir, but I don't know if that's going to work."

Hagen looked at him. "Fire cures all ills, John."

"Normally it does," Bookman admitted, "but this is different. These boys will get mighty sick if their laudanum supply burns up. Maybe the few that are new to the pipe will get over it, but the boys who are too far gone will be completely useless to us. I've seen what men go through when they don't have the money for a smoke and it ain't pretty. If they're too sick to work your mines and tend your stock, it'll cost us a lot in the long run. Some of them might even die."

Hagen was accustomed to being right, but he imagined John Bookman had a point. Hagen had never even tried the stuff and knew little about its toll on the human body.

"Anyone who decides to take up laudanum smoking deserves to pay the price for their weakness in my book," he declared. "But this problem seems to be far more difficult than I thought."

He drummed his fingers on the desk as he weighed all his options. Damn Adam and his blasted revenge!

His anger burned through the problem and revealed a solution. "How big a piece do I own of the Crooked C in Ogallala?"

Bookman had to think about it. "I think you own it outright, sir. I remember you bought out Calhoun lock, stock, and barrel, but you might want to check with Mr. Montague on that."

Hagen would make a point of doing that. In addition to being the president of the Blackstone Bank, Montague also handled all his business matters for him. In fact, he was only the bank president because of his association with Hagen.

But there was no time to lose. "I want you to make a list of all the ranch hands who are too far gone to do us much good. Then I want you to head into Laramie and send a telegram to the Crooked C, telling them we need some of their men to come work here. We'll increase their wages and pay for their train fare here. I'd like to know how many we can expect by the end of business tomorrow."

Bookman said, "I can set to writing that list right now if you give me something to write on, sir."

King Charles shoved some paper at him and a pencil.

"As soon as those replacements arrive, we'll show my nephew just how dangerous the laudanum trade can be."

Chapter 5

The next day, Trammel was walking into Robertson's General Store to buy some coffee for the jail just as Emily was coming out.

Both stopped when they saw each other.

Trammel touched the brim of his hat as he stepped aside. "Morning, Emily."

She composed herself and walked past him after closing the door behind her. "Good morning, Sheriff."

He could almost feel his heart breaking as she passed him without another word. He had become accustomed to her coldness to him in recent months, but on that particular morning, it hurt him deeply.

"What happened between us, Emily?" he asked. "What made you hate me all of a sudden?"

She stopped walking but did not turn to face him. "I don't hate you, Buck. I don't think I could ever hate you. But I can't allow myself to love you either. You take too many chances. Too many risks. My husband's death took the ground out from under me and I can't allow myself to go through that again."

Trammel had heard her say that before, and hearing it again did not make him feel any better. "I can change, Emily. I really can if you'll just give me the chance."

Now she turned to face him, and he saw the tears in her eyes. "You can't change who and what you are. I wouldn't dream of asking you to even try. This town needs you, especially with the trouble that's brewing between the Hagens. They need you more than I do." She looked down at her basket of goods. "You'll always be a lawman, Buck. Whether or not you've got a star pinned on your chest or a gun in your hand, you'll always try to protect people, and that means you'll be in danger."

"We're all in danger," Buck told her. "Living out here is dangerous business."

"Even more so for you. And that's too much for me to handle. I can't go through the pain of missing someone I love again. I don't think I'd make it next time."

He was finally seeing cracks in the ice that had formed between them over the long months since the Stone Gate business, and he sought to chip them to pieces. "We could leave town. We could go live somewhere else. I could do something else. Another line of work, maybe?"

She laughed as she wiped away a tear. "Like what? Work in a saloon? Ride shotgun for the stage line? Dig coal?" She sadly shook her head. "None of that would change who you are. Besides, the town needs us. If we left, who would take our places? I'm the only doctor they've got and you're all the sheriff they've got."

"Hawkeye could take over for me," he answered. "He's grown up a lot since he started working for me."

"He's still a boy and he'll never be you," she said. "And if anything happened to him after we left, you'd never be able to forgive yourself."

He wanted to tell her that she was wrong. He wanted to tell her that he was tired of taking on other people's burdens, tired of being alone.

He was about to tell her all these things when a horrible shriek came from the canvas tent just behind the Pot of Gold Saloon.

Trammel instinctively stepped between Emily and the trouble while he looked to see what had happened.

He saw four men spill out from the tent

and run toward Main Street. Two of them were shaggy and filthy and looked like they had slept in their clothes for a week. The other two were Chinese toughs paid to keep an eye on the laudanum den behind the saloon. And each of them was holding a cleaver.

Trammel turned to tell Emily to get back in the store where she would be safe, but she was already hurrying up the street toward her house.

Glad she was out of harm's way, he ran toward the brawl that had broken out on Main Street.

The Chinese were yelling and brandishing their cleavers at the two men who were just getting to their feet. One of the men was about to charge the guards when Trammel grabbed him and pulled him back.

The sheriff stood between the two sides and kept them each at bay. "Everybody just calm down and tell me what this is all about."

"They took our money, Sheriff," one of the men said. He looked familiar to Trammel, but he couldn't quite place him. "They said we didn't have enough to smoke and kicked us out without even giving us our money back."

"And we did have enough to smoke," said

the man Trammel had pulled away from the fight. "They flat-out robbed us, Sheriff. Rolled us like drunks in an alley."

Trammel looked the two men up and down. "From the looks of both of you, I'd say that's exactly what you are." Trammel realized the second man looked familiar, too. "Where do I know you two boys from?"

"We worked the Blackstone," the first man said. "I'm Joe Allan, and this here's my brother, Sam."

Now he remembered who they were. "What are you boys doing down here? Shouldn't you be working the ranch?"

"We would be," Sam said, "if Bookman hadn't cut us loose. He paid us off for the rest of the week and sent us on our way."

"Yeah," Joe agreed. "Five years of working that place and all we get for it was a kick in the pants and ordered off the ranch." He ran his fingers across his nose, and they came up bloody. "Now we've got no jobs and can't even soften the hurt with some smoke."

The brothers tried to rush the Chinese again, but Trammel grabbed both of them and easily pushed them down.

He remembered these boys from a while back. They were solid workers for the Blackstone Ranch and hardly ever caused any trouble when they came to town. They had been strong, hearty men then, but now they were shadows of their former selves. Beneath the dirt, their clothes were filthy, and they looked like they had aged at least ten years since the last time he had seen them.

"You boys had best stay down if you know what's good for you," Trammel told them. "Next time I won't be so gentle."

He turned to face the two Chinese, who had drawn closer to the Allan boys. And they were still holding their cleavers. The blades were caked with a brownish film Trammel took to be blood and dared not think what kind of blood it might be.

These men were not the coolies who ran around the den and cleaned up the place. They were both tall. One was bald and one had his hair tied behind his head in a queue style. Both of them sported long, droopy mustaches and looked like they knew how to use the cleavers they held for more than just cooking.

Some men treated the Celestials as if they were different from the rest of humanity, but Trammel knew better. He had seen enough dead Chinese to know they were the same on the inside as much as any other man.

He pointed at both of them and said,

"Now it's your turn to tell me your side of it. And don't play like you boys don't know how to speak English because I know you do." He looked at the bald one. "I've heard you speak to Hagen as clear as I'm speaking now, so you go first."

"They paid," the bald man said, "but got angry when we wouldn't give them extra dope. We said, 'No money, no dope.' They said they're good customers and lost their jobs and should get more than they paid for. Boss Lady said no, and they caused trouble. They threatened Boss Lady, so we threw them out."

This was exactly the kind of trouble Trammel had worried about when Hagen started selling that stuff in town. He was only surprised it had not started earlier. "They started trouble and you threw them out. That about right?"

The man with the queue said, "That's right."

Trammel had figured as much. "And what about their money? You give that back to them?"

From behind him, Joe yelled, "You deaf, Sheriff? We already told you they didn't."

Trammel ignored Joe and waited for the Chinese to answer. "Well? Did you give it back to them or not?"

"They caused trouble," the bald man said. "They broke things. We need the money to pay for that."

Trammel was beginning to see why the boys were so angry. "The place is a tent full of pillows. How much damage could they have done?"

The man with the queue leered at him and gripped his cleaver tighter.

Trammel saw it, too. "Don't do anything stupid. Just answer my question."

The bald man cursed in his native language as he dug coins out of his pockets and tossed them at the Allan boys. They scrambled in the dirt like dogs to pick up the money.

"Look at them," the bald one sneered. "Like pigs digging in their own dirt for a few lousy coins."

His arrogance annoyed Trammel. "Your dope made them that way. Don't you forget it."

"No one made them smoke. They chose. Now look at them."

The man with the queue spat in their direction, but the boys were too busy gathering up their coins to notice.

Trammel pointed at both of them again. "You two best get back inside while they're distracted."

The bald one said, "They can't come here again. You tell them that."

"I will," Trammel agreed, "but if they do, you send someone to get me." He pointed at the cleavers they were holding. "I find they're missing or cut up somewhere, I'll hold both of you responsible."

The two Chinese spoke to each other in their native tongue as they turned to go back inside the tent. Trammel did not understand Chinese, but judging from the tone of their voices, they were not singing his praises. He did not particularly care as long as they went back inside.

Trammel was about to tend to the Allan boys when he felt a hard tug at the Colt holstered on his right leg. He looked down and saw Sam Allan trying to pull the pistol free.

Trammel slammed an elbow hard into Sam's face, sending him tumbling backward into the dirt.

Joe lunged at him next and delivered a blow that caught Trammel just under the chin. The world tilted for a moment, but the sheriff kept his feet.

"You can't let those low-down scums treat us that way," Joe yelled as he closed in for another punch. "They can't just shut us out like that. We need it."

Trammel recovered in time to dodge Joe's next wild punch, and the one that followed that.

Trammel connected with an uppercut that lifted Joe off his feet. He was out cold before he hit the ground.

Trammel saw Sam's face was a bloody mess, but he had managed to get Trammel's gun out of its holster as he fell back. He was blinking hard, trying to fix his aim on the sheriff as Trammel ducked out of the way. A single shot rang out, which missed Buck by a country mile. He rolled on his shoulder and found his feet under him, ready to charge the remaining Allan boy, when he saw Hawkeye come from across the street and bring the butt of his heavy revolver down on Sam's head. The blow was hard enough to lay the man flat.

Hawkeye plucked the Colt from Sam's hand and gave it back to Trammel butt forward. "You hurt, boss?"

Trammel took the pistol and tucked it back in the holster where it belonged. "Glad to see you're finally awake," the sheriff said to his deputy.

"One of us has to work nights," James "Hawkeye" Hauk told him. "I came running when I heard all the yelling in the street. Sorry for not getting here before he took a shot at you."

"He didn't come close to hitting me," Trammel said, "but while you're here, you can help me get these two to the jail."

As was his way, Hawkeye did not protest. In fact, Trammel could not remember hearing a single complaint from him since the day he pinned the deputy star on his chest. The boy was about twenty and seemed grateful for the work. Trammel hoped his love of the job lasted a little longer; he could certainly use the help.

Trammel looked around for a wagon to load the Allan boys onto but didn't see any available. "Looks like we're dragging them," he told Hawkeye. "You grab Joe and I'll grab Sam."

"Hey!" Hawkeye called out. "This is Sam and Joe Allan. Good boys."

Having grown up in Blackstone, Trammel figured there weren't too many people Hawkeye didn't know. "That's who they told me they were. And now they're prisoners."

He grabbed hold of Sam's left leg and began to pull him along Main Street down to the jail. Hawkeye did likewise with Joe, but did not let the extra burden keep him from talking. "I've known these boys my whole life, boss."

"So you said." He was glad the laudanum had made Sam Allan so skinny. He was easier to pull.

"They never caused any trouble," Hawkeye continued. "They kicked up a fuss on a payday now and then, but nothing like this. I can't even remember a single fight they started in all the years I've known them."

"Well, they sure as hell started this one," Trammel told him. "We're just lucky we were able to finish it."

He hoped Hawkeye would let it go until they reached the station, but he was a talkative boy and figured he wouldn't. His deputy did not disappoint. "What do you think got into them to make them do this?"

The street had filled in some with curious townspeople stopping the course of the day to watch the sheriff and his deputy drag two men along the dust of Main Street.

"Laudanum is what got into them," Trammel told his deputy. "It can make a man do some mighty strange things, including going for my gun. That's why I've always warned you to stay away from that stuff. It's no good for you."

"You know me, Sheriff," Hawkeye panted as he began to feel the effort of dragging Joe Allan. "I don't even like tobacco, much less laudanum."

He looked back and saw his deputy struggling and decided to give him a hand. "Let me drag them both while you run up ahead and unlock the jail. We'll put them in separate cells. These boys will be having a rough couple of days without their dragon smoke to help them. Best make sure we have plenty of buckets for when they do."

Hawkeye looked like he had a million questions, but Buck was glad he had the good sense to hold on to them until they got to the jail.

He ran ahead toward the jail while Trammel ignored the stares he drew from the good citizens of Blackstone as he dragged two men past them.

CHAPTER 6

Trammel looked up from his paperwork when he heard Hawkeye clear his throat. The deputy was standing by the entrance to the cells. "You getting sick or just trying to get my attention?"

"Sorry, boss, but I think you need to come back here and take a look at the prisoners," Hawkeye said. "They look mighty sick to me."

Trammel went back to finishing his report on the dustup with the Allan boys earlier that day. "I've seen men get the shakes before, Hawkeye. It happens when the drug begins to wear off and the body gets to missing it. They'll be like that for a couple of days. It'll be a messy business before it's over, but it's part of the job."

Hawkeye seemed less than pleased about the possibility of cleaning up not just one but two cells of men with dope sickness.

"You think we ought to send for Doc Emily?"

Trammel really wanted to get this report done before Rhoades came around asking for information for the next day's paper. "Not much she can do for them except give them a little more laudanum to ease their suffering. All that'll do is delay the inevitable, so best to leave her out of this for now. If they get worse, we can always call for her then."

Trammel hoped that would be enough to ease the deputy's mind, but it wasn't. He still stood there, looking in at the prisoners and back at Trammel like a confused puppy. He finally said what was on his mind. "How will we know when it's bad enough to call her?"

Trammel had lost his temper enough for one day and did not want to lose it with his deputy. "If one of them quits breathing or turns another color, we'll get her. Until then, I don't want her bothered for the likes of them."

"Nonsense," Adam Hagen said as he strode into the jail. His dark gray suit clashed with his maroon brocade vest, but he managed to pull off the look. "I'll pay for the good doctor's time in attending to the Allan boys. They're good customers of mine and I intend to see they're tended to."

Trammel slammed down his pen. At this rate, he would never get that damned report done. "Don't you ever knock?"

"Why should I?" Hagen asked as he sat down and pulled out a silver cigarette case. "I pay taxes in this town. I own the hotel right next door and most of the furniture in here came from there. I'm not asking for a key to the front door, of course, but I'm still entitled to come in whenever I want."

Trammel wanted to throw him out, but not in front of Hawkeye. Emily had told him that Hawkeye looked up to both of them. And although Trammel hoped the young man turned out different from Hagen, he didn't want to demonize Hagen either. It might have the opposite effect and Hawkeye would feel sorry for how Hagen was treated.

Hagen selected a cigarette and held out the case to Trammel. "Would you like one?"

The sheriff shook his head. "God only knows what you've put in it."

"I can assure you that it's only tobacco," Hagen said. "I wouldn't waste anything more exotic on your puritanical tastes." He looked back and held open the cigarette case to Hawkeye. "What about you? You're old enough now. Want a smoke?"

"He most certainly does not." Trammel thought of a good reason to get Hawkeye out of the jail, especially while Hagen was around. To his deputy, he said, "I forgot to pick up some coffee from Robertson's this morning. Why don't you head over there and have him grind some for us, then put on a fresh pot when you come back?"

He looked at Hagen. "Maybe our guest will be gone by then."

"Don't be silly." Hagen grinned. "I love it here. Surrounded by old friends and the most stimulating conversation one could hope for."

Hawkeye clearly wanted to stay and listen to the sheriff and the dandy spar with each other, but Trammel was his boss and he had given him an order. Reluctantly, he went about his chore and closed the jailhouse door behind him.

Hagen thumbed a match alive and lit his cigarette. "I certainly hope you didn't send him away on my account."

Trammel had no choice but to set aside his report for the moment. "What the hell do you think you're doing by offering him a smoke?"

"He's at least twenty or twenty-one," Hagen said. "He's old enough to drink, kill wild Indians, and help you corral a couple of dope fiends in the main thoroughfare. If working for you hasn't gotten him killed yet, a cigarette won't do the trick."

"He's a good kid, Hagen, and I want to keep him that way."

"You mean keep him your way," the vice peddler said. "As in you would disapprove if I hired him on and asked him to follow in my footsteps."

Trammel had no claim on Hawkeye whatsoever. But he had grown fond of the kid and felt a certain responsibility for him. "Anyone who follows in your footsteps risks getting shot in the back."

Hagen laughed. "This coming from the man who courts trouble simply by getting out of bed every day. Which reminds me, where are you sleeping these days?"

"You tell me," Trammel said. "You see everything from that grand balcony of yours, don't you?"

Hagen snapped his fingers, as if he had just remembered something. "That's right. You're back at the Oakwood Arms, aren't you? Guest of Mayor and Mrs. Welch." He sucked his teeth. "It's a shame, really. Not only have you had to grow accustomed to the fact that Dr. Downs threw you over, but you have to trek all the way to that ghastly old barn each night after work."

ing about you being the sheriff of Laramie. I run one side of the fence while you run the other. I keep my side down to a dull roar and innocent casualties to a minimum and all you have to do is agree to look the other way from time to time."

Trammel sat back in his chair and regarded Hagen. His fair hair and neatly trimmed Vandyke were the same, but the man who sat before him now was nothing like the Adam Hagen he had once considered his friend.

"This your idea of our friendship, Adam? You go on breaking the law and I go on letting you."

"Don't look at it like that." Hagen pitched forward in his chair as he pleaded his case. "Look at it as a way to keep a lid on the territory. Laudanum is frowned upon, but it's not illegal."

"Yet," Trammel cautioned.

Hagen grinned. "You just let me worry about that. We both know everything in the territory begins and ends in Laramie. Lucien Clay and I already have most of the saloons and brothels sewn up throughout the territory, but we're looking to expand our reach beyond Wyoming. With only a little help from you now, we'll be in a position to help you in the future."

"By kicking out Rob Moran and giving me his job in Laramie," Trammel concluded. "And just how do you plan on doing that? You can't buy him off and you can't scare him off, so that leaves only one option."

"Kill him?" Hagen shook his head. "Why kill what you can buy? Moran's a good man. An ambitious man, too, from what I've heard about him. Getting on in years, and I imagine he'd take the territorial marshal position if we could get it offered to him."

He flicked his ash into the cuspidor and pointed the cigarette toward Trammel. "That'll give you a clear shot at Moran's job. I know they'll think about one of his deputies taking his spot, but none of them are the Hero of Stone Gate."

Like a lawyer who had just finished making his case, he sat back in his chair, rather pleased with himself. "So, there it is. My grand plan all laid bare for you to feast your eyes upon. What do you say?"

At certain times, usually on sleepless nights, Buck Trammel stared at the ceiling and cursed the chances he had not taken. If he had just stayed in Manhattan and done what they wanted, he'd have a nice life for himself right about now. Maybe a wife and kids. And if he'd just stuck with the Pinkertons a little while longer, he might have had a nice office in Chicago or an easy job as a railroad detective.

But for one reason or another, he had closed all those doors behind him forever years ago. He had quit the cops and the Pinks because he would not do another man's evil. He could not be another man's puppet then. And despite all the hardship his stubbornness had caused him, nothing had changed.

"You want my answer now?" he asked.

Hagen said he did not. "Take your time. Lucien and I are still working out some details, but soon Blackstone and that ranch out there will be mine to do with as I please. When the dust settles, Laramie is our next stop."

"And you think Lucien will keep going along with all this?"

Hagen allowed some smoke to escape through his nose. "He will if he knows what's good for him. With Madam Peachtree rotting in her shallow grave, everyone who's anyone in power in this territory answers to me now, and they find me much more generous than she ever was. Lucien serves his purpose for now. But if you join up with us, you and I will be partners, Steve. Just like we used to be."

Trammel's eyebrows rose. "Steve, is it? You must really need me pretty bad."

Adam Hagen's eyes narrowed. "I don't need anyone. Not even you. I'm doing you a favor right now, you big dummy. You've passed up opportunities before. Don't let this be another one of them. Take a couple of weeks to think it over. The picture will be pretty clear by then."

But Trammel did not need a couple of weeks. He did not even need a couple of seconds. "You've got a real crooked idea of friendship, Adam. The answer is no."

He had expected Hagen to be angry. He half hoped he would lose his temper and try something stupid. It would give Trammel the excuse to end Hagen's plans right now, once and for all.

But he did not look angry. His placid expression did not change a bit. "I knew that would be your first answer. That's why you're the man for the job." He finished his cigarette and dropped the remains in the cuspidor as he rose to leave.

Trammel sat back in his chair and put his hand on the butt of his Colt. Just in case.

Instead, Hagen looked at his reflection in the mirror beneath the regulator clock on the wall. He fixed his hat to a jaunty angle. "You've always been a brave, tough man,

Buck, but you're blunt. You need to see things before you believe in them. You do things your way and I admire you for it. But when the seeds of destruction I've planted begin to flower and blossom, you'll see I'm right. And when that blessed moment comes, I'll accept your partnership with open arms."

The latch on the jailhouse door sounded, and Trammel got to his feet and drew his gun. Out of the corner of his eye, he saw Hagen already had his in hand. Even left-handed, he was still fast on the draw.

They both knew Hawkeye never opened the door without knocking first.

The jailhouse door swung open and John Bookman walked in. Upon realizing he was staring down the barrels of two pistols, he raised his hands slowly.

"Easy, boys. I came here to talk, not fight."

Trammel holstered his Colt. "Damnit, Bookman. Didn't anyone teach you to knock first?"

"Why should I?" the ramrod said. "This jail and the whole town belong to my boss."

"Not everything," Hagen said through clenched teeth.

It was only then that Trammel realized Adam had not holstered his gun. "Put it away, Hagen. He's here to talk."

But Hagen didn't budge. "You forget this man tried to kill me? Smother me in my bed like an infant."

Bookman sneered. "I should've done that when you *were* an infant. Would've saved your family a whole lot of trouble and grief."

Trammel had been in enough fights with Adam Hagen to know that look in his eye. He acted the high-talking dandy and gentleman gambler when it suited him, but at his core, he was a stone-cold killer.

Trammel slowly came around the desk and stood off to the side of both men without getting between them and Hagen's gun. "I told you to put it away, Adam. You just spent a whole lot of time telling me there's a time for everything. There's a time for killing Bookman, but this isn't it." He put iron in his voice as he said, "Put the gun away. Now."

The look in Hagen's eyes did not fade, but Trammel was glad when he began to lower his gun.

Bookman grinned. "Glad you listened to reason for once in your life, boy."

Now Trammel moved between the two men. "Shut your mouth, Bookman. He's still liable to kill you, and I'm of half a mind to let him. Say what you came to say or get out. But if you've come to get the Allan boys, you're out of luck. I'll be holding them for a while longer, until the poison is out of their system."

"You can keep them until hell freezes over for all Mr. Hagen cares," Bookman said. "They don't work for us anymore. No, I just came here at the request of Mr. Hagen." Bookman looked around Trammel at Adam. "The real Mr. Hagen. He sent me here to give you a warning."

Trammel turned to face him directly and took a couple of slow steps toward him. "A warning? That sounds like a threat to me."

Bookman leaned against the doorframe and hooked his thumb in a belt loop, real relaxed. "No threat, Sheriff, but a true warning. You've got big trouble coming your way, and soon."

"What else is new?" Trammel stopped a few feet in front of the man. "What kind of trouble are you talking about?"

Bookman nodded toward Adam. "His kind. The laudanum kind."

"Quit talking in riddles, Bookman," Adam said. "You don't have the brain for it."

"Then I'll speak plain. Mr. Hagen is letting go all the men who got themselves hooked on Adam's dope. He's cutting them loose today, and we imagine the first place they'll hit is here, for their smoke." A thin smile appeared on his face. "We're giving them all two weeks' pay, which is more than they deserve. But we figure they'll spend it all on whores and pipe smoke. Your friend back there will make a pile of money. We have no doubt of that."

Bookman looked up at Trammel. "And you're going to have your hands full with twenty men hopped up with no place to go and no money in their pockets."

"That's nonsense," Adam said. "That'll leave the ranch with only ten hands. The Blackstone's got too many cattle and horses for ten men to handle. My father isn't that stupid."

"He's not your father," Bookman reminded him. "But you're right about him not being stupid. We're hiring on twenty new men from a ranch back East. It's more than we need, but we figure some trouble might be coming our way, so they might come in handy."

"Splendid!" Adam cheered. "My dens are always happy to welcome new customers." He walked toward Bookman, his Colt still at his left side. "And they will come to me. You know that. The sweet smell of my pipes drifts far and wide."

Trammel held out an arm to keep him from getting too close to Bookman, especially with that gun still in his hand. "That's far enough, Adam."

Adam did not try to get around him. "Tell me something. How does he like the production of his mines dropping off thanks to my customers? By my estimation, he's probably off by twenty percent or more."

"Mines aren't my concern," Bookman said, "but those new hires are. And they'll be given strict instructions to stay away from those dens of yours. Any man who comes back from town smelling of pipe will be fired on the spot." It was his turn to look happy. "And these boys have traveled a long way for a good-paying job to risk that on your nonsense."

Hagen forced a laugh. "Oh, John. Your gullibility is almost endearing. Whole empires have been gained and lost because of the allure of my product. Emperors have fallen to the smoke I provide. King Charles Hagen will be no different."

Bookman shook his head. "All them pretty words in such a rotten mind." He looked at Trammel again. "We expect you'll be on our side of all this, Sheriff. It's no secret that you hate his dens as much as we do. We know you've had your differences with us in the past, but Mr. Hagen is willing to set all that aside for the sake of justice."

Trammel took another step closer to Bookman. "He stuck a shotgun in my face. You held a gun to my head. You might be willing to let that slide, but I'm not."

Bookman shrugged. "We know you and your friend over there are mighty close, so Mr. Hagen also wanted me to tell you that if you don't handle the dens, we will. Our own way."

Trammel snatched Bookman by the shirt and pulled him off the doorframe. "Seeing as how you're so good at delivering messages, you be sure to tell him this from me. I'm paid to enforce the law in town, and anyone who breaks it winds up dead or in a cell. Their choice. That goes for Adam's customers or whatever lynching party you send down here. You got that?"

Bookman looked brave for a man who had almost been lifted off his feet when he said, "Anything else?"

Trammel gripped him tighter. "As a matter of fact, there is." He shoved the ramrod hard and sent him spilling off the boardwalk and into Main Street. "Next time, knock."

Trammel reached back and slammed the door.

Adam rushed to open it again, but Trammel kept his hand on the door.

Adam screamed at Bookman anyway.

"You tell that old buzzard his days are numbered, Bookman. You hear me? Numbered!"

Trammel shoved Hagen flat against the door and pinned him there. "What I said to him goes for you, too, Adam. You break the law, you get a bullet or a cell. Understand me?"

Hagen held up his hands to show he was calm, and Trammel let him go but kept his hand on the door.

The dandy straightened his coat and fixed his hat. "You'll have no trouble from me, at least nothing worse than I'm already doing. And if my plans fall into place, the only gunshot you'll hear is my beloved uncle blowing his brains out." He glared up at the sheriff without a hint of fear or hesitation in his eyes. "That's a promise."

Trammel pushed him aside as he opened the door to look outside. He was glad to see there was no sign of Bookman anywhere.

He opened the door fully. "Time for you to leave, Hagen."

"So now it's back to Hagen again, is it?" The man laughed. "That's fine, Buck. Have it your way. But before all is said and done, you'll be back at my side, which is right where you belong."

Hagen touched the brim of his hat and

began to leave the jail, but Trammel gave him a parting word. "You'd better do something about that hate in your belly, Adam. It'll hollow you out until you've got nothing left. I've seen it happen to men before. I'd hate to see it happen to you."

Hagen stopped without turning around. "It's touching to know you still care. But don't worry about me. I was born hollow."

Trammel was relieved when he turned left and walked back to the Clifford Hotel. There would be no showdown between Adam and Bookman. At least not that day.

"Hey, boss!" Hawkeye called out as he crossed over from the other side of Main Street. He was carrying a sack of coffee from Robertson's store, along with some other provisions. "What'd I miss?"

"Plenty," Trammel told him. "Nothing that would've done you any good to see."

"Well, speaking of seeing things," Hawkeye said as he walked into the jail, "did you see all the excitement in town?"

Trammel let out a heavy breath. He'd had his share of excitement for one day. "Let me guess. We're surrounded by Sioux."

"Of course not," Hawkeye said as he set down the provisions on the desk. "The Sioux never came this far south, at least according to what I know."

Trammel knew he had never been good at sarcasm, and Hawkeye's reaction only proved it. "What is it, then?"

"A fancy lady just rode into town," Hawkeye told him. "Didn't come in on the stage either. Came in riding a freighter packed to the gills with stuff. Has this big black fella with her, too. Bigger than you, even. He doesn't talk much, but his face says plenty on its own. All scarred up and such. Scariest man I've ever seen."

Given that Hawkeye had spent his entire life in Blackstone, Trammel did not think much of his judgment on that score. Still, a new arrival made him curious. "Know what they're doing here?"

"They've moved into one of those new buildings Mr. Hagen opened up the street," Hawkeye said. "Mr. Robertson said they rode into town a little while ago."

Trammel was less than pleased. The last thing Blackstone needed was another saloon. He walked over to the stove and poured himself another cup of coffee. It was still hot, and now that they had new grounds, he could make himself a fresh pot. "What'll they call this place?"

"I knew that even before Mr. Robertson did," Hawkeye boasted. "I saw the sign they're going to hang over the door. It was lashed to the side of the wagon. It's a pretty name, too. 'The Gilded Lily.' "

Trammel almost dropped the cup. "What did you just say?"

"I said it's called 'the Gilded Lily.' " Hawkeye looked at his boss. "At least that's what the sign said. Why? You know it?"

"Know it?" Trammel said as he grabbed his hat off the rack and pulled it on his head. "I used to work there."

He slammed the jailhouse door as he went to see if it was really her.

Just when he thought his life couldn't get more complicated, Lilly comes back into his life.

He cast a look up to the sky and spoke to whoever might be listening. "You sure like to keep things interesting, don't you?"

Chapter 7

He saw Miss Lilly Maine standing on the boardwalk at the new section of Main Street that Adam Hagen had bought and built upon. It was a corner building that Hagen had built with a saloon in mind if he could find the right tenant for it.

It looked like Hagen had done precisely that, only this time he reached back into their shared past and chose her.

Trammel was glad she had not changed much in the year or so since he had fled Wichita. He imagined a year was not very long, but the journey from Kansas to Wyoming was not an easy one. So much time spent traveling and camping could take a toll on someone as delicate as Miss Lilly. She still sported a nest of black, curly hair pinned up beneath a violet hat that matched the color of her dress. Her complexion was what some might call dusky and she had been mistaken for Mexican many times while Trammel had worked for her. She told everyone her grandparents were from a place called Belgium, and although Trammel knew it was over in Europe, he did not know exactly where. He did not care where it was, though he had always been grateful that her ancestors had come to America.

The Gilded Lily Saloon had been a refuge for Trammel when he had left his old life behind and headed west. Miss Lilly had given him a job as the bouncer in the saloon that bore her name. He had only worked there for a year before his troubles with the Bowman clan forced him to run. But that year had felt like a lifetime to Trammel. It had allowed his conscience to heal and reminded him that there was more to life than killing. He had feared he might forget that upon coming to Blackstone with Hagen, but he had not.

He remembered the kindness she had shown him when others only feared him. A gentle breeze along Main Street carried the subtle scent of the rosewater she favored since the day he had told her he liked it.

And although they had never been lovers, Trammel had always thought of them as being together.

It was not until she turned and looked his way that he realized he had been standing there gawking at her like a fool.

Her entire face brightened, and he felt himself smiling. "Steve? Is that you?"

She was running to him before he could answer her and wrapped her arms around his middle. "It is you!"

Although they were in public, he returned her embrace. She was half his height and the feather from her hat grazed his chin.

Lilly pulled away from him. "Oh, it's so good to see you again." She pulled him down and planted a kiss on his cheek. "I hope you won't hold it against me, but Adam and I wanted this to be a surprise."

He remembered Hagen had told him there would be some new surprises in town, but he had never counted on Lilly being one of them. "I certainly wasn't expecting to see *you.* What made you leave Wichita?"

"Business dried up," she said. "Your run-ins with the Bowman family set the whole town against me. At first it was good for business. Everyone wanted to have a drink at the saloon where Trammel and Hagen once were. But after your dustup with the Pinkertons, the Bowman family cursed me and told everyone to stay away from my place. They still had a lot of sway in town, so that meant I was all finished in Kansas. I'd heard Adam was building up the town and looking for a couple of new saloon keepers for Main Street. So I packed up the whole place, loaded the sign on a freighter, and here I am."

He took a closer look at her and could not believe what he saw. "You don't look like you've just spent a lot of time on the trail to me."

"Oh, I didn't," she told him. "Adam paid for me and Big Ben here, to load our freight on the train to Laramie. We unloaded the freighter and came straight here."

That was when Trammel noticed the large Negro man unloading the sign from the side of the freighter. For once, Hawkeye had not exaggerated what he saw. The man was at least Trammel's size, maybe bigger. He hauled the long sign into the saloon as if he was carrying a single piece of wood.

"He sure is strong," Trammel observed.

"He had to be. I had to find someone to replace you after you left me in the lurch like you did." She linked her arm through his and pulled on him to follow her, which he gladly did. "Come, let me introduce you to him and show you the new place. We've only just begun to unload our things, of course, but we should be ready to open in a day or two."

She pressed her face against his biceps and

gave him a good squeeze. "God, it's good to see you again, Steve."

She made him glad to be seen. "They call me Buck around here. That was Hagen's idea. Said no one was afraid of anyone named Steve."

"Then Buck it is, except when we're alone." She remained close to him as they walked past the vacant buildings Hagen had just built. The air was thick with the pleasant smell of fresh-cut wood and sawdust. "Adam told me you've had quite a rough time of it since you got here. One bit of trouble after another."

Trammel was curious. "Sounds like Adam told you a lot."

"You know him. Drunk or sober, he was always talking about one thing or another. Sometimes I think he talks just to hear the sound of his own voice. But he writes the most charming letters. He should write a book one of these days. He's got quite a gift for storytelling."

"And for causing some of that trouble he wrote you about," Trammel said. "What kind of place are you planning on opening, anyway?"

"Same as back in Wichita," she told him. "Plenty of good whiskey and card tables. Might even put in a roulette wheel if Adam can get one for me. He said he knows of an old paddle wheel in New Orleans that's no longer fit for the water. He put in a bid on it for me and we should know if we got it any day now." She squeezed him again. "Oh, it's just like old times again, isn't it, Steve? You and me and Adam together again. Only this time it'll be better. Quieter and happy."

But Trammel knew the old times were not so old. He had only worked for her for a little more than a year, and Hagen had only lived at the old Gilded Lily for a short time before they got run out of town. He remembered it as a bland, endless time of minding drunks and gambling tables. It had been a healing time for him, so if that was something she considered good, it was just fine in his book. Her moods had always been infectious for him, especially when she was happy.

But her dealings with Hagen concerned him. "Sounds like you and Adam have gotten awfully close."

She stopped walking and pulled him up short. She had a mischievous look in her hazel eyes. "Why, Sheriff Trammel. Did I just hear a hint of jealousy in your voice?"

He did not want to offend her on her first day in town. "No. Just curious, is all."

She let out a heavy sigh and pulled him along with her again. "I see we still have to work on your more charming qualities. And to answer your question, any connection between Adam and me is on a strictly business basis. He needed a saloon keeper and I needed a saloon, so here I am." She dropped her voice to a whisper as she said, "But knowing you were here was all the inducement I needed to come to Wyoming."

He felt himself blush and was glad to see Big Ben walk out onto the boardwalk and stop when he saw them.

"Ah, perfect timing!" Lilly exclaimed. "Steve — I mean Buck Trammel — meet Big Ben London, your replacement."

Now that they were closer, Trammel could see just how big the man was. He stood about six-feet-eight-inches tall and was built like a mountain. He saw the scars on his face that Hawkeye had told him about, and imagined each one of them hurt. His left eye was clouded over, and he wondered if he could still see through it. His neck bore a nasty set of scars that Trammel knew was either from a rope or a chain around his neck. He would have wagered the man had once been a slave or had been lynched at one point in his life. Trammel did not know which and did not need to know. Either way, this man had seen his share of pain in his life and had survived it.

Trammel extended a hand to him and said, "Pleasure to meet you. Hope you've been taking care of Lilly, here."

Ben shook his hand, but applied more pressure than Trammel had counted on. Seeing it clearly as a test of strength, Trammel replied in kind and saw a flash of pain on the big man's face.

They let go at the same time.

Lilly had seen the contest, but clearly chose to ignore it. "Don't hold Ben's silence against him. He hasn't been able to speak since before he fled Georgia." She rubbed the big man's arm. "He's been my special project, though. Taught him how to read and write. Now he writes beautifully, don't you, Ben?"

He nodded to her and offered what Trammel figured was his version of a smile. "Why don't you go back to unloading the wagon? Mr. Hagen is supposed to send some men along to help us in a while."

Ben gave Trammel a final look before going back to work. It was not a vicious look, but it was not a look of deference either. After all the man had endured, Trammel doubted he gave ground to any man.

Lilly pulled Trammel into the saloon.

"Don't let his demeanor fool you. He's actually a gentle giant. Harmless most of the time. Well, almost gentle, unless trouble starts."

Trammel did not doubt it. "A man his size has a way of stopping trouble before it even starts."

"Some of my customers in Kansas objected to his presence on account of him being black, but I didn't mind losing their business. Adam said the people of Blackstone are far more open-minded."

"Depends on who you're talking about," Trammel said. "We've got good and bad here, just like in any other town."

She led him through the doorway of her new saloon and finally let him go. "Well? Take a look at her and tell me what you think."

Trammel had always thought saloons all looked alike, but he had never seen one as brand-new as this. The bar looked to be made of mahogany, as was the frame of the mirror behind it. The brass footrail gleamed, and the floor did not have a hint of sawdust. The green felt on the card tables was clean and devoid of cigar burns or liquor stains.

The banister that led to the rooms upstairs sported a newel post with a cherub carved on top of it. Several chandeliers sporting cut glass hung high above the place. As his eyes continued upward past the rooms upstairs, he saw the roof had clear windows that allowed light to shine down into the place during the day.

Trammel knew he was looking at something special, for the moment the place was opened to the public, it would never look this good again.

He said the first thing that came to his mind. "Beats the hell out of what you had in Kansas."

"Doesn't it, though?" Lilly beamed. "This is going to be a real classy place, Steve. The kind of place I've always wanted, and now I have it." She hugged him again. "God, I can't remember ever being this happy."

And as she looked up at him, he forgot about all that had happened with Hagen and Bookman and Mike Albertson's rabble-rousing. Kissing her felt like the most natural thing in the world, and that was exactly what he did.

He was glad when she slipped her hand behind his head and pulled him down to her, kissing him deeply.

He didn't know how long they had been kissing, though he was dizzy when they stopped.

He felt himself redden. "Sorry about that.

I don't know what came over me."

She placed a slender finger to his lips, just as she'd done the day he had fled Wichita with Hagen. "That kiss was a long time in coming, Sheriff." She ran her finger along his jaw. "Too long. When I watched you two ride away, I promised myself I'd show you how I felt about you the next time I saw you. That promise helped me get through some awfully rough patches this past year."

Trammel did not know what to say because he had never heard those words before, at least not from anyone directing them his way. The words of dance-hall girls and painted doves did not count. Their affections were fleeting and stirred by the money in his pocket that would soon be theirs.

But Lilly had no reason to say such words unless she meant it. And he was awfully glad she had.

She arched her back to look up at him. "What's that look for? You seem troubled." An idea dawned on her. "There's not someone else, is there? Because if there is, I'm not asking you to leave her."

"There's no one," he admitted. "Not anymore."

She put her head against his chest over his heart. "Good, because her loss is my gain. There's no reason for anything to come between us now. Not the Bowman family or Pinkertons or even those damned Earp boys. Blackstone belongs to us now. Just you and me."

He held her as tightly as he dared, the feather in her hat be damned. If it were only that simple.

He hated ruining the moment, but knew he'd never be able to sleep that night if he did not speak his mind. "There is one thing that's bothering me."

"I already know what you're going to say and don't worry," she said sleepily. "I found us a great big bed that'll be plenty comfortable for both of us. And you can hate me for being too sure of myself, but I don't care."

He gently eased her away from him and held on to her shoulders. "That's not it. When I asked you what kind of place you were planning on running here, you didn't really answer me."

"Sure, I did," she told him. "It'll be a much better place than the old one. Table games. A roulette wheel if Adam can get one for me. I've got a source for better liquor that'll be shipped here all the way from San Francisco. After we open and I see how the place is doing, I plan on having a few girls working the floor if I can find the right sort. If not, I'll rent out the rooms upstairs to upstanding folk. Why do you ask?"

Trammel was growing frustrated with his inability to speak his mind. "I'm not talking about that either. I'm asking about your arrangement with Hagen. What are the details you agreed to with him?"

Lilly thought about it for a moment. "He's not charging me rent for the first two months until the place gets up and running, if that's what you're asking. After that, it'll be forty percent of the take. If that take goes above a certain number, I won't have to pay rent. I don't know the exact dollar amount, but it's not much." She ran her finger along his jaw again. "Why the concern?"

"Did he say anything about pushing laudanum here?" Trammel finally managed to spit it out. "He's been selling laudanum out of the Pot of Gold down the street and he's got a laudanum den set up in a tent behind the saloon. Has he talked about having you run anything like that here?"

"Not a word," Lilly said, "and he'd better not try. I hate those places. Damned smoke always gives me the worst headache."

Trammel smiled, really smiled, for the first time since Emily threw him over. "Good.

I'm glad to hear you say that. Just make sure you don't give in to him. You know how he can be. He could sell salt water to a sea captain."

"Don't worry, Sheriff. There's only one man in town who could talk me into anything, and I'm looking at him."

She went on her tiptoes and whispered in his ear, "You know, I can get some of the boys to set up the bed right now if you want."

Trammel kissed her again and let her go. "What I want and what I've got to do are two different things. Right now, duty calls. But I'll be back later on tonight to check on things."

He smiled as he touched the brim of his hat to her. "Afternoon, Miss Lilly."

She curtsied. "And to you, Sheriff Trammel."

He walked out of the new Gilded Lily and saw ten of Hagen's men had shown up to help Ben unload the wagon. They were in awe of how easily he moved the barrels of goods that took two of them to carry.

He caught Ben's eye and nodded to him as he passed. He thought Ben nodded back but couldn't be certain.

Chapter 8

Adam Hagen flexed his right arm before he pulled on his shirt. It was the first time he had attempted to dress alone in months. One of his painted doves had been helping him dress since the shooting, but today was a special day. He had serious business to discuss with a serious man.

The constant pain that had been with him since the shooting had begun to dull over the past month or so, and his strength had returned. He imagined Dr. Downs would have been impressed by his progress had he allowed her to examine him, but he had not. He had other plans for his own recovery that served his purpose beyond the fair Miss Emily.

His right hand shook as he began to button his shirt, but he willed his fingers to work. He was drenched in sweat by the time he was done and had to dry himself with a towel. A wave of dizziness from the pain caused him to sit in a chair until it passed.

He'd never imagined something so routine as buttoning a shirt would be so taxing, but he had never been shot in the shoulder before.

When he opened his eyes, he was glad the room had stopped spinning. He found himself looking out his front window and at the Hagen ranch house in the distant hill-side. The very sight of the place was enough to spur him on to finish getting dressed. Adam Hagen had learned the hard way that hate was an effective painkiller.

Pulling on his pants had proved less try-ing than the shirt, but trying to pull on his boots almost killed him. It took him more than half an hour of trying a variety of angles before he got them both on. He counted the fact that he had not ruined their shine as something of a victory.

He removed the Colt Thunderer from its holster and placed it on the bureau. The absence of the gun made the belt lighter and easier for him to buckle. By the time he had finished tying down his holster, he found his right arm ached less than it had in a long time. The endless hours he had spent squeezing the bag of sand had worked.

He held out his right hand before him and tried to keep it steady. He was able to do so for about ten seconds before it began to shake and the pain returned. *Tomorrow I'll try for twenty seconds. After all, Rome wasn't built in a day.*

He took the gun from the bureau and holstered it. The sound of gunmetal against fine leather almost made him feel whole.

He checked his reflection in the mirror one final time before he went downstairs to greet his guest. He looked better than he had since the shooting. His skin looked healthier. His eyes were brighter, and his cheeks weren't as fallow as they had been only last week. One would have to look especially hard to see the white bands of hair among the blond. He would be wearing his hat the whole time anyway, so his guest would be none the wiser.

He straightened his tie and straightened his vest and made sure his suit coat fell just right. He was still thinner than he ought to be and the clothes looked big on him. He was glad his guest was a cunning man but not necessarily an observant one.

Hagen raised his chin and spoke to his reflection, something he had not done since his days as a cadet at West Point. "You are not sick. You are the picture of health. You are the topman. You will win."

His voice was strong. And his wink was as

sharp as ever. It should be enough to win the day.

Deciding he looked as good as he could manage, he went downstairs to greet his guest. He had kept him waiting for more than half an hour, which was by design. If their partnership was to work, Lucien Clay would need to know his place.

As expected, he found Lucien Clay pacing in the lobby of the Clifford Hotel. Hagen smiled, though not for Clay's benefit. It was for himself, and the fact that making him cool his spurs waiting for him had produced the desired result.

"Lucien, my friend," Hagen said as he reached the final step. "Forgive me for being late, but I had important business that needed tending to."

Clay stopped pacing and looked him over, as if he was one of the prospective sporting gals he hired to work for him in Laramie. "Good to see you up and around, Adam. You're looking well."

Clay seemed surprised that Hagen offered to shake hands. Hagen was glad he was able to mask the spike of pain when they did.

"I've never been better," Hagen lied. "The rest did me some good. Gave me the chance to do an awful lot of thinking, and I know you'll be happy with the results." He gestured toward the door. "Shall we begin our tour?"

Hagen followed Clay out onto the boardwalk, and they began walking toward the section the locals had already taken to calling New Main Street.

He saw Clay take his measure again as they walked, only this time he was more subtle about it. "I've got to admit that I didn't expect to find you in such good condition, Hagen. How are you? And tell the truth. Don't try to put a shine on it."

Hagen had no intention of telling Clay the truth, especially because the truth would only benefit Clay. "I've been shot before, Lucien, but will probably be shot again. It hurt like hell, but believe me when I tell you, I'm the better for it. The entire experience has served to make me sharper and stronger in the long run, as you'll see in the course of our visit."

Hagen spotted a black coach with gold trim and a four-horse team parked just in front of the hotel. It bore a gold "LC" on the black door. He took this to be Lucien Clay's private coach. "I assume that one's yours?"

"It certainly is," Clay said proudly. "I got it last month. Figured a man in my position deserves a bit of luxury. After all, what good is having all this money if you don't spend it?"

"A wonderful sentiment," Hagen said. *Put a beggar on horseback and he'll ride to hell.* "I'm glad you're already enjoying the fruits of our partnership. If our luck holds out, you'll be able to have one of those waiting for you at the train station at each of the towns we control."

"Luck?" Clay repeated. "This isn't about luck. This is about us doing what we want to do. Controlling what will happen before anyone else does it for us."

"There's always a certain amount of luck required in any successful enterprise," Hagen said. He loved talking to Clay in a fancier manner than usual. He hoped it served as a subtle reminder that he was just a jumped-up saloon keeper and that was all he would ever be. "But I suppose you're right. Luck doesn't acquire property or drive nails into wood. It takes money and men to do that." He nudged Clay with his left shoulder. "Men like us."

A ragged man stumbled toward them on the boardwalk, and Clay managed to move out of the way just before he walked into him. "Don't like to see that kind of thing, though. Saw half a dozen just like that as we rode in here. A thing like that pulls down a town like this, Adam. I don't like it."

"But you like the profit they bring us, don't you?" Hagen answered. "It's all part of our plan, Lucien. I believe there's an old Chinese saying, 'Out of chaos comes opportunity.' Or something like that."

Clay did not look impressed. "Hope you didn't get that from one of the Chinamen who are supposed to be selling our dope. They should keep their mind on business, not fancy sayings."

"Never fear," Hagen assured him. "Our Celestial friends are keeping their nose to the grindstone. How being surrounded by laudanum fumes all day and night hasn't baked their brains is beyond me, but they seem to be managing nicely."

By then they had reached the Pot of Gold and Hagen stopped walking. He gestured down the alley to the canvas tent. "Would you like to see it for yourself?"

Clay squinted as he looked down the alley and scowled. "With all the building we're doing in town, I'd expected you to build them a better setup than that."

"I certainly offered," Hagen told him. "I even insisted, but our Celestial friends declined. They said they own the canvas and everything that goes on in it. I was hesitant at first, but they're making more money for us than ever before, so I'm inclined to let them have their own way for now."

"And where's all this new money coming from anyway?" Clay asked. "Your letters have been pretty vague on details."

"But our balance sheet is decisively clear," Hagen reminded him. "My father fired twenty of our best customers. He paid them a generous wage, which most of them eventually spent in our saloon, drinking our whiskey and using our women. Whatever they had left over was spent in that canvas tent you look down upon." Hagen looked down the alley with the pride of a new father. "Yes, sir. You may see filthy canvas, but I see a golden palace down there. It's bigger than it looks, too. They've had to double the size of the place in the past month."

Clay did not look impressed. "Those wages he gave them must be all dried up by now. Cowhands have never been good at holding on to their money, thank God. Where's the rest of it coming from?"

"Miners in the hills are our best customers now," Hagen said as they resumed their walk. "Father has forbidden anyone in his employ from visiting our saloons and our laudanum den, but he allows them to frequent the Queen Victoria and the Firebrand

Saloons."

Clay looked puzzled. "But we own them, too, don't we?"

"Most certainly" — Hagen grinned — "but my father doesn't know that." He hated referring to Charles Hagen as his father, but Lucien did not know the truth, and Hagen saw no reason to enlighten him. "His hold on the town is on the wane and he knows it, not that he'll ever admit it. Besides, his attentions are required elsewhere."

"That so?" Clay asked. "Like where? Not Laramie, I hope."

Hagen almost laughed at the ignorant fool. "Don't worry, Lucien. He has cast his gaze at prizes far from this humble patch of land. My brothers are representing his interests in steel and railroads. One of them is even down in Texas on a venture to bring up oil from the ground. Not even King Charles himself can run everything by himself, so we have been able to use his distraction to our benefit."

Clay glowered at a townsman who looked at them too long. The man quickly stepped off the boardwalk and into the thoroughfare as they passed by. He lowered his voice when he said, "That's another thing you've been awfully vague about. Just how do you plan on pulling him off his throne. He still seems to be dug in pretty deep in these parts."

But Hagen would not be rushed and had no intention of discussing the topic on the street, where anyone could hear. "Patience, my friend, patience. Let us enjoy our first steps on New Main Street and bask in the warmth of what we have wrought."

Clay's failed attempts to mask his confusion over what Hagen was saying was priceless and made his right arm ache a little less.

He gestured toward the Queen Victoria Saloon, which was doing a fair business although it was not yet noon. "This is the first of our contributions to Blackstone's entertainment needs. The locals call it 'the Vic,' which was unintended, but has a certain charm. Here, we peddle mostly beer and whiskey, and the occasional laudanum now and then."

"Why not laudanum?" Clay asked.

"Because it's a substance that can quickly get out of hand, as you saw earlier when one of our customers almost walked into you. The Celestials like to keep it contained."

"Trammel wants it contained, too." Clay grinned. "See, you're not the only one who hears things, Adam. I've got eyes and ears in places, too."

Hagen had never doubted it for a moment. In fact, he had a pretty good idea who it might be, too, though only time would prove if he was right. "I'm sure you do. It's only prudent that you would want an independent report on your investments."

They walked a bit farther, past a vacant storefront, to the Firebrand Saloon. "This place caters to a more rustic crowd. No gambling in here either. Only at our last stop on the tour. The locals refer to it as 'the Brand,' and I must admit I like it, too. The customers are often of the harder luck variety. I laid it out in a particular order."

He gestured Clay to follow where he was pointing. "The Clifford is strictly a hotel and caters to a more refined crowd. Mostly people who come to town to do business with my father. The mining concerns and the like. Then we come to the Pot of Gold. A decent place, but the main attraction is laudanum. When they can't afford whiskey in the saloon, they end up at the Vic in between their trips on the dragon's back. When their prices become too dear, they wind up here at the Brand."

"And where do they go after that?" Clay asked.

"The gutter, which is according to the plan we'll discuss over a bottle of fine whiskey at our final stop." He motioned toward the Gilded Lily. "Shall we?"

But Clay would not be rushed. He pointed at the empty storefront between the two saloons. "Why's this space empty? What are you putting in there?"

Hagen had not forgotten about it. He just had not counted on Clay caring enough to ask. "That is where I plan to have the doctor's office."

"Doctor's office? This town's already got a doc in the Downs widow. How much medicine does a place this size need?"

Hagen placed his hand on Clay's back and gently urged him forward. "Miss Emily is a fine doctor, but she's not really a doctor. She's a fine nurse. An apprentice doctor at best, and was a good student of whatever her late husband taught her. She may be the town doctor, but she isn't our doctor. My new man will belong to us. Part and parcel owned by us."

Clay did not look any less confused. "What the hell do we need with a doctor?"

Hagen grinned. "All part of that plan I told you we'd talk about in a bit."

Hagen saw Michael Albertson, the rabble-rouser, out for a stroll with Old Lady

Higgins. They spotted each other at the same time and, with a pat of Mrs. Higgins's hand, Albertson stormed toward them. And judging by the fire in his eye, he was about to give them a loud lecture about corrupting the town.

Hagen decided to have some fun with the blowhard before he got started. "Mr. Clay, I beg you to pause for a moment and behold a truly righteous man. The cornerstone upon which our humble village has built its conscience and turns to in times of moral corruption and strife."

Albertson stopped in the middle of the thoroughfare and waggled his finger at the two men. "Don't you dare mock me, you vulture. How can you show your face in the light of day? Just look at what you've done to this town. You, with your whiskey and women and laudanum. Poisoning the minds of good men with good jobs only to pull them down to your level. You're a scoundrel, sir. And I'd call you worse, still, if a fine woman of substance wasn't within earshot of my words."

Hagen admired the old fool's bravery. He told Clay, "Listen to him and listen to him well. For this man is the very embodiment of Michael, the archangel himself, sent by the Good Lord above to smite us sinners in

His holy name. An old freighter hand who lay down his reins in the hopes that he might one day reign at His right hand in Heaven above."

Albertson spat in their general direction, but, Hagen noted, not too close. He wasn't a complete fool.

"A pox on you, Mr. Hagen. A pox on you and your house." He looked at Clay. "And to any man who joins you. I take it this man's a friend of yours."

Hagen knew Clay's temper and did not want to risk it getting the better of him. Albertson certainly deserved a beating, but it would only serve to make him more popular than he already was. People loved a martyr.

"Let's go, Lucien. Sinners like us are not fit to be in the presence of such pious company."

Hagen was glad Clay seemed more amused by Albertson than annoyed by him, especially when the man continued to wish a pox upon them as they walked away.

"Mouthy old coot, isn't he?" Clay observed. "He really gets people following him with that fire-and-brimstone nonsense?"

"Thirty or more last I counted," Hagen told him. "In a town this size, that's a good number. They can't do much on their own, but the *Blackstone Bugle* covers their marches. It's only a matter of time before his antics get picked up by one of the Laramie papers, and when it does, we might find ourselves tripping over Bible thumpers wherever we go."

"I've got a handle on the press in Laramie," Clay said. "I'll make sure any mention of Albertson's antics gets stopped quickly. I'll have a word with the editor as soon as I get back to town."

Funny, Hagen thought. *I never mentioned Michael Albertson's last name.* Maybe it was nothing. Maybe it was everything. "Come, let's forget about him, and let me show you the houses we're building on Buffalo Street. It'll help us change the town forever."

An hour later, as they shared a bottle of fine whiskey in the refined surroundings of the Gilded Lily, he could tell Lucien Clay was impressed. Not just with the interior of the saloon, but by all that he had seen that day.

"I've got to hand it to you, Adam. I didn't think much of your plan when we joined up, but now that I've had the chance to lay eyes on it, I sure do like what I see."

Hagen was glad. Clay's opinion meant nothing to him, but his continued participation in their partnership did. For without it, he would be hard-pressed to pull King

Charles Hagen from his throne. But once that happened, Lucien Clay's opinion would be worthless.

"I'm glad you're pleased," Hagen said. "Those houses should attract a lot more people to town when they're finished. People we'll need on our side in the months to come."

Hagen looked around to see if anyone was close enough to hear them. No one was there except for Big Ben London, helping the bartender stock new bottles behind the bar. And his father's attorney and president of the Blackstone Bank, Mr. Frederick Montague, having a quiet drink by himself at a table close to the bar.

"But I still don't understand the reason for building all them new houses. And the saloons, too, for that matter. This place is beautiful, and I get why you built the other two dumps. But where are all the people going to come from? Your father's cowhands and the miners can only drink or smoke so much. We've paid for an awful lot of new buildings here, Adam. I'd like to know why."

Hagen decided he had kept his partner in the dark long enough. Any further delay would only agitate him, perhaps make him withdraw his support. Hagen may have inherited Madam Pinochet's collection of corrupt officials and businesses, but influence only went so far without something to back it up. Hagen had no choice but to level with him.

"The best way to destroy a house is from beneath it," he explained. "Ruin the foundation and the whole thing becomes unstable. Cracks begin to form and the building will fall in on itself. That's what we're doing now with my father's hold on the town."

"You keep saying that, but I don't see how."

Hagen was only too glad to tell him. "He fired twenty men and hired on thirty from a ranch he controls in Nebraska. He's paying them twice what he paid the old hands, which not only galls him to no end but also makes him spend more than he planned. My father is nothing if not a planner. He's also threatened to fire all the miners in his employ, but that didn't go as planned. Miners are a close bunch, and the lot of them threatened to strike if he dared fire a man just because he happened to smoke laudanum. He's still trying to force the issue, but continues to meet resistance, which only frustrates him further."

"Yeah, but —"

Hagen talked over him. "The rest of the mines in the area are owned by smaller concerns, or by men who have independent claims. None of them are as big as my father's holdings on their own, but together, they're more than enough to compete with his production." He raised his glass and toasted Clay. "And we're going to own them. All of them."

"How?"

"By having them sign the titles of their mines over to us in exchange for credit at our gambling houses and the laudanum den at the Pot of Gold. Their vices are our reward."

"That's it? That's your grand plan?" Clay lost all color in his face. He downed the remaining whiskey in his glass and quickly poured himself another. "You mean to tell me you've put our money at risk on the chance that all of this might happen the way you say it will?"

"Don't be ridiculous," Hagen said. "I only started after we already controlled a good number of the mines. I've been a gambler long enough to bet only on a sure thing. I'm hurt you'd think otherwise." He winked. "I think I might even cry."

Clay shook his head, as if to clear it. "Are you telling me we're already in the mining business?"

"My friend, you've been in the mining

business since the moment you agreed to work with me," Hagen told him. "We had a quarter of the deeds to good mines back then. We own more than half of the independents now, with the promise of more to come by the end of the month. Word has spread among them that I'm very fair to deal with. I let them work their claims for a ridiculously low fee and let them drink and smoke all they want for free. The whiskey and laudanum are overpriced anyway. The Celestials complained when businesses started issuing chits for free smokes, so I let them have a larger share. They're stealing from us anyway, but the vices are but a means to an end. As things stand, The Blackstone Mining Company is already the second-largest mining concern in the territory. When the rest of them sign over their shares to us, we'll be bigger than the Hagen Mining Company, and the tide will begin to turn in our favor."

Clay looked at him from across the table as all he had just learned began to settle. "So that's where the extra money has been coming from. The mines we own. I was wondering why the numbers didn't add up."

"We've gotten them hooked on our vices so we can gain control of legitimate businesses. Father has lost twenty good men and is overpaying for good hands far away from home. Despite his edict, a fair number of them have visited the Celestials. I've made sure our friends from the Far East moderate their consumption. We don't want to use them up quite yet."

"But now you've got another problem," Clay said. "The town's full of men high on our product."

Hagen was not surprised Clay was so slow to grasp the situation. "That's not our problem. That's Trammel's problem. He's so busy trying to sweep the dirt off the streets that by the time we're ready to take down my father, he'll be in no position to stop us. He's a good man. A big man, but he's still only a man, and everyone has their limits. The busier he is cleaning up after us, the better off we are."

Hagen enjoyed watching Clay ponder all the news he had just given him. His partner was a blunt and deliberate man. He did not have the mind for nuance, which was exactly why Hagen had thrown in with him. He was like the meat cleavers the Chinese bouncers used to protect the den, while Hagen was the dagger that pierced the heart of the beast. Both had their own roles to play, depending on the situation.

Clay still did not appear to comprehend

the situation. "So, what does all of this have to do with the houses we've built? Or these saloons? And how are you going to bring down your father?"

Hagen knew they would eventually get around to discussing this, the most delicate part of his plan. He had spent many hours wondering how much he should tell Lucien Clay. He ultimately decided that holding anything back from him could cost him Clay's support just when he needed it most. It was a gamble, but he laid his cards on the table.

"The Blackstone Ranch runs cattle and horses," Hagen reminded him. "The biggest herds of each in Wyoming. While cattle and horses are profitable, they're quite susceptible to conditions of the lungs. All it takes is one infected animal to spread it to the rest of the herd." He examined his nails. "It's been known to ruin even the biggest ranches in a matter of weeks. I'm afraid a similar fate will befall my father's ranch very soon, courtesy of the efforts of our Celestial friends. The Chinese are an ancient and deadly people, particularly when there's a profit in it for them."

Clay's reaction surprised him. "Are you out of your mind?" Hagen noticed Montague and Ben look over at them and he gestured for Clay to lower his voice.

Clay complied. "What happens when he brings all that livestock to market? They'll infect every other animal they're penned in with. You'll kill off an entire industry!"

Hagen shook his head. The poor slob was so ignorant, it was almost comical. "My father will cull his herds and bring them down to be shipped out of Laramie next week. A large number of his ranch hands will go with them, leaving the ranch relatively unguarded. Our Celestial friends will poison the drinking water for the cattle and for the horses. Only the remaining animals will be affected. His best breeders."

Clay sat back in his chair. "Oh."

"Some of them will undoubtedly survive," Hagen admitted, "but not nearly enough to save him. A former cavalryman like me hates the thought of hurting an animal, particularly the horses, but I'm afraid it can't be helped. A greater purpose and all that."

"Your old man will be in a fine fix after that."

"To say the least," Hagen said. "Some of these diseases have been known to jump to humans and I hope it'll happen in his case, but I doubt it. That old varmint won't have the decency to die so easily, but that part of this is my affair." He fixed Clay with a steady glare. "I'm afraid I'm going to have to insist on keeping that part from you, Lucien."

"Of course," Clay said absently as he picked up his glass but didn't drink from it. He was too deep in thought to drink just then. Hagen imagined he was digesting all he had just heard, trying to find a flaw in it. He envisioned his partner's mind to be like a maze where a mouse hunted in vain for the cheese he could smell but could not see.

Clay sipped his whiskey, which seemed to revive him. "You're going to need muscle to pull this off in case something goes wrong. This plan of yours has a lot of holes in it and you'll get caught short if things get rough. You were a hell of a gunfighter for a gambler in your day, Adam, but with that right arm being as it is, you'll need some help. I've got some real choice boys I can send up here to help you. No offense, of course."

"None taken," Hagen lied. For when all this was over and he was finally in charge of his family's kingdom, Lucien Clay and the rest of the world would know that his injury had only made him more dangerous than he ever was.

"But I think I'll decline your generous offer for now, Lucien. Your concerns have been noted and are already well in hand."

Clay set his drink on the table. "I sure hope you're not going to rely on those Chinese characters to have your back if things get tough. They stick to their own."

Hagen chanced a glance at his ace in the hole. Big Ben was busying himself behind the bar, ever the loyal employee to Miss Lilly Maine. But before he had worked for her, Ben had served as his bodyguard, back when he worked the riverboats on the Mississippi. He had remained loyal to Hagen since the day Hagen had killed the man who had once owned him and still considered him his property. He had even been loyal enough to travel to Wichita and work for Lilly when Hagen had asked him to.

"Like I said, Lucien. I appreciate the concern, but it's all well in hand." He filled their glasses and proposed a toast. "To a future of our own making."

Chapter 9

Up in Lilly's room, Trammel stood by the window that looked out on Main Street. He saw the fancy black-and-gold coach parked up near the jail and wondered whose it might be. It was not a funeral coach and it was not the regular stage that ran from Laramie to Blackstone and farther north to Dutch Springs. That meant it must be a private coach, which baffled him. Why would anyone who could afford their own coach be in Blackstone?

There was only one reason why: Adam Hagen. As for who the owner might be, Trammel intended to find out right now.

"What time is it?" Lilly asked sleepily from the bed they had shared.

Trammel tucked his shirt into his pants. "Time for me to go to work. Go back to sleep. You've still got a few hours left before the evening rush begins."

"Then why are you leaving?" she asked. "I

thought you and Hawkeye switched shifts so you could have days with me."

"I did, but something's come up that needs tending to." He patted her leg after he shrugged into his shoulder holster. "Rest. I'll come back up here before my shift starts if I can."

He had switched shifts with Hawkeye in the month since Lilly had come to town. When he was not working, he was with her for as long as he could manage it. He began to feel guilty about leaving the young man with so much responsibility so suddenly, but it could not be helped. Lilly had a hold on him now that would be mighty tough to break. He did not care any less for the well-being of the town, but he found himself caring more for her with each passing day.

He gave her one last look in the darkened room before he headed out to do what the good people of Blackstone paid him to do. And as he shut the door quietly, he felt a powerful sense of guilt overwhelm him. Lilly had made him greedy and selfish. She had made him think of himself for a change, instead of only the town. No one else had ever affected him this way, not even Emily Downs. Maybe it was because Emily and he were both equally interested in the well-being of the town and its citizens, whereas

Lilly only cared about her saloon. As long as Hagen got his piece of the profit from the place, nothing that happened beyond the front door of the Gilded Lily mattered to her.

As he walked down the stairs to the saloon, Trammel wondered if he was becoming the same way. Had his focus narrowed so much that all he cared about was Lilly? Did he care too much for her to do his job properly?

He rounded the last flight of stairs and heard the unmistakable cackle that could only belong to Adam Hagen. He continued down the remaining steps, fully expecting to be noticed by Hagen and whoever he was drinking with.

He was not disappointed.

"Now would you just look at that," Hagen boomed to the empty saloon. "Our fearless champion rising at the crack of noon to tend to his duties. After an evening of many splendors with the proprietress of this establishment, no doubt."

He had no choice but to go see what Hagen was up to. He walked through the saloon and saw that it was not completely empty. Big Ben was helping the new bartender set up the place for the evening. Fred Montague, the bank president, was there, too. He was drinking alone at a table by the bar. That was all wrong to Trammel. Montague liked his whiskey as much as the next man in town, but he never came in before noon. Seeing him drinking alone so early in the day seemed strange. But maybe not so strange, because Adam Hagen was there.

He walked to the table where the fair-haired Hagen was sharing a bottle of whiskey with the darker and dour Lucien Clay. At least now he knew where the fancy coach had come from. Clay had always been about as subtle as a dead dog in the middle of Main Street. As unavoidable as it was unpleasant.

"What are you doing here, Hagen?" Trammel asked. "It was a lot quieter around here when you were sick in bed."

"Perhaps, but it was a lot duller without me out and about." He gestured toward the dour man sitting across from him. "I'm sure you remember my guest and business partner, Mr. Lucien Clay of Laramie."

Trammel did not like the way the dark-eyed man looked up at him. He had never liked Lucien Clay to begin with. "Same question I asked Hagen goes for you, too, Clay. What are you doing here?"

"Your mind must be elsewhere, Sheriff." Clay flicked the bottle of whiskey. "What does it look like we're doing?"

"I mean what are you doing in Blackstone. I take it that fancy coach outside belongs to you."

"It certainly does," Clay sneered. "Partnering with your friend Hagen, here, has made me a very rich man. I'd tell you to smarten up and get in while the getting is good, but you're not smart enough to listen, so I won't bother."

The sass from Clay was beginning to annoy him. Trammel knew he was baiting him but did not care. "He's not my friend and neither of you have answered my question. I won't ask it again."

Hagen said, "We're discussing business, Buck. The kind of business I've already discussed with you. You're more than welcome to pull up a chair and join us. Just ask Ben for another glass and a bottle and we'll be more than happy to tell you all about it."

Trammel did not entertain the idea for a second. "No thanks, Hagen. I'm much better at fixing messes than causing them."

"Yes." Hagen looked genuinely disappointed. "I was afraid you might still think that way."

"Who needs him?" Clay said. "Besides, I got a good look at the girl who runs this place when she got off the train in Laramie.

And if I had a chance with a gal like that, I wouldn't care about much either." He looked up at Trammel. "How much is she anyway? Or does she give you a discount on account of you being the sheriff?"

Hagen slammed his fist on the table just as Trammel's temper began to rise. He was admonishing Clay for his crassness and for talking about Miss Lilly in such a deplorable manner.

But Trammel only heard bits and pieces of it over the sound of his own blood rushing in his ears.

He felt Fred Montague and Ben looking at him, which broke the spell of rage that had fallen over him.

Hagen was spilling over with apologies for Clay's behavior when Trammel's left hand shot out and snatched Clay by the throat. Trammel's hands were big enough to get a good hold of his neck on the first try.

Clay gurgled as the sheriff pulled him out of the chair, toppling it over. He tried to get his feet under him while Trammel dragged him across the saloon toward the front door. Clay held on to Trammel's arm as his heels scraped across the floor, trying in vain to wriggle free from his grip. But neither Trammel's grip nor step faltered.

Once out on the boardwalk, Trammel

pointed to the coach driver down Main Street in front of the jail.

Clay's struggles began to grow weaker as Trammel pointed at the driver and yelled, "You!" He pointed at a spot in front of him on Main Street. "Here! Now!"

The coachman released the brake and snapped his four-horse team to life. They sped along Main Street until the driver brought them up short on the spot Trammel had indicated.

The coachman was as wide-eyed as the team he drove, but when he began to climb down to help his employer, the sheriff said, "Don't!"

Trammel jerked Clay to his feet as if he were a rag doll before hurling him against the coach door. The impact was hard enough to send him bounding off the door and straight into a punchTrammel threw that connected squarely with his jaw. Clay landed flat on the boardwalk, out cold.

Trammel flung open the coach's door, grabbed Clay by the back of the pants and collar, and tossed him into the coach like he was a sack of barley. Trammel shut the door and went around to the front to confront the driver. "You as stupid as you look?"

"I — I don't think so."

"Good, because when your boss wakes up,

you be sure to give him a message from me. Tell him if he mentions Lilly again, I'll kill him. If he comes back to Blackstone, I'll kill him. If I see him in Laramie, he'd better get inside or I'll kill him. You be sure to remind him of that if his pride sets to eating at him in the next day or so. You get all that?"

"Y-y-yes, sir," the coachman stammered. "I'll remember it. All of it."

"Good. And if I see this coach in town again, I burn it, and you along with it. Now get out of here before I change my mind."

The last word had no sooner left Trammel's mouth when the coachman cracked the reins and got the team moving again.

Trammel flexed his left hand as he watched the wagon speed away on the road back down to Laramie. He was pretty sure he had not crushed Clay's windpipe but did not especially care if he had. Sheriff Moran down in Laramie would be glad to be rid of him, and he doubted the territorial marshal would raise much of a fuss over the death of a cancer like Lucien Clay.

But Clay was only partly to blame for what had just happened. Hagen was the one who had brought the man to Blackstone in the first place. He needed to learn his lesson, too. Maybe not as harshly as he had taught Clay, but hard enough for it to stick.

Trammel turned to go back into the saloon but found Big Ben London standing in his way. He almost filled the doorway.

"It's all over now," Trammel told Ben. "I'm going in to see Hagen."

But Ben did not move.

Trammel caught the hint of a challenge in his eyes. "I'm the sheriff of this town and I'm telling you to get out of my way."

Still, Ben did not move.

Trammel slowly closed the distance between them until they were less than a foot from each other. He imagined the day when they had to face off would come, but he had not expected today to be that day. "We going to do this already?"

Ben balled his fists at his sides until they cracked.

Trammel figured now was as good a time as any until he heard Lilly scream from inside, "Stop it, both of you." She was small enough to squeeze past Ben and the doorway he blocked. She was clutching her nightgown closed as she got in between them and pushed both men farther away from each other. "Stop this nonsense right now. What the hell has gotten into you two? You're friends, remember?"

Trammel and Ben kept glaring at each other. "Ask him. All I was trying to do was get back inside to talk to Hagen."

Ben did not look away as he made some motions with his hands that Lilly seemed to understand. "He said you started trouble in the bar, so you don't get to come back in."

"Remind him I'm sheriff of this town and I go where I please."

Lilly translated another series of motions from the bouncer. "He said this place is different. No one starts trouble in here. Not even you."

Trammel was more than willing to keep up the staring contest. "Tell him to move or he's going to jail. And I'm going to take him there. One way or another."

She placed both hands on Ben's face and pulled his head down to look at her. "Let him by, Ben. Everything is fine. No more trouble. Please."

Ben gave Trammel a final look before he went back inside. The sheriff could have sworn the big man was grinning.

Lilly pushed Trammel. "What's wrong with you? Acting like that?"

From inside the saloon, Hagen said, "It's not entirely his fault, Lilly. Lucien goaded him into it by saying something ugly about you. Buck might've been a bit harsh, but I don't blame him one bit. Buck, I hope you'll accept my apology on his behalf."

"I don't understand any of this," Lilly said. "First I get woken up by hearing Buck yelling in the street, then I come down to find this mess. How did it all start?"

"Doesn't matter how it started," Trammel said. "It's how it ends, and it ends right now." He pointed at Hagen, who was standing alone in the middle of the saloon. Fred Montague was nowhere in sight. "You and me are going to have a talk. Right now."

"No, we're not," Hagen said. "Not until you've calmed down some."

The anger that had begun to ebb in him started to flow again. "I'm in no mood for your games or your mouth, Hagen. Get out here. Now."

But Hagen remained still. "Not until I know you won't hit me. I warned you about what would happen the next time you laid a hand on me, Buck, and that still goes." He placed his left hand on the pistol holstered at his side.

Lilly screamed as Trammel pulled her behind him as he yanked the Colt Peacemaker from under his left arm. He aimed it at Hagen, whose gun was already out and aimed at Trammel.

"I'm just a little bit slower with my left hand than my right," Hagen said, "but I'm still faster than you. You're entitled to answers and I'll be more than happy to give them to you, but not when you're like this. You name the time and I'll meet you at the jailhouse. But now is not the time."

Trammel knew Hagen was every bit as deadly as he thought he was. He would shoot if it came down to it, and he would shoot to kill. Trammel doubted the first bullet would kill him before he got a shot off, but he was not eager to test that theory.

Lilly placed her hand gently on Trammel's arm. "Please, Steve. He's right. You're too angry right now to have a sensible conversation. Let everything calm down for a while before you talk to Adam." She pressed herself closer to him and laid her head on his back. Her hand remained on his arm but did not move. "Please. If not for you or for Hagen, do it for me."

As if on cue, both men lowered their pistols at exactly the same time. Hagen slid his Colt in its holster and Trammel tucked his away in the holster under his arm.

Lilly wrapped her arms around Trammel's waist as tight as she could, but Trammel was still too focused on Hagen to notice. "I'll be down at the jail for the rest of the day, Hagen. I'll expect you before nightfall. If you don't come to me, I'll come looking for you."

"I'll be there well before dusk," Hagen said. "You have my word."

"Your word," Trammel repeated. "That just makes everything better, doesn't it?"

He kissed Lilly on the top of the head and walked toward the jail. He had work to do.

CHAPTER 10

John Bookman could not remember the last time he had seen Charles Hagen laugh so hard or be so happy. He had asked Bookman to repeat the events that had happened at the Gilded Lily three times. Each time he seemed to find something new to laugh about. This was especially rare because Bookman knew he was not a particularly good storyteller. He was just repeating the gossip he had heard from the ranch cook, who had been in town at the time, buying supplies.

King Charles wiped tears of laughter from his eyes. "The only way that could've been better is if the two of them wound up killing each other at the end. And you're absolutely certain you don't know if Clay is dead or alive?"

"Cookie said he had a good angle on the whole thing from Robertson's store," Bookman told him for the third time. "He said he'd never seen a man get hit so hard by another human being, which is saying something, because Cookie's seen his fair share of the world."

Mr. Hagen puffed on his cigar as he sat back in his chair, looking up at the ceiling. The picture of a happy man. "Remind me to send word to Fred Montague tomorrow. I want him to head down to Laramie to find out Clay's condition. I'm sorry my nephew and the sheriff didn't kill each other, but I'd settle for knowing that whoremonger was dead." A new thought came to him. "No, not dead. Incapacitated. Crippled would suffice. Actually, crippled would be preferable." He smiled at Bookman. "Can you imagine their partnership then? A one-armed dope peddler and a mute whoremonger."

He slapped the arm of his chair and howled at his own joke. Bookman figured if the wind was right, they could probably hear him all the way down in town.

After this round of laughter was over, Mr. Hagen composed himself. "Sorry about all this hilarity, Bookman, but there's been damned little enjoyment around here of late. Let's get back to the business at hand. How are the new men working out?"

Bookman hesitated to tell him because he

knew this part would kill his good mood. But Bookman was a worse liar than he was a storyteller, so he told him the truth. "I hate to have to tell you this, Mr. Hagen, but they're not much for saddle work. The ten original hands we've got left have been working extra to bring the twenty new men in line. I don't know what they were up to back on that ranch they worked in Kansas, but it's a miracle that patch made as much as a cent."

"What exactly is the problem? Are they surly? Shiftless?"

"Can't say that about them, sir," Bookman reported. "They're as polite as you could expect and get to whatever I ask them to do as soon as I ask it. They do their best, but wrangling livestock isn't their strength. They're comfortable in the saddle, but it's the little things that show they don't know what they're doing. And not one of them can handle a cutting horse. The poor horse does all the work and that's just out of pure habit. It'll only be a matter of time before they get lazy and forget what we taught them. Then we'll be stuck with worthless workhorses, and worthless horsemen, too."

Bookman had expected Mr. Hagen to lose his temper. Instead, he just kept puffing on the cigar, as content as a calf pulling from its mama's teat. Bookman was beginning to wonder if his employer was starting to go a little funny in the head.

Mr. Hagen cut loose with a snootful of smoke and watched it trail up toward the ceiling. He flicked his ash in the ashtray on his desk before looking at Bookman. "Well, I suppose the time has come to tell you everything, John. You're a hard, loyal worker for me and you deserve the truth. You see, those boys we hired from Kansas weren't brought all this way for their roping skills. True, I was led to believe they were better ranch hands than they've turned out to be, but I'm not surprised by their performance."

Bookman had never thought of himself as a particularly clever man, but he knew he was not stupid either. He understood what Mr. Hagen was telling him. It was just that what he was saying did not make any sense. "If you didn't hire them to tend the livestock, what did you hire them for?"

"They're here because we'll be needing them," Mr. Hagen said. "Especially after tonight. Because tonight is the night when my nephew learns what happens when you prod a bear once too often."

Now Bookman understood him fully. "Just

tell me what you need done and it's done, sir."

"Good man. I need you to take three of the new boys with you. I'm told every single one of the new bunch has killed more than his share of men in his time. I want three of them to ride the fastest horses we have into town. I want them at the mouth of the alley where the laudanum den is located. I want you around back of the den, setting fire to the canvas. And I want the three in the alley to shoot every single one of them that comes running out. Heathen and white man alike, I don't care. When they've emptied their rifles, they're to hop on their horses and ride back here. You too. I want you out of there as soon as the flames take to the canvas. When Trammel comes around asking questions, which he undoubtedly will, I'll tell him all of my men were present and accounted for right here on the ranch that night. He probably won't believe me, but that'll be just too bad for him. He won't have any proof that it was us and besides, he'll have enough trouble dealing with the dead and dying as it is, not to mention the damned fools who'll be roaming the town begging for whiskey once their laudanum burns up."

Bookman knew he had to choose his next

words most carefully or risk Mr. Hagen losing patience with him. "You can consider that place burned, sir, but even that won't be enough to make Adam go away. He still owns all the saloons in town, and those new houses on Buffalo Street. He'll miss what he makes off the smoke, sure, but the rest will be enough to keep him afloat for a while."

Bookman saw a flash of annoyance in his boss's eyes and feared he had pushed him too far. But his annoyance was quickly replaced by patience. "You're absolutely right, John. He has many interests in town, but none as lucrative as his laudanum trade. And the heathens he employs will be angry that my nephew failed to protect them, as promised. They will likely turn on him and may take his life. One can only hope. If they don't, Lucien Clay will, as he and my nephew are partners. Perhaps it will only be a minor inconvenience for Adam. If so, your efforts will still be worth it. Any way it goes, it will remind my nephew who really runs Blackstone."

Bookman was not sure anything short of a bullet to the head would remind Adam Hagen of anything, but he kept that opinion to himself. He figured Mr. Hagen must have his reasons for wanting to keep his nephew alive. Reasons that were none of his concern. Mr. Hagen did not pay him to think. He paid him to do what he was told.

Bookman figured their conversation had come to an end, so he stood as he said, "I'll go pick out three of the new men and we'll be ready to ride as soon as it's full-on dark. That way, no one will see us riding into town and no one will see us leave."

"You're a good man, John Bookman," Mr. Hagen called after him. "And you're doing good work this evening. For us and for the town."

Bookman thought it would be nice if it was only that simple.

CHAPTER 11

Frederick Montague was deep in thought, examining the bank's ledger for the day, when he heard a familiar voice say, "Afternoon, Fred."

The banker almost jumped out of his skin, fearing he was being haunted by a ghost. He quickly calmed down when he saw it was not a ghost, but a demon instead.

"How in the world did you get in here, Adam?"

Hagen grinned and held up a set of keys. "My father left these to all the buildings in town at the Clifford. Now that I own it, I have the key to your back door. Don't worry. No one saw me come in."

Montague gestured toward his office door, and Hagen went over and locked it. "Now we can conduct our business in private."

The thought of being forced to betray Charles Hagen had been a tough one to swallow. He cursed himself for putting himself in a position in which Adam could use his failings against him. Being blackmailed for his indiscretions was bad enough, but knowing his fate and good name rested in Adam Hagen's hands was almost too much to bear.

"I want to repeat, once again, how much I loathe and despise you for doing this to me, Adam."

Hagen opened the humidor on Montague's desk and helped himself to one of his Havana cigars. "Nonsense, Fred. No one's holding a gun to your head. Why, if you order me out of your office right now, I'll gladly go out the way I came in and we'll never have to do business again. Just keep in mind that we won't be in the position to do business again because you'll no longer have a job. My father isn't a very forgiving man, even in the best of circumstances, and you may rest assured that he will frown upon the knowledge that you corrupted the morals of a young lady from such a prominent family. A Southern member of Congress, no less. He was always uncomfortable with the gaggle of 'nieces' you traipsed in and out of here from time to time, but when confronted with the letter the poor young woman's father wrote you? Well, that may be the straw that breaks the camel's back."

Montague had wanted to ask him how he had gotten hold of that letter from the girl's father many times but had refused to give Hagen the satisfaction. He had it and that was all there was to it. "I was only one in a long list of corruptors, I assure you."

Hagen used the cutter to snip off the end of a cigar and did not trouble himself when the end missed the ashtray. "I know, but Father won't care about that. Especially when he reads it in the *Bugle.* Those newspapermen can never refuse a story like that. It'll be in all of the Laramie papers, too. Who knows, they might even write about it back East. Wouldn't that be a fitting end to your career? An entire life spent as my father's lapdog only to be booted out into the cold like a common cur. Oh, I'm sure you'd find work eventually. You're a survivor. Your type always finds a way to live. You're an attorney, so you could probably get work in a couple of years, once the scandal dies down. Perhaps as a clerk in a land claims office somewhere small, where they'd welcome a man of your talents."

He grinned as he thumbed a match alive and lit his cigar. The dancing flame cast nasty shadows on his face as the tobacco was lit. "Curse me all you want, but never say you don't have a choice, because we both know you do."

Montague never thought he would see the day when the smell of one of his own cigars would turn his stomach, but it did. And so did the man smoking it. He had only one weapon to use against his tormentor and he used it now, whatever the cost. "Please stop referring to that great man as your father. We both know he isn't. He's barely even your uncle."

Hagen waved the match dead and tossed it into the general direction of the ashtray. It fell short and skittered onto his desk. "I may forget many things, old friend, but I'll never forget that. It's the whole reason why we're doing business today, isn't it? Speaking of which, I trust you enjoyed my conversation with Clay? I hope it was enough to satisfy any lingering questions you might have about our partnership."

Hagen had told Montague to be in the Gilded Lily so he could see that he and Clay were, indeed, in league with each other. "Yes, it did. I also saw what Trammel did to Clay afterward. And I saw you two almost shoot it out over the matter."

Hagen blew a smoke ring up toward the ceiling. "From the safety of the back door of the saloon, no doubt."

Montague hated the fact that Adam

Hagen was as smart as he thought he was. "I know you think you can handle him, but you can't. One day you'll get too arrogant and push him too far. You'll have to kill him then, but not before he takes another piece out of you."

"I sincerely hope that day never comes," Hagen said, "but today was not that day." He looked at the banker. "Have you prepared the document we discussed? You said you'd have it done by today. I hope you didn't forget."

Montague cursed Hagen as he fumbled to get the keys from his pocket and unlocked the bottom drawer of his desk. He unlocked the drawer and jerked it open. He found the two documents and tossed them on the desk in disgust. "There they are, just as you ordered. It's an exact copy of your father's — I mean your *uncle's* — last will and testament."

Hagen looked down at the documents but did not reach for them. "Not an exact copy, I trust."

Montague gritted his teeth. He never thought he was capable of hating any man as much as he hated Adam Hagen now. "It's an exact copy that includes all of the revisions you wanted."

He waited until Hagen took the documents in hand before telling him, "But there's been a slight difficulty."

Hagen's eyes flicked to him. "Not too much of a difficulty, I hope. For your sake."

Montague thumbed a bead of sweat from his forehead. "A fairly substantial one. I was unable to successfully duplicate Charles's signature. It's fairly distinctive, as you know, and difficult to copy. That is by design. I tried to duplicate it dozens of times and none of my attempts even came close. I even tried to trace his signature from his actual will, but as you can see, the legal stock I use is not thin enough for easy tracing."

Hagen ran his fingers over the document. "I suppose that was by design, too."

Montague smiled. "You're not the only unsavory character in this world, Adam. Many people have tried to do what you intend to do, and they almost always get caught."

He had hoped that concern might give his tormenter pause, but it did not. "Then I should count myself lucky that I have the cooperation of the man my family trusts most of all with their business affairs. And we should count ourselves especially lucky, because copying my uncle's signature is child's play."

Montague felt any hope he had of foiling

Adam die in his chest. "It's what?"

"Child's play," Hagen repeated. "Don't tell me your hearing is starting to go. You're a bit too young for that malady to plague you. As for being unable to copy his signature, it's to be expected. Spending all day in a saloon like you do. It's a miracle you're even awake. Best thing for the shakes is a bit of the hair of the dog, my friend. Trust me, I know."

Montague was about to protest the implication that he spent his days drinking when Hagen flipped to the last page of one of the copies, where the signature was to be placed. Montague knew all about Adam's ruined right arm and doubted it was steady enough to hold a pen, much less forge such an elaborate, distinctive signature as that of Charles Hagen.

But his right hand was perfectly steady as he took one of Montague's pens, dipped it in the inkwell, and proceeded to create a perfect copy of the elaborate signature of Charles Hagen. Montague did not need to compare it to any of the other signed documents he had from King Charles. He knew the signature by heart and knew Adam had produced a perfect copy. Right down to the elaborate swirl of the C in his name.

Montague let out an uneasy breath. "I

don't want to know how you came to learn how to do that, especially with your right arm in the state it's in."

Hagen grinned as he blotted the signature and signed the second copy exactly the same way. "Necessity, old friend, necessity. You forget that my livelihood was often at the mercy of the king's whims. I've lost count of how many times he cut me off over the years. Fortunately, I knew where he kept his accounts and was always able to find a way to finance my life."

He blotted the second signature as he had the first and blew on both documents to ensure the ink was dry and would not smudge. "As for your question about my right arm, I'm genuinely touched by your concern. But don't worry. It's getting stronger every day. And it's just recently become strong enough for me to hold a pen and forge a signature I know as well as I know my own."

Hagen obviously saw the disappointed look on Montague's face and laughed. "Oh, poor Freddy. You put all your chips on the hope that the signature would stop me, didn't you? Well, sorry to disappoint you. Like I said, necessity and all that."

He surprised Montague by folding the

documents and slipping them both into his pocket.

"What do you think you're doing?" Montague asked. "I need one for the official record in my safe."

"Of course you do," Hagen said. "And you'll have it, too, after I've had the chance to read both copies. Unless you'd prefer me to stay here and do it. But I'm an awfully slow reader and I'm afraid you'd be stuck in here with me the entire time. We wouldn't want anyone to see me here if you opened the door, now would we?"

Montague ran his hand over his mouth and fought back the words he wanted to say.

Hagen looked at him closely. "You haven't tried to pull a fast one on me, have you? Maybe changed the wording of a clause here or there to weaken my claim? Something subtle that might cause my endeavor to fail? I won't hold it against you if you tried, but now's the time to tell me. Because if I get back to my room and find you've done anything like that, I'll be mighty cross with you."

Montague could not hold on to his anger any longer and banged his desk in frustration. "No, damn you. You'll find everything is exactly as you wanted it to be. But I'll need one of those copies back before you do whatever it is you're planning to do. And I'll need that letter from the girl's father, too."

"All in due time, Mr. Montague," Hagen said as he picked up his cigar and headed for the back door. "You'll get your letter after the will has been read and the estate is settled. It'll help give you focus in the confusion that lies ahead. Make you remember that you work for me now."

Montague had never been cornered like this. He had always been able to find a way to get out of whatever trouble he or his clients found themselves in. Someone to pay off. Someone to kill. A threat of some kind.

But here he sat, completely at the mercy of the vilest human being he had ever known. He could not allow this man to leave him without at least one last attempt to strike him where it hurt most. "I don't know how you plan on getting that document in his safe up at the ranch and I don't want to know. But even if you do, his sons will never stand for this. Or their sisters. They know how much he hates you and they'll do everything in their power to contest this will. I won't be held responsible if the courts are involved and this gambit of yours fails."

Hagen stopped just short of the door and stood completely still, as if he had been slapped. Montague knew that had gotten to him and took no small amount of pleasure that he had finally pierced Adam Hagen's thick skin.

"My sisters will never want for anything as long as they live," Hagen said. "As for my brothers, they're weak and stupid. I'll find a way to buy them off. As for you, just keep doing what I tell you and all will be well. If not, the publication of an angry letter from an aggrieved father will be the least of your concerns."

Hagen opened the back door and left as quietly as he had come in. He even had the courtesy to lock it from the other side.

Frederick Montaguc was left alone in his office, staring at the spot where Hagen had stood only moments before, wondering what he had done to deserve such a burden, especially at this point in his life.

CHAPTER 12

Adam Hagen was a happy man. He carried the means to destroy the man who had ruined his life in his coat pocket. A few strokes of the pen had been the key to opening an entirely new world for him. A world he hoped would bring him riches beyond his wildest dreams and a peace he had never known. If the copies of the will were as true as Montague said they were, all that was left was to do what needed to be done.

He made a point of tipping his hat to everyone he passed, much to the giggling delight of the women and children. He did not mind their laughter. He was too happy to allow anything to spoil his mood now, not even the nasty conversation he was about to have with Trammel.

If anything cast a shadow over his mood, it was the idea that his happiness depended on betraying his friend. He could not begrudge Trammel his resentment of him.

Trammel was a fair man who believed in things like justice and the law. He had seen enough of the ugly side of life to know it was never that easy or that decisive, but he held those beliefs dear anyway. He truly believed in the notions of good and evil. He could not fault the man for that. If anything, he envied him.

Which was why he had decided it was time to meet him at the jailhouse and take whatever medicine the sheriff decided to dish out. Montague had been right about one thing. One day he may push Trammel too far, and it would mean the end of one of them. Which one did not matter, because Hagen knew if one of them survived, a piece of him would die, too.

As he crossed Main Street on his way to the jail, he saw the stagecoach from Laramie had arrived in front of Robertson's store. That must mean it was close to five o'clock. A quick check of his pocket watch proved him right.

During his convalescence on his balcony at the Clifford Hotel, Hagen had spent the time becoming familiar with the ways of the town. The comings and goings of people on their way to work or to the store.

The arrival and departure of the stagecoach had held a particular fascination for him because it was, surprisingly, always on time. No matter the weather, the stage from Laramie always arrived promptly at five in the afternoon whenever a passenger was due.

And given the magnitude of that day's events, Adam Hagen had forgotten about the passenger he was expecting on that day's stage. Had he not seen it arrive, he might have forgotten about him entirely, but fortune had intervened on his behalf.

Hagen decided Trammel would have to wait a little while longer while he greeted the man he had sent for.

The town's new doctor, Jacob Moore, late of New Orleans.

Hagen was glad the doctor had not changed much since their friendship along the mighty Mississippi. He was still skinny, and still wore the thick spectacles and a thatch of dark hair on his head.

"Jacob!" Hagen called out when he got close enough to Robertson's. "There you are. I was beginning to think you'd had the good sense to change your mind."

"Hello, Adam," the doctor said as they shook hands. "Has it really been two years since we've seen each other?"

"Seems like much longer if you ask me," Hagen said. "Let me be the first to welcome you to Blackstone, your new home."

Moore looked around the place and frowned. "Not much to it, is there? Seems to be a far cry from New Orleans, doesn't it?"

"Not yet, old friend, but I'm working night and day to change that," Hagen confided. "But first, let's get you settled. I'll take you to your office. There's also an entire floor upstairs for your own private rooms. I think you'll find it all quite satisfactory. Where is your luggage?"

Moore lifted the single bag he already had in his hand. "I'm afraid this is all I have."

"Which is why you're here," Hagen said as he took him by the arm and brought him across to New Main Street to where his office and living quarters were, between the Vic and the Brand Saloons. "I know you'll think I'm mad for building a place for you between two raucous saloons, but there's a purpose, I assure you."

"Only a fool would doubt you, Adam," Moore said. "I've never gone wrong yet by following your lead."

As long as it stays that way, Hagen thought.

He used his key to open the door of the vacant building between the two saloons and ushered Dr. Moore inside. He was glad to see the medical man was immediately impressed.

"Adam, this place is enormous," Moore said as he set down his bag and walked through the space. "You've already got a waiting room set up, two offices in the back for examining rooms."

Hagen called after Moore, who had already started looking at everything. "You'll see the pump for the well is in the back room, so you won't need to go outside to fetch water. You'll find that mighty handy in the winter. The winters are more severe here than in New Orleans."

"I'm originally from Boston, remember?" he answered from the back. "I'm used to bad winters."

Hagen had been to Boston in the winter. It was cold and had a fair amount of snow, but it was nothing compared to the suffocating blanket of ice and misery of a Wyoming winter. "I'm sure you'll manage just fine. The only thing I was not able to procure for you were medical supplies. Scalpels and such. I assume you brought your own."

"I managed to save those despite everything else, thanks to you." Moore walked toward him from the back and ran his hand along the banister that led up to his rooms. The place still smelled new. He looked at Hagen with tears in his eyes. "Thank you for this, Adam. You have no idea how bad things got for me after you left."

But Hagen had a very good idea of what had happened. Hagen and the good doctor had helped each other many times during Hagen's time in New Orleans. Dr. Moore had repaired the various wounds Hagen had suffered following any number of scrapes he had gotten into following games of chance. Hagen, in turn, had helped cancel the numerous debts the doctor owed to a number of unsavory characters in the parishes around the city. Moore had something of a gambling problem, which he'd seemed to have in hand when Hagen was forced to leave New Orleans. But in the two years since, Dr. Moore fell back into his old habits and had been at risk of being killed by his numerous creditors.

The doctor's misfortune was Hagen's gain. "No need to thank me for anything, Jacob. I owe you my life, many times over."

Moore wiped at his eyes and remembered something. "Speaking of which, how is your right arm fairing? I'd forgotten all about it when we shook hands. Come to think of it, you had a surprisingly normal grip." He began walking toward Hagen. "I can take a look at it if you want."

"You can look at it tomorrow, after you've

settled in," Hagen said. "I used that old sandbag trick I saw you prescribe for others. I have to admit I didn't imagine there'd be much to it, but it's helped me regain some of my strength."

"I'm glad I could be of help, even if only as an influence." He looked at the floor and said, "I know I've made a lot of mistakes, Adam. I promise to mend my ways. I mean it this time. You have my word."

Hagen did not have the heart to tell him that the only reason he had been brought to Blackstone was because of his weakness. "Chin up, man. You're a doctor, for God's sake. A man of medicine with his own practice in a town that's on the cusp of greatness."

When Moore looked up, his mood had brightened some. "There," Hagen said. "That's the spirit." He decided it was time to gradually introduce him to the realities of his situation. "Now, as I discussed in my letter, there are some conditions that come along with our arrangement. First, the saloons in town are closed to you. Not all of them have gambling, but given certain frailties, you are forbidden from entering any of them. That's nonnegotiable, Jacob."

"I understand, Adam. It's for the best."

"You may have a drink or two at the Clifford Hotel or when you're in my presence, but no more than that. I know whiskey was never your weakness, but intoxication leads to other evils. Do we agree?"

"Yes, Adam."

"Good. You'll continue to work here and accept patients as soon as you are ready," Hagen went on. "The sooner the better. See whomever you want and treat them as you see fit, but remember that my interests come first. When I send for you, you are to drop everything and come to me immediately."

"Unless I'm in the middle of a procedure that requires me to complete it," Jacob said.

Hagen saw he had a point. "Let's hope those instances are few and far between. You will occasionally have people come here asking you for laudanum. Although you will be well stocked, you will not give them any unless they have a note from me. Is that clear?"

"Certainly."

"I also want a weekly list of who you treated and why," Hagen went on. "I know there's a certain implied confidentiality between a doctor and his patients, but not here. I want to know everything for reasons of my own."

"And you will."

Hagen had intentionally saved the most

important part for the end, as if it was an afterthought. "One more thing. You will also serve as the town's chief coroner and assist her until she decides otherwise. Signing death certificates and things like that. Most of our deaths are from laudanum poisoning these days, so it won't be a demanding task at all. You'll also get a small stipend from the town for each certificate issued, so that'll help with things."

"Adam, about that —"

"What I said in my letter still holds," Hagen told him. "I will not charge you rent and you can keep all of your fees from your patients. All of your expenses will be charged to my account at Robertson's store, as will all of your meals at the Clifford Hotel. I must insist on that."

"But that's not right, Adam," Jacob Moore protested. "I can't just live off you for free."

Hagen smiled warmly. *You're right, old friend. Nothing in life is free. And you'll pay me back for everything I've done for you with a simple stroke of the pen.* "It won't be forever, I assure you. Once you're up and running, I'll be charging you a pretty penny to rent this place. And you'll be able to afford it, too."

Hagen was not surprised when Moore embraced him and sputtered his thanks. His enthusiasm almost made Hagen feel guilty for using him like this. Almost, but not quite.

As Hagen began to leave, Moore surprised him by saying, "I understand there's another doctor in town. A woman named Emily Downs."

Hagen turned. "Who told you about her?"

"Someone on the train mentioned her," the doctor said. "She seems like a remarkable woman. I would like to talk to her, maybe even work with her if it's possible."

Hagen saw no harm in it. She would not be around much longer anyway. "I shall introduce you to her tomorrow. Until then, go upstairs and get a good night's rest. You're going to need it."

As he walked along Main Street to meet Trammel at the jail, Hagen considered himself a lucky man. Just when he did not think he could feel any better, he'd had the good fortune to meet Jacob Moore's coach. Hagen took that as a good omen of better things to come in the days ahead.

His path to glory was now clear. He had King Hagen's lawyer cowed, his own doctor in place, and the Celestials on his side. Each of his saloons was already full and it was not even sundown yet.

Now, if Lucien Clay had the decency not to succumb to the beating Trammel had given him, he could pull the lever, and the gears of his great scheme could be put into motion within a matter of days. His vengeance was at hand.

Hagen knew he would need all the good feeling he could muster to help cushion the anger Trammel was sure to hurl at him in the jailhouse. His ire would be worth it in the long run.

Despite the closed door, Hagen could hear raised voices coming from inside the jail. These were not the moans of anguish of the laudanum addicts who now crammed his cells but the voices of men in argument.

Hagen smiled as he knocked on the heavy door. Yes, everything was certainly falling into place at exactly the right time.

"Come in," Trammel barked. "It's open."

Hagen opened the door and saw the reason for the shouting.

It was a packed house. Mayor Jonah Welch, the proprietor of the Oakwood Arms, was on his feet before Trammel's desk. Rhoades, the newspaperman, was also there, taking copious notes in his notebook.

Even Dr. Downs was in attendance, sitting next to Rhoades. Her arms crossed and her eyes closed, as if she was waiting for a storm to blow over.

That storm was a fury of words from the mayor.

"I've said it before and I'll say it again, Trammel: We cannot have this kind of conduct take place in broad daylight on Main Street!" A tall, hatchet-faced man with a high, stiff collar and brown hair, Welch glowered down at Trammel over round, wire glasses perched on the bridge of his nose. "As if we don't have enough to worry about with these hordes of mindless men wandering the streets at all hours of the day and night, we have to contend with our sheriff practically beating an innocent man to death. We will not abide this, sir. Not one bit!"

Hagen slipped into the jail and quietly closed the door, but he was not quiet enough to escape the mayor's wrath.

"And there's the man who is the culprit behind it all." Welch pointed at him. "This liar, this proprietor of iniquity, this fiend who fouls his family's name with every breath he takes."

Hagen laughed. "A fine speech, Jonah, but I'm far from the only sinner in this room. You'd been known to monger a few whores yourself in your day. One in particular who used to work at the Painted Dove before it closed down."

Welch's hatchet face only reddened. "My indiscretions are my business, Hagen, not yours. They never inflicted any harm on the town; not to any magnitude that matched your efforts, anyway. You've turned a nice, quiet town into a reflection of yourself, a wretched slum as bad as any in the Old Testament."

Hagen laughed again. "Good Lord, Jonah. Did one of your tenants leave behind a dictionary? I never knew you possessed such oratory skills. This is quite a revelation."

"And a revelation it will be for this fair town if we don't get some law and order around here, and by thunder, I mean the Book of Revelation!" He turned his fury back toward Trammel, who had continued to sit calmly behind his desk during the exchange.

"That part's your business, Sheriff. You're paid to keep the good people of this town safe from the likes of Hagen over there. In their name, I demand to know how you plan to go about doing just that."

Hagen watched Trammel closely. He knew the sheriff's temper well, and knew he did not like being spoken to like this. He was slow to rile under the right circumstances, but Mayor Welch seemed to have been pushing Trammel mighty hard for quite a while. There was no telling how the big man would react. Hagen was glad he would be there to see it, whatever his reaction.

Hagen noticed Dr. Emily looked concerned, too. She knew Trammel's temperament better than anyone.

But the sheriff's reaction was to do nothing. Trammel did not blink. He did not move. He barely even breathed. He simply sat behind his desk and watched the mayor's breathing calm down after his rant.

"Well?" Mayor Welch asked after a solid minute went by. "What do you have to say for yourself, Trammel? Or have you grown content with doing nothing these days?"

"I was just giving you a moment to calm yourself," Trammel told him. "I was hoping the silence would show you all that ranting and raving didn't get you anywhere but worn out. Your face is redder than hell and you're panting like you just ran a mile. You want Doc Downs here to look you over before I give you my answer?"

The concern over his health only served to stoke the fire of the mayor's temper. "I'll have my answer now, by God, because the people of this town deserve action."

"And they've been getting action," Trammel said. "You want to know what me and

Hawkeye have been doing? Why don't you go back to where the cells are and see for yourself? I've got them packed with men in various states of delirium from the laudanum Hagen's Celestials serve up. They don't have a cent in their pockets to pay for their fines, and seeing as how they're all ranch hands or miners, I can't hold them or send them to Laramie for thirty days because I don't want to cripple the few businesses we've got around here."

He pointed at Emily. "Dr. Downs has been good enough to check in on the prisoners daily to make sure none of them die. We've had a few close calls, but so far, they've all made it. But the doctor's time is worth something, so it's costing the town money every time she walks through that door." He looked at Emily. "That's not a complaint. You know that. You're entitled to get paid for what you do. That medicine you give them isn't free."

Emily continued to look down. Hagen was glad she seemed completely content to remain clear of this fight.

Trammel looked back at Mayor Welch. "As for you not being happy with the job I'm doing, that's your decision." He pointed at the star pinned to his vest. "This comes off as easy as it goes on. It's yours whenever you want it. You want me to apologize for beating the hell out of Lucien Clay this afternoon? You'll have a long wait, because I'm not sorry. That man's had a hand in every crooked deed I've handled since coming to Blackstone, and today he got some of the justice he's been avoiding."

"I heard about how he looked when you threw him in his coach," the mayor said. "He was in a bad way. If he dies —"

"Wyoming will be a better place," Trammel said.

"And you'll be facing a murder charge," Welch said, finishing his thought. "Making excuses for you with Mike Albertson and the Citizens' Committee is one thing, but my influence in Laramie is limited at best."

Hagen cut loose with a sharp laugh. "So's your influence here in town. No one listens to you except those poor creatures who work for you in that miserable hovel you have the audacity to call a hotel."

Welch glared at him and looked even more bitter than normal, but he did not say anything. Hagen knew there was nothing to say, for Welch was not a fool and knew Hagen had spoken the truth.

The mayor turned his attention back to Trammel. "There's got to be something you can do about this, Buck. You know I've always supported you, and so has the town. But these dope fiends wandering around, disrupting lives. Breaking up homes. We've never encountered anything like this. What can we do?"

"I've told you before that I can only enforce the laws we've got on the books," Trammel said. "You want me to stop Hagen's laudanum den, pass a law that makes it illegal."

Hagen had heard that one before. "Laramie will never allow it."

Trammel kept talking as if Hagen was not there. "Or pass a law saying all places of business have to be shut down at midnight. Nothing good ever happens after midnight anyway. That'll go for the Celestial den, too. Probably go a long way to getting men off the streets once they've had their smoke, especially first thing in the morning."

"I suggested that at the last county meeting and got laughed at." Mayor Welch looked at the door that led to the cells in the back. The moaning and cries of pain from men slowly emerging from the oblivion the laudanum had provided. "I wish they were here now. They wouldn't be laughing."

"They wouldn't care either," Hagen said, drawing all the eyes in the jail to him. "And please don't look at me with such righteous indignation, everyone. You may hate men like me and Lucien Clay, but we provide as much of a public service as the good Dr. Downs provides to her patients."

"How dare you!" Mayor Welch spat.

"I don't dare," Hagen replied. "I speak the truth. You expect those men to herd cattle and horses and break their backs in the mines without some measure of entertainment? Those men are going to do something when they're not at work and need something to look forward to when they are. They're not the type to crack open a Bible and read the Good Book by candlelight before they go to sleep, for if they were, they wouldn't be frequenting our establishments in the first place. They need companionship. They need to forget about their lot in life for a while. Someone's going to provide it. If I don't, someone else will. Madam Pinochet did it before me, as did Lucien Clay."

"Your laudanum rots men's souls, Hagen," Welch said.

"So does whiskey, Jonah. It just gets them there faster, and only if they abuse it. Most of my clients don't. I've seen more men destroyed by whiskey than laudanum. I'd be more than happy to provide other releases if I could. Cocaine, for instance. But it's difficult to obtain, and my Celestials have a hold on the laudanum trade. Why, even the good doctor here provides laudanum to relieve the pain of her patients. Isn't that right, Emily?"

Dr. Downs came to life. "Prescribing laudanum is different than a laudanum pipe and you know it."

"Perhaps," Hagen allowed, "but the desired result is the same. A temporary relief from pain. I just provide it in a different form."

"And for a different reason," Trammel said. "But that's going to be part of a separate discussion between you and me." He looked at Rhoades, the mayor, and Emily. "If you will excuse us, I've got some business to talk over with Adam."

Hagen held up his hand as the three began to rise. "Not before Adam has finished what he came here to say."

Once again, he had their attention.

"I live here, too, and despite what you all think of me, I'm not immune to your concerns, Jonah. I've seen the men wandering around our streets after our clients have finished their time with us."

"Clients." Welch sniffed. "That's an awfully nice way of putting it. That help you sleep better at night, Hagen?"

Adam chose to ignore him. "That is why I

have secured the services of one Dr. Jacob Moore of New Orleans. I brought him here at considerable personal expense due to his expertise with treating those who have become addicted to the drug. I've witnessed his methods firsthand and can attest to their effectiveness."

"You never struck me as a laudanum man," Trammel said.

"I'm not," Hagen admitted. "I've always managed to effectively defile myself with whiskey. Preferably gin, when I could find it. But I've known many people from across the social strata who lost themselves to the smoke and I can assure you that Dr. Moore's methods work. I'm not a medical man, but I know the good doctor would be more than happy to talk to you, Jonah, and you, Emily, at your earliest convenience, maybe even agree to an interview Rhoades."

Trammel spoke first. "When's this Dr. Moore supposed to be in town?"

"He's already here," Adam told them. "In the store between the Vic and the Brand. He'll be more than happy to tend to the ailments of the other residents in due time, of course, but for now, his explicit purpose is to cure this town of its laudanum problem."

Mayor Welch and Emily traded glances, with Welch saying, "Want to go see this doctor now?"

"Of course."

Hagen beamed. "Never let it be said that Adam Hagen is not civic-minded."

Mayor Welch got up first and opened the door for Emily, followed by Rhoades. "Even if this doctor is everything you say he is, it doesn't change my opinion of you, Hagen. If you brought him here, it's to serve your own purpose. I don't know what that is yet and I hazard to guess what it is. Just remember that the longer this goes on, the more powerful Mike Albertson and his marchers become. You might not like dealing with me, but if he manages to get himself named mayor, you'll be sorry."

"Mike Albertson will never be mayor of Blackstone," Hagen said. "On that, you have my solemn promise."

But Mayor Welch was not through. "I'll be taking this matter up with the county at our meeting next week, and I'll use every ounce of influence I have to have them move against you."

Hagen remained seated and gave the politician his best smile. "As you only have an ounce of influence to use, I suggest you use it wisely, Jonah."

Emily gathered her shawl around her and left the jail, with a perturbed Mayor Welch and Rich Rhoades close behind.

That left only Hagen and Trammel together in the jail. The sounds of the ailing prisoners now seemed louder than they had before.

Trammel looked at him but said nothing. If looks could talk, the sheriff's expression had nothing nice to say.

Hagen threw open his hands. "What did I do now?"

"Get up," he said as he grabbed his hat off his desk. "You and me are going for a walk."

But Hagen did not get up. "A civilized walk, remember."

"As civilized as a stroll through Union Square on a spring day." Trammel pulled his hat onto his head. "Now get going."

Hagen saw no reason why he should not comply.

CHAPTER 13

The sun had already begun to settle in for the night and cast wide ribbons of blue and pink across the sky. Night was on its way, but this day looked like it was going to give ground in spectacular fashion.

Trammel normally did not like to leave the prisoners alone but figured this was a good exception. He needed to talk to Hagen in private and Trammel could not abide hearing those men suffer any longer than he already had. He did not consider himself an especially compassionate man, but he hated seeing people suffer. He hated it even worse when it was their own doing that put them in such a state.

He steered Hagen to walk behind Main Street, walking behind the buildings and along the edge of town. The only structure that stretched this far back was the canvas of the laudanum den.

It was the reason why Trammel had chosen this route. "Place has expanded some."

"Don't tell me this is the first time you've noticed," Hagen said. "You don't miss much and you certainly didn't miss that."

"Never claimed otherwise," Trammel said. "I stood right there and watched your Celestials set it up. They're an efficient bunch, I'll give them that."

"They're efficient when there's something in it for them," Hagen said. "They're no different from anyone else in that regard."

"What's in it for you, Adam?" Trammel looked at him as they walked. "I mean it. Besides money, what are you doing this for? The laudanum, I mean. It can't be about money. It's causing more trouble than it's worth. The mayor was right about Albertson. His march last week had fifty people, and they weren't all from town either. People came down from the hills. Miners' wives and some up from Laramie, too. The next one will be even bigger."

"I'm looking forward to it," Hagen said. "More business for me after their march. Nothing like a shot of whiskey to make the long ride back to Laramie bearable."

"That's what I'm talking about," Trammel said. "You already made a nice bundle with the saloons and the Clifford. Hell, I can even understand why you expanded Main

Street and built all those new houses. You're planning something. Word has it you're thinking about building a lumber mill."

"Assuming this goes no further than the two of us," Hagen said, "that's exactly what I'm planning on doing." He pointed at a spot past the end of New Main Street. "It's going to be built right over there. Big enough to put fifty men to work, maybe more. It'll change this town forever, Buck. I plan on making this place in my own image."

"Then why not give up the laudanum, Adam?" Trammel had tried threatening him and knew that did not work, so he gave sincerity a try. "Why pull down the same place you're trying to build up? It doesn't make any sense to me. You're giving Blackstone a reputation that'll be awfully tough for us to shake. I figure it's got something to do with your fight with your father, but —"

"My uncle, you mean," Hagen corrected him. "The same one who tried to have me smothered to death?"

"Your uncle," Trammel agreed. "You know you can't take him on, don't you? Not directly. Not even if you and Clay are gobbling up all the mines in the area."

Hagen stopped walking. "So, you know

about my gambit, eh?"

Trammel stopped walking, too. "I've heard about it. Mostly from the men I've arrested when they sober up enough to talk. And if I know it, chances are your uncle knows it, too. He's probably already working on a way to stop you."

"And he'll fail." Hagen resumed walking, and so did Trammel. "While he was distracted with his holdings elsewhere, I've snuck in and acquired all of the mines he doesn't already control. I'll be able to influence the market now, every bit as much as he can. He won't be able to stop it. It's only a matter of time before my production outpaces his. You'll only find his workers in your jails. They don't come to town to smoke. My miners smoke elsewhere."

Trammel caught that. Come to think of it, all the men in his cells did work for King Charles. "You give your miners their own supply?"

"In a fashion," Hagen allowed. "The Celestials have opened another den up in the hills, closer to the mines. Not as fancy as this canvas palace before you, but enough to get the job done, and without the same problems as Blackstone."

"Addled men are bad enough on horseback," Trammel said. "Having dope sick men wandering around a mine is dangerous business."

"Indeed, it is," Hagen agreed, "which is why they only get a quarter of the amount for the same price."

"Is that so?" Trammel said. "You crafty sidewinder."

"Shrewd is more like it. I own the claims they work and they get free laudanum as long as they work. It's diluted, so they don't get sick but remain bound to me. Everyone's happy."

"So why not do the same thing in town?" Trammel asked. "Cut the amount you give people without cutting prices?"

"Because it doesn't serve my purposes," Hagen told him. "Look, I've never had a poor opinion of you, Buck. I've never treated you poorly or insulted your intelligence. You've stuck by me in the past and have always been the better for it. I'm asking you to trust me now. I've brought Dr. Moore to Blackstone to treat the worst cases. He's a good man and he'll do what I've said he'll do. But my purposes and methods are legal and my own doing. Please don't press me any further on the subject. I don't want any more difficulty between us than what already exists."

Trammel knew Hagen well enough to see

he had already gotten as much truth out of him as he was liable to get. Pushing him for more would be a waste of time and result in a lot of hot air and verbal sparring Trammel knew he would likely lose. Hagen was as deadly with his mouth as he was with his gun, even if his right arm *was* damaged.

"I know you won't tell me what you're planning against your uncle and I'm not going to waste my time trying to find out," Trammel said. "But whatever it is better not mean killing. Because if it does, you and me are going to find ourselves on opposite sides again. And I wouldn't like that."

"Neither would I," Hagen said.

They passed by the back of the canvas tent. The stench of laudanum smoke turned Trammel's stomach. "Wouldn't like to have to kill you if I could avoid it."

Hagen kicked aside a rock in his path. "Same here."

CHAPTER 14

Trammel let Hagen walk into the Gilded Lily on his own. He would come back later to see Lilly once he knew Hawkeye was ready to take control of the prisoners. He planned on letting a bunch of them go in the morning, which should cut down on the noise in the jail, not to mention the stench. Poor Hawkeye had to clean up a few times a day, which was no pleasant task, but nothing Trammel had not done many times in his day. As he told the young man when he pinned the deputy star on his chest, the job had its ugly side, too.

As night slowly settled over Blackstone, he was glad to see almost all was in order. No one was lingering on the boardwalks. The Vic and the Brand were doing a good but quiet business. He looked through the window of the new doctor's office and saw the mayor and Emily in close conversation by lamplight. He hoped Adam was not lying about Moore handling the laudanum smokers. The town needed the help. It was just like Adam to provide the answer for a problem he had started. He was a gambler who preferred to control the outcome whenever he could. Sometimes he admired his former friend for his cleverness. But that admiration disappeared quickly when he had to haul another of his clients out off the street and into the cells. At this rate, Trammel was going to have to ask Mayor Welch for money to expand the jail. He did not want to do that, for to do so would be giving in to the problem. Trammel had hoped that once word spread about the miserable conditions of the jail, smokers would think twice before risking a night behind bars.

But he knew the allure of the dragon was stronger than any fear a jail might have once a man's cravings kicked in. He would make a point of asking Welch for that expansion money the next time he saw him.

By the time he reached the jail, he found Hawkeye had already finished with his latest round of cleaning. The place smelled decent for once, almost clean.

"What's that smell?" Trammel asked as he closed the door behind him.

"Mint!" the young deputy exclaimed. He was quite happy with himself. "Mrs. Welch gave me the idea yesterday. Said you fill a bucket of water and drop in some mint leaves, cover it, and let it sit overnight. So that's what I did, and it works great. I don't think the place has ever smelled better."

Trammel only wished Mrs. Welch used the same trick at her own place. He had been staying there since things had cooled between him and Emily. The air inside was always humid and musty. His window did not open, and he was tempted to break out a pane or two just to air the place out a bit. "I'll tell her that you put her idea to good use."

"I'm thinking I might use some other flowers next time," Hawkeye said. "Maybe change the smell up some."

Trammel smiled as he took his seat behind the desk. That was Hawkeye. Give him a task or an idea and he threw himself into it.

That's when he saw the notice on his desk. "What's this?"

"Someone was handing that out on the street when I was coming here," Hawkeye said. "Figured you'd want to see it. They're supposed to start hanging them up all over town tomorrow."

Trammel read the notice out loud, not that it made him feel any better. " 'Come One, Come All, to Prevent Blackstone's

Fall! March on Dens of Inequity This Saturday Afternoon. All Committed to Fighting Evil are Welcome.' " Trammel set the notice back on his desk and asked Hawkeye, "Who gave you this?"

"Mrs. Higgins was handing them out in front of Robertson's store. She only had a few left, but I made sure I got the last one. Like I said, they'll be posting them all over town tomorrow."

"All over the territory is more like it," Trammel said to himself. That notice spelled bad news for him. The march with fifty people had been tough enough for him and Hawkeye to cover. A march like this could stir up twice that amount. Suffragettes and people from the temperance movement were bound to show up, too. People loved nothing more than a chance to get together and yell about something. He had seen his fair share of marches turn ugly in Manhattan and Chicago. "You see Albertson anywhere while Mrs. Higgins was giving these out?"

Hawkeye thought about it. "Can't say as I did. I haven't seen him in a couple of days, come to think of it."

And now that he thought of it, neither had Trammel. He wondered why that was. What could a retired freighter possibly do inside all day long? He was not a drinker. He never frequented the saloons, and he had never heard anyone say they had seen him buy a bottle, much less drink. Mrs. Higgins was a temperance woman from way back. He doubted she would allow him to have any liquor in her house.

Trammel got up from his desk and took the flyer with him. "I'm going to find Albertson and put a stop to this nonsense," he told Hawkeye. "Lock the door behind me."

It was already full-on dark by the time he walked over to Mrs. Higgins's house. It was a delicate-looking place with a white picket fence in the front and a tended lawn all around it. The house was white and the shutters were blue, though it was tough to see this detail at this time of night.

Soft oil light cast easy shadows on the ground around the property, making it easier to find in the dark. He knocked loudly on her front door, knowing her hearing was not what it once was.

She opened the door, scowling. "No need to pound like that, Sheriff. I'm not deaf."

He shook his head. He had managed to annoy just about everyone he had met that day. "Sorry about that, Mrs. Higgins. And I'm sorry to bother you like this, but I'd like to have a word with Mr. Albertson."

"I'm sorry, too, young man. About your manners and about Mr. Albertson. He's not here."

"Not here?" Trammel repeated. "Well, do you know where I could find him?"

"He's doing the Lord's work wherever he is," Mrs. Higgins said proudly. "He's a blessing, that man is. A true blessing. I'm sure you know about the march we're planning on Saturday. We're expecting a lot of people to come out to denounce the wickedness you've allowed to descend on this town."

Trammel was disappointed Albertson was not at home but decided he might be able to use that to his advantage. "I was hoping you might let me take a look in his room for a moment."

"I most certainly will not," she said with a fair amount of iron in her voice. "He is a good man. Pays his rent on time and has never given me a lick of trouble. He even pays more rent than he needs to when he can. Blackstone should have more men like him instead of men like you, who just strut around all day with big words, doing nothing."

Trammel hung his head. He was getting the strap from everyone today, even from old Mrs. Higgins.

But then a thought came to him. "I was actually hoping to get a look at his room as a favor to you, Mrs. Higgins."

"My benefit?" she asked. "How could you searching his room benefit me?"

"Well, I was hoping I didn't have to mention it, but there have been some nasty rumors spreading around about Mr. Albertson. The kind of rumors that cast you in a bad light."

The old gossip's eyes narrowed. "What rumors? I've heard nothing but praise for Mr. Albertson."

"The kind of rumors that don't circulate in refined circles, ma'am. Rumors that involve a delight in the consumption of spirits."

"Never!" She rose to her full height of five feet. "Not a drop of liquor has passed this threshold since my Thaddeus died, God have mercy on his besotted soul."

"I don't pay them any mind myself," Trammel said. "But I'd hate for anyone to be able to drag your name through the mud. That's why if you'd allow me to just take a quick look at his room, I'll be able to put those ugly rumors to rest before they take root."

She hesitated for a moment, and Trammel

took the opportunity to ease past her into the house. "You know what they say about weeds and all. Now, if you could just tell me which room is his, I'll be out of here in no time at all."

She was so taken by the hint of a scandal that might involve her that she forgot all about her protest. "It's the first door on the right at the top of the stairs. But you won't find anything, I assure you. And don't you go making a mess, now. Mr. Albertson is mighty particular about how his things are kept."

Trammel took the stairs two at a time and found Albertson's door unlocked. He opened the door and saw that Mrs. Higgins was right. He kept everything nice and orderly. Perhaps *too* orderly. At first glance, it looked like no one lived there.

He left the door open as he began a quick search of the place. He checked under the bed and saw it was clear. Not even so much as a ball of dust.

He got up and moved to the dresser. Each drawer only had an article or two of clothing. No one would ever accuse Albertson of being a dandy, but he'd expected him to have more clothes than these. Strange.

He moved to the wardrobe next and opened it. Only a few shirts and a pair of pants. Not even an extra coat or boots.

On the top shelf of the wardrobe, he saw a pile of neatly stacked newspapers. Trammel thought they were probably copies of the *Blackstone Bugle* that featured some of the marches he had organized. Even the righteous liked to see their names in print. He took one down and saw it was not the *Bugle,* but a copy of the *Laramie Ledger.* And it was dated from the day before. Trammel took down some of the other papers, all of them from Laramie and all of them from the previous month. He knew he did not have time to read through each paper, but the fact that Albertson had them at all was strange enough. Blackstone only carried the *Laramie Daily.*

That meant Albertson had been to Laramie fairly frequently. Or had someone who kept the newspapers for him. But why would a Blackstone rabble-rouser care about what happened in Laramie? And why would he visit the place so often?

Trammel put the papers back in order and closed the wardrobe as he had found it. He moved to the nightstand beside the bed next and began opening drawers. Besides the *King James Version,* there was nothing of interest.

That was, until he saw something tucked

beneath the mattress. He grabbed it and pulled it out. It was a thick notebook, and Trammel knew he had hit paydirt. Why would a pious man like Albertson take the time to hide something like this? Surely not from Mrs. Higgins. He had her complete trust and she would not stoop so low as to search a tenant's belongings. Especially a good man like Mike Albertson posed to be.

Trammel opened the book and was trying to make sense of what was written there when he heard Mrs. Higgins begin to ascend the stairs.

"You've been in there far too long, Sheriff Trammel," she sang out. "I'm going to have to ask you to leave now."

He tucked the book in the back of his pants and pulled down his vest to conceal it. He carefully shut the door behind him as he left.

"You were right, Mrs. Higgins," Trammel said as he passed her on the stairs. He wanted to get out of there before she realized his excuse for being there was ridiculous. "There was nothing to the rumors at all. I'm glad this is one bit of slander I'll be able to put to rest."

"See to it that you do," she called after him as she followed him to the door. "And you should think about taking a page from that man's book, Sheriff Trammel. Might give you renewed purpose in making this town safe for womenfolk and children again."

"Don't worry," Trammel said. "I intend to read every page in his book from cover to cover."

"See to it that you do," she said as she closed the door behind him.

He waited until he was clear of the house and on his way back to the jail before he checked to make sure the book was still there. He had never been much of a thief, and given how this day was going, he would not have been surprised if it had fallen out on the staircase.

But it had not. It was still exactly where he had placed it.

At least one thing has gone my way today, he said to himself.

But he changed his mind quickly when he heard the gunshots ring out along Main Street.

Chapter 15

John Bookman brought his sorrel mare to a halt just outside of Blackstone.

The three men following him into town did the same, fanning out on either side of him so they could hear his orders.

"Like I told you boys back up at the ranch," he said amidst the growing darkness of night. "You'd best not stray too far from your horses. Stay mounted if you can, because you'll need to ride out of town fast once the shooting ends. You'll be close to your targets, so when the fire flushes them out, go to work with your rifles first and end with your pistols. When you run dry on bullets, get yourselves back up to the ranch as soon as you can. First one back makes a report to Mr. Hagen about what happened. If we're lucky, all four of us will be there to tell him at the same time."

"And if we're not?" one of the men asked. Bookman did not know his name, which had been by design. Knowing a man's name was dangerous business. His death might weigh heavy on his conscience, and Bookman preferred to keep his conscience clean. These three men had been with the ranch for little more than a month. Considering they might be going up against Trammel before the night was over, there was a chance they might not be alive much longer.

"It's like I told you when you volunteered to ride down here with me," Bookman reminded them. "Once you boys cut loose with those rifles, it's every man for himself. Don't go wasting time looking for me to tell you what to do because I'm gonna be too busy. Don't even worry about one another. When your gun clicks dry and you've killed just about as many as you can, put your spurs to your mount and keep your head down while you ride like hell for home."

"I won't shoot any kids," one of the other new men said. "Not even Celestial kids. Any man who pulls on a pipe's got whatever comes to him, same as a man who can't hold his liquor. But shooting kids is bad business, and I won't do it."

The lines men like these refused to cross simply amazed him at times. Bookman was almost fifty years old and people still managed to amaze him.

"No one's asking you to shoot kids or mothers," Bookman reminded him. "Just customers. You don't even have to shoot the ladies if you can avoid it, but if you can't, don't let it bother you much. No one in that tent is a hostage. Every single one of them is in there of their own accord, and Mr. Hagen wants them gone. You just remember that whenever doubt sets to creeping in. It might not seem like it now, but you boys are doing good work. Just remember to hold your fire until they start running into the alley."

It was too dark to tell if any of the men actually believed that, but they went about their business like he told them.

Bookman heeled his mount around the wide end of New Main Street and brought his horse to a gentle trot as he rode behind the buildings. The air was crisp and he could still smell the varnish and fresh-cut wood from the new saloons. From the sounds he heard coming out the back, every one of them was doing a good business, especially the Lily. He did not hold out much hope for the lives of the men he had sent to shoot up the alley. They would probably be gunned down by customers from the saloons, or by Trammel once he heard the ruckus. Adam Hagen would probably kill them, too, if he was able. Ruined arm or not, he was still a dangerous man.

But the shootings were not the main point of Bookman's mission. That part was up to Mr. Hagen to figure out later. The fire was the thing. The fire would destroy the canvas and a fair amount of the laudanum that the Chinese were selling. He did not doubt the canvas would be replaced in a matter of hours, but the laudanum would not be replaced so easily. It would be a while before a new shipment reached town. Even if it was sent up from Laramie, it would put a dent in Adam's operation, which was all Mr. Hagen wanted to do. He wanted to remind his nephew that there was only one Hagen in charge of Blackstone, and his first name was not Adam.

Bookman pulled the torch from his saddle and checked to make sure the rag wrapped around the tip was still soaked in kerosene oil. One whiff in the darkness told him it was. Knowing the flame would frighten his horse, he climbed down from the saddle and tied the animal to the nearest porch post behind the Pot of Gold.

He found the matches he kept in his waistcoat. One flick of his thumb and the vengeance of King Charles would be at hand.

But while Bookman was taking a match from his waistcoat pocket, a powerful blow knocked the torch from his hand and bent his arm back behind him with frightening speed. He would have screamed out in pain as he felt his right shoulder separate from the socket had he been able to scream. A heavy rope around his neck prevented him from doing that.

Bookman struggled as he felt himself being lifted off the ground and wondered how he could have missed a rope being flung around his neck. He wondered what he was being hung from. He knew the back of the buildings on Main Street well. There was no overhang that could pull him up.

But as he clawed at the rope around his neck, John Bookman realized it was not a rope at all. It was flesh. An arm, in fact. And he was being lifted by a man.

He knew he could not reach his gun on his left arm, so he fumbled for the knife he kept in his belt as he desperately tried to kick free. His heels found something behind him. The man's legs. As breathing became harder, he put all of his failing energy into kicking the man who was slowly choking him to death. He kicked again and again until he heard a crack.

For the briefest of moments, Bookman

thought he had busted his attacker's kneecap and forced him to lose his grip on him.

But as he felt himself fall to the ground, he knew the sound he had heard had not been a kneecap but his own neck.

He tried to get to his feet, to get as far away from this powerful man as he possibly could. But his feet would not work, and neither would his arms. Only his eyes could move, and they grew wide as he realized he was paralyzed.

He felt a great fist grab hold of his hair and pull his head from the ground. He looked up to see the horribly scarred face of the black man who worked at the Gilded Lily. The one they called Big Ben London.

He was holding something in his hand for Bookman to see, but he could not make out what it was until the tip of it came alive with fire. It was a match. And when he used it to light the torch that was on the ground, Bookman knew what the monster was about to do.

He forced his eyes shut with all the strength he had left and hoped to whatever God there was that he would not feel himself burn alive.

Ben dropped the torch on the dying man's back and left him there. A white man once had tried to burn him alive with a torch. He knew well the fear of the flame. At least this one would never be able to hurt anyone again.

He went to Bookman's horse and pulled the rifle free from the scabbard on the saddle. He had seen the men ride into town from his post at the front door of the Lily and saw them scatter like wolves in the darkness. When he had seen the one they called Bookman break off from the others, he knew they were up to no good. When he saw Bookman take hold of his torch, Ben knew he had been right.

The flames began to spread on Bookman's back and the smell of the smoke was beginning to make the horse nervous. He untied the animal from the porch post and slapped it on the rump, sending it running back to the Blackstone Ranch.

If Ben had anything to say about it, it would be the only member of the ranch who survived that night.

He went through the back door of the Pot of Gold Saloon and made his way inside. The place was packed with drinking men and sporting ladies plying their trade. The tables were full of gamblers playing cards and upping antes.

He knew all of them were looking at him,

surprised by the sight of the large, scarred black man with the rifle in his hand as he moved past them on his way to the front door. He did not bother to look back at them. He had seen such looks before.

Out of the corner of his eye, Ben saw the bartender come out from behind the bar and head to the back, undoubtedly running to Mr. Hagen's office in the back of the place to tell him what was going on.

The few customers by the door scrambled out of his way as he levered a round into the chamber of the Winchester and walked outside.

There, at the mouth of the alley, were the three men who had ridden into town with Bookman. One was on his side of the alley, one in the middle, and one at the opposite end. All of them had rifles in their hands. All of them were waiting for the flames and the screams that would signal them to start shooting the men fleeing the flames.

But Ben knew the flames they were waiting for would be much smaller than expected.

One of them said to the others, "Hey, boys. You smell that?"

Ben smelled it, too. The unmistakable smell of something other than canvas burning.

The man in the middle of the alley seemed to smell it, too, and aimed his rifle at the tent. "You think that's the start of it?"

The other two brought up their rifles as well and aimed them at the tent. "Could be. Best get ready."

Ben brought his Winchester up to his shoulder and shot the closest man to him. The shot caught him in the side of the head and pitched him forward into the alley.

The rifleman at the mouth of the alley turned to look at his partner but kept his rifle trained on the tent.

Ben racked in a fresh round as he shifted his aim. By the time the second rifleman realized what was happening, Ben fired. His bullet hit the man just below the left cheek and sent him spinning to the ground.

Ben ejected the spent round and took aim at the third man, who, by then, was almost in his saddle.

Ben fired and hit him high in the chest. The blow knocked him backward, but he did not fall. It took two more shots to make him pitch forward and drop to the ground, dead.

Ben heard people cry out and spill out of the saloons behind him, but he did not turn around, for he saw another man round the corner on the other side of Main Street and yell at him, "Drop the rifle. Now!"

Ben saw the star on his vest and the Peacemaker in his hand and knew from the size of him that this was Buck Trammel. And in that fraction of a moment, he remembered how the big man had threatened him in front of the Lily. They both knew all this would ultimately come down to the two of them fighting each other, so Ben decided to address the problem before it became one.

He shifted his aim to Trammel as he levered in a fresh round and fired.

Ben watched the sheriff fall backward before the bullet tore a hunk out of the porch post where Trammel had just been standing.

Ben felt a sting in his right shoulder that rocked him backward and caused him to drop the rifle. It was the first time Big Ben London had ever been shot, and he did not like the feeling.

Adam Hagen rushed into the street between them, pistol in hand, yelling, "Don't shoot, Buck! It's just Ben. He shot at you by mistake."

"Like hell he did," Trammel said as he got to his feet and stormed across Main Street toward them.

Adam Hagen took a look at Ben's shoulder and said, "Good work, old friend. Trammel's bullet went straight through and didn't hit anything vital. It'll sting for a bit, but you'll be fine. You and I will talk later, when things quiet down, but for now, just follow my lead like always."

Ben did not doubt his former employer for a second. He had always followed Mr. Hagen's lead in New Orleans and had always come out ahead. He was as smart as he was brave, which, in Ben's experience, was a rare combination for a white man.

He watched Adam move to head off Trammel in the thoroughfare. "Calm down, Sheriff. Ben shot at you by accident. It was in the heat of battle. I saw the whole thing."

But Trammel kept coming and pushed Hagen out of the way. "Save it, Hagen. He looked at me for a full second or two before he took a shot at me. He did it on purpose."

Hagen recovered and got in front of the sheriff once again. "You've got it all wrong, Buck. I was right behind him. It was a mistake. His blood was up and he shot at the next thing he saw. You can hardly blame him under the circumstances."

Ben saw Trammel had stopped coming toward him, but he still had the same fire in his eyes. He knew. And he wouldn't forget.

Trammel looked at Ben's shoulder. "I do that?"

"You most certainly did." Adam grinned. "And with a pistol, too. Quite a shot for a city boy."

Trammel did not celebrate. "I was aiming for his head."

Ben heard the crowd behind him part as a man with a medical bag rushed his way.

"Let him through," Hagen told the crowd. "That's our new doctor come to treat Big Ben's wounds."

Ben remembered the doctor from his time with Hagen in New Orleans but did not react when he saw him. For his part, neither did Moore.

The doctor stretched and went on tiptoe to see the wound, which was bleeding through Ben's fingers.

Doc Moore put his hand on Ben's back. "If you can walk to my office, I'll take a look at that wound for you."

Ben was all too glad to go with the doctor. It gave him a good excuse to get away from the angry sheriff. He did not doubt he could take Trammel if he had to, but he knew he was in no shape to do so the lousy way he felt. It was best to rest up and be ready for another day.

"Make sure you keep him there until I

come for him," Trammel told Moore. "I'll hold you responsible if he's not."

"He's not going anywhere, Sheriff," Moore assured him as he led Ben toward his office. "That hole you put in him will require quite a bit of attention."

Ben turned around when he heard a wagon approaching and saw the lady doctor pulling the horse to a hasty halt in front of the saloon. She grabbed her medical bag and began to climb down. He saw Trammel take her by the waist and help her down. She acted like he had done it before.

Looks like the sheriff and the lady doc are more than friends, Ben noted. He would have to make sure Miss Lilly knew that.

"What happened?" he heard her ask Trammel. "I came as fast as I could when I heard the shots."

Mr. Hagen did not give the sheriff the chance to answer. "I'm glad you were delayed, Emily, for you would've been caught in the middle of a heroic action. Big Ben, here, subdued three robbers who were looking to attack my place."

"Bull —" Trammel was about to say when Ben Springfield, the bartender from the Pot of Gold, rushed onto the boardwalk. "Miss Emily. You'd best come quick. Someone's been burned pretty bad out back. And I think he's still alive!"

Ben watched Trammel push through the crowd as he led Miss Emily and Mr. Hagen into the Pot of Gold.

He followed Doc Moore through the crowd toward his office. He had not expected John Bookman to still be alive.

He did not care much either.

Chapter 16

Trammel winced as he watched Emily work by torchlight. Bookman was too badly burned to move him, so Trammel and Springfield, the bartender, held the torches for her while she tended to the man.

The stench made him gag, but he held the light in place for Emily's sake. "You sure he's still alive?"

She checked his eyes and nodded. "He's still breathing, but barely. His face is the only part of him that wasn't burned. Where the hell is Mr. Hagen? Bookman won't last much longer."

The only words Bookman had been able to speak since they found him had been, "Get Mr. Hagen." Trammel had sent Hawkeye to go fetch him. That had been about a half an hour ago. "He'll get him here as fast as he can. Should be here any minute. Just hold on, Bookman. Hold on."

Trammel fanned away the smoke that was

still rising from his body. How a man could still be alive after such an ordeal was beyond him. The human will to live never ceased to amaze him, and he had a newfound respect for the dying man. He was only sorry he had acquired it at the end of the man's life.

Trammel tried to distract himself by thinking of other things. He asked Springfield, "You said Ben did this?"

Springfield held the torch but looked away from the scene. "I said I thought he did this. When that big fella came into the saloon, toting that rifle, I knew there'd be trouble, so I ran to the office to tell Mr. Hagen. When Mr. Hagen went to see what was going on out front, I smelled something burning out back here. That's when I found him. I ran back inside and grabbed a couple of blankets from the closet to stomp them out. Old Bookman must be a tough one, on account of him never letting out a peep. I'd say his horse must've thrown him because it's nowhere in sight."

Trammel had seen Emily treat all sorts of wounds and injuries since he had come to Blackstone, but he had never seen her care for someone in this condition.

"It doesn't make any sense," she said as she stroked Bookman's forehead. "Why did he just lie here like this? Why didn't he get up and try to put himself out? Even if he got thrown from his horse, he should've been able to flip over. Or cry out. Something."

But Trammel had a good idea why and surprised himself by saying it. "That's because his neck was already broken when he caught fire. He probably couldn't feel it."

"Bad bit of business," Springfield said as he gagged on the stench. "Never figured Bookman would ever get bucked off a horse. I always thought he'd been born on a saddle."

"He didn't get bucked off," Trammel said. "Just like he didn't get burned by accident either. Big Ben did this. And he'd better have a damned good reason why."

Trammel turned when he heard several horses riding his way and saw King Charles Hagen leading Hawkeye and five other men from the Blackstone Ranch.

Hagen absentmindedly handed the reins of his horse to Hawkeye as he slowly climbed down from the saddle. The proud man took timid steps toward the burned thing on the ground that was all that remained of his right-hand man.

He took off his hat and whispered, "John. Is that you? Good God."

Trammel knew there was no time to waste. "He's fading fast, Hagen. You'd better get over here and speak to him now while you've got the chance."

Hagen quickened his pace and reluctantly knelt beside Bookman, wanting to touch him but unsure of where he could place his hand without hurting him.

Emily moved away as she said, "He's been asking for you, but his voice is weak. You'll have to get in close to hear him."

Hagen surprised Trammel by lying flat on the ground next to the dying man and putting his ear close to him. "I'm here, John. Tell me who did this to you."

Trammel was too far away to hear what Bookman whispered, but he saw his eyes flutter open and shut from the effort. When he was done, he did his best to turn his face away from his boss and cough a deep, rasping cough before continuing.

Trammel watched King Charles Hagen's eyes dim as Bookman finished rasping to him. The cattleman got to his feet and wiped the tears from his eyes before drawing his pistol.

"He wants me to end it for him," Charles told the crowd. "Please stand back and allow me to grant him his wish."

Springfield was only too glad to move

away and take his torch with him.

Emily moved behind Trammel, who remained where he was, providing enough light for Hagen to do what everyone knew needed to be done.

The cattle baron's hand shook as he aimed the pistol down at Bookman. His voice cracked as he said, "God bless you, John. You were the finest friend I ever had."

Hagen's hand stopped trembling just before he fired and put John Bookman out of his misery.

The solemn moment was shattered by the sound of clapping.

Trammel looked up to see Adam Hagen standing at the back door of the Pot of Gold.

"How touching," Adam mocked. "Fitting, though. A loyal dog should be put down by his master."

King Charles did not react, still too taken by the smoldering sight of his best man.

Trammel quickly moved between the two men. "Get inside, Adam. Right now."

"And miss such a touching moment?" He dabbed at his eyes with a handkerchief before loudly blowing his nose into it. "After all, it's not every day a man gets to see a king laid so low."

Trammel noticed Hagen's left hand was already resting on his belt, close to his pistol. "I told you to get back inside. Don't make me tell you again."

Charles Hagen was still looking at Bookman's body when he said, "You." His voice was low, like the sound of distant thunder rolling across the plains. "You did this to him. You're responsible."

"Me?" Adam said, feigning shock. "I did no such thing. I didn't even know he was back here until Springfield told us about it. Ask Trammel and the good doctor over there if you don't believe me. He was already crispy by the time I got here."

Charles began to turn, raising his pistol as Trammel grabbed him and forced his hand down. The older man was much stronger than Trammel had expected him to be. "No, sir. Not now. Not this way."

"Step aside, Trammel," Charles growled. "This is none of your concern."

"Yes, Buck," Adam encouraged. "Step aside. Let's end this now while the moment's fresh."

Trammel struggled to keep hold of Charles while he told Adam, "Will you shut that damned mouth of yours for once?"

Trammel tightened his grip on Charles's gunhand and kept it pointed away. "Let me handle this my way. The legal way."

"How dare you talk to me about laws

when a good man has been burned to death like a pig?" The rancher's voice trembled with rage. "I don't give a damn about you or your laws. I care about Bookman. Now he's dead and that rat is to blame. Get out of my way and let me do what needs doing." His eyes dimmed as a new thought came to him. "Or should I have my men do it instead?"

Trammel heard the sound of guns clearing leather and hammers being cocked. Out of the corner of his eye, he saw Hawkeye had turned to face them and already had them covered.

"Let's not do anything hasty, boys," his deputy warned.

Charles Hagen told Trammel, "You'd best get that idiot out of the way if you don't want him killed."

Emily surprised Trammel by walking past them both, into the middle of the fray and stepping onto the porch in front of Adam Hagen.

"Come, Adam," she said. "It's time to go inside. You're being cruel."

Trammel held King Charles's glare, willing Adam to do what Emily had said and go inside. He almost allowed himself to breathe again when he heard their footfalls on the boardwalk as she eased him back into the saloon.

He was relieved to hear the cacophony of hammers being lowered as the men from the Blackstone Ranch put away their guns.

But none of the anger had left Charles Hagen yet.

Trammel was not accustomed to pleading, but given the circumstances, he decided to give it a try. "Let the law handle this, Mr. Hagen. Let me handle this."

"You?" Charles sneered. "You're his friend. You're in this with him."

"No, I'm not," Trammel told him. "You know that."

The elder Hagen searched the sheriff's eyes and, finally, some slack came to his gunhand. "I know."

Trammel slowly released his grip on the man and put his pistol back in its holster.

"Now, I've got a good idea of what happened here tonight," the sheriff told him, "but I need you to let me find out for certain. Give me a day — two at most — and you'll know everything I do."

"The truth," Charles said, as if it was a threat.

"And nothing but the truth," Trammel confirmed. "You'll get it all. If Adam or any of his people are guilty, he'll stand trial for it. I can promise you that." He looked at him closer so he could see his sincerity. "You've got my solemn oath on that. And my personal promise. If Adam's guilty, he'll hang."

Charles Hagen glared past Trammel at the back door, where Adam had been standing. "You know this isn't over. You know I won't let this stand."

Trammel moved to block his view. "And neither will I."

Charles Hagen looked back down at Bookman's smoldering corpse. "He deserved better than to die like this."

Trammel did not think so. The man had threatened to kill him on more than one occasion, but now was not the time to open old wounds. There were more than enough fresh wounds to tend to. "There are three more dead men to see to at the mouth of the alley. I'd wager they were your men, too. Hawkeye, here, will escort you around to take a look at them and collect them if you want. You can leave a man here with Bookman until you're ready to take him away. I'm asking you not to bury John until Emily has had a chance to look him over in the morning. She'll be there first thing and I'll be with her."

"Come whenever you want," Charles Hagen said as he walked back toward his horse.

"I won't sleep tonight anyway."

Trammel caught Hawkeye's eye and gave him a nod of approval. The young man nodded back. He had shown more grit than Trammel thought he had.

Hagen ordered one of his men to stay with Bookman while the rest of them rounded the corner to head back toward Main Street to collect the others.

The young man looked at Trammel and swallowed hard. "You won't have any trouble from me, Sheriff. I promise."

"Good," Trammel said as he headed into the Pot of Gold. "There's been enough trouble tonight already."

Chapter 17

Trammel checked Hagen's office at the back of the saloon, but there was no sign of him or Emily. He shoved his way through the crowd around the bar and got Springfield's attention. He was already telling his customers what he had done and looked unhappy about the interruption.

"Whiskey," he told him. "And not that panther piss you serve these idiots. Something good from Hagen's stock."

Springfield looked at him. "Never took you for a drinking man, Sheriff. You sure?"

Trammel glared at him until the bartender realized the sheriff was most definitely sure.

Springfield took a decanter from the top shelf and the sipping glass that was next to it and set both of them in front of him. Trammel took the glass top from the decanter and sniffed it before pouring it almost up to the rim. He put the container back on the bar and sipped his drink.

It was indeed the good stuff, and he felt the smokey burn hit the back of his throat before the warmth reached all the way down to his gut. The taste should have turned his stomach, especially after the grisly scene he had just witnessed with Bookman, but it did not. It had been a long time since he had needed a drink, truly needed it, but that night had called for it.

Trammel could feel events getting ahead of him, and the liquor was the only thing he knew that could slow it down. Tempers were running high all over town and he could not afford to let his own get in the way of doing his job. An element of fear and danger rippled through the Pot of Gold that night. By tomorrow it would be a tangible thing felt throughout the entire town. Everyone would be on edge, waiting to see what King Charles did next. Adam Hagen's saloons would be waiting for something to happen and one cross word could kick the whole thing off.

It galled Trammel because this was exactly what Adam had been working for since the day they had come to Blackstone. He had done everything he could to poke and prod Charles Hagen every chance he got. And what chances did not present themselves, he had created. He had been prodding the old man long enough and now it had come to a head. Mike Albertson's marches. The hopheads wandering the street. The corruption of the men from the Blackstone Ranch. The buying up of available mines. Bringing Lucien Clay and his Laramie bunch into the thick of it.

Trammel knew this was what Adam Hagen wanted and it was up to him to stop it from happening. Him and a single, raw-boned deputy.

He felt his mind beginning to race again, so he took another sip of booze to slow it down.

One of the men Trammel had pushed out of the way to get to the bar cleared his throat and said loudly, "Hey, boys. Is it me, or do you all smell something burning?"

Some of the drunks suppressed laughter, which only encouraged the idiot to keep talking. "It's a familiar smell that I can't quite figure. Can you, boys?"

More boozy snickers.

The man snapped his fingers. "I know what it is. Smells like a pig roast. Yes, sir. Barbecued Bookman is what it smells like."

The snickers broke out into full-blown laughter all around Trammel.

The sheriff ignored it and sipped his whiskey.

He heard the loudmouth sniff loudly. "I couldn't tell where it was coming from, but I think I've got it figured out now. It's coming from our big, old sheriff over here."

Encouraged by the laughter of his friends, the man leaned on the bar next to Trammel. Judging by the coal dust on his face and beard, the sheriff figured him for a miner. He only came up to about Trammel's shoulder, but he had the thick, powerful build of a miner. "What about it, Sheriff? That Bookman dust you washing down with that fine whiskey?"

From his spot behind the bar, Springfield looked nervous. "Mister, if you want to kill yourself, do it somewhere else. I'd leave this man alone if I were you."

But Trammel put Springfield at ease. "Why would I be mad? He's not wrong. He knows what happened out back." He turned his head and looked down at the man. "Why don't you go out and take a look at him for yourself. That'll cure your hunger pretty quick."

"Didn't come here to eat, Sheriff," the miner persisted. "I came here to drink, and that's a mighty hard thing for me to do with you reeking of dead man like you do."

Trammel looked him up and down before turning back to his whiskey. "Then drink.

No one's stopping you."

"Now, see," the miner continued. "That's where you and me have what you might call a disagreement on account that I was doing that very thing when you pushed me out of the way without even a word of apology. I don't think that's polite, and this here is a polite place, ain't it, boys?"

His friends agreed with him, though judging by the sound, Trammel heard fewer of them do so this time.

"So, Mr. Lawman, I'd like for you to apologize to me and my friends for disturbing our evening."

Trammel sipped his whiskey and filled the glass again. "No, you don't."

"What was that?" The miner cocked an ear in his direction. "I'm afraid I didn't catch that. Guess working for a living in the mines has dulled my hearing some."

Trammel put the top back in the decanter and motioned for Springfield to take it away, which he quickly did.

"You don't want an apology," Trammel said as he looked at his glass. "You want a fight. You and your friends have a bellyful of whiskey and not an ounce of common sense between you. You figure you can ride me until I set to swinging, so all of you can join in. Maybe you'll win." Trammel shrugged.

"Maybe I'll win. But either way, you'll lose."

Trammel heard the men behind him back away even farther, but the loudmouth remained next to him.

"Well, now, Sheriff. I know you might not think much of us working men, but even I'm not dumb enough to pick a fight with a man with a star on his chest and a gun on his hip."

Trammel sipped his whiskey and set the glass back on the bar. "The star comes off easy enough. The gunbelt, too. So, if that's what you want, just say the word. I'll be more than happy to put them both on the bar and your friends can enjoy their drinks while they watch me beat you to death."

The miner clearly had not expected that.

Trammel enjoyed his confusion and remained focused on his whiskey. "You think you're the first little man I've come up against in a saloon? Some gasbag who was just drunk enough to think he could get over on me. Well, I've got news for you, friend. You're not. And no amount of goading or prodding from you is going to make me lose my temper and start swinging. So, if it's a fight you want, I'm in the mood to give you one, but be a man about it."

Trammel looked at the man for the second time. "But you'd best make sure your affairs are in order, because when I start in on you, I won't stop until you're dead."

He went back to his drink. "So, either call it or go away."

Trammel did not give the miner another thought. And by the time he had finished with his second glass of whiskey, the miner and his friends were gone.

Trammel pushed the empty glass toward Springfield. "Where's Hagen?"

But the bartender was still taken by his run-in with the miner. "Sheriff, I thought that was going to go another way."

"I didn't," Trammel said. "Hagen. Where is he?"

Springfield swallowed hard. "He and Doc Emily went to Doc Moore's place to check on Big Ben. It's the new storefront between the Vic and the Brand."

Trammel pushed himself away from the bar and walked out of the saloon. And this time, no one got in his way.

Trammel found Hagen and Emily at Doc Moore's office. Lilly was there, too, clutching a shawl around her bare shoulders.

"Steve!" she exclaimed and threw her arms around him. "Thank God you're all right. I was worried."

Trammel could not swear to it, but he

thought he saw Emily roll her eyes.

"I'm fine." Trammel nodded toward Ben. "He going to live?"

He had seen the place being built, but had not known what it was for. Hagen was always cagey about it when asked and now he knew why. Dr. Jacob Moore had not just stumbled upon Blackstone. He had been sent for by Adam Hagen, which meant he was there for a reason. One of Hagen's reasons.

Hagen and Emily were in the back, watching Moore sewing up the hole Trammel had put in Ben's shoulder. The silent man glared at him through the pain.

"You've missed the show, I'm afraid," Hagen greeted him. "As you can see, the good doctor here is almost done cleaning up after you. The wound was a bit more serious than we first believed. A few hairs to the right and you may have nicked an artery."

"Like I said," Trammel reminded him, "I was aiming for his head."

"Buck!" Emily and Lilly chided him in unison.

Hagen perked up as he smelled the air. "Have you been drinking?"

Trammel nodded. "Whiskey."

Hagen continued sniffing the air. "It smells terribly familiar."

"It should. It's yours."

"I thought so." Hagen frowned. "My private stock. How much did you have?"

"Enough."

"I hope not too much. That was shipped to me all the way from Scotland."

But Trammel had more on his mind than Hagen's booze. "He tell you what happened?"

"Of course not," Hagen said. "You know he can't speak."

"I know that," Trammel snapped, and looked at Lilly. "I mean to you. Those things you two do with your hands. Did he tell you what happened?"

"How could he?" Lilly said. "The doctor's been treating his wound."

Trammel looked at Moore. "You almost done?"

"In a moment, Sheriff," the doctor told him. "We want to do this right to reduce the possibility of infection. But Ben will be fine. It's not the first time I've —"

Trammel saw Hagen and Moore exchange a glance before the doctor finished his thought. "It's not the first time I've stitched up a bullet wound."

Trammel took his first good look at Ben's wound. The bullet had hit just below the clavicle and went out the back. Moore had been right. A bit higher and he might have hit something vital. It was a mistake Trammel knew he would live to regret based on the way Ben had glared at him from the moment Trammel had entered the office.

"The wound is a long way from his hands," the sheriff observed. "Lilly, ask him what happened."

The doctor did not give her the chance to answer. "I told you, I will be done here in a moment, Sheriff Trammel. I don't see the need for the sudden urgency. The facts of the matter will continue to be the facts when I am done in a few minutes. You can talk to him then."

"I don't know about you," Trammel argued, "but I'd call saving our hides a pretty good reason for urgency."

Doc Moore stopped stitching the wound. "Don't be so melodramatic, Trammel. It doesn't suit you."

"But staying alive does," Trammel said. "We've got five armed men from the Blackstone Ranch in town right now collecting four of their dead friends." He pointed at Ben. "Charles Hagen had to put his foreman out of his misery personally. The rest of them are out on Main Street right now, collecting the men Ben killed. I got Charles to give me two days to investigate, but his word won't mean much when he finds out the disposition of the man who killed his cowhands. He's liable to come in here and try to lynch Ben, and if he does, he's liable to have a whole lot of help with him. Too many for me and Hawkeye to stop for long."

"Lynching?" Lilly said as she slowly backed away from him. "Because he's a Negro? How could you say such a thing? Ben has been a dear and loyal friend to me since you left. I always knew you had your faults, but I never took you for a bigot."

"Trammel's not a bigot," Hagen told her, "but King Charles is. And so are many of the men who work for him. Trammel's right. We don't know how they're going to react when word spreads that it was Ben who did the killing, so we'd better get the story out quick."

Ben began motioning again with his hands, but Hagen spoke aloud. "Ben was working the door at the Lily when he saw a group of four men ride into town after dark. One of them broke off from the others and rode around back of Main Street while the other three rode on and stopped at the mouth of the alley of the Celestial den. Ben didn't like the looks of it, so he went out back and saw a man behind the tent trying to light a torch. The man lit it and tried to attack Ben. There was a struggle, the man fell on the torch, and it caught fire. In fear for his life, he grabbed a rifle he found in the man's saddle and ran out front to face the three men in the alley. He quickly dispatched them and accidentally fired on the sheriff here, whose return volley is the reason why we're all here in Dr. Moore's office now. He didn't know it was Bookman or that those men worked for the Blackstone Ranch, though the fact that they did speaks volumes as to motive, if you ask me."

Hagen held out his hands as if he was a stage actor who had just finished reciting a sonnet. "That's how it happened. I'll be more than willing to sign a sworn statement to that effect."

Trammel looked at Hagen, then at Ben, and asked him, "That the way it happened?"

The big man nodded, and although he could not speak, Trammel could sense the truth in his affirmation. Hagen seemed to have gotten it exactly right.

"How?" the sheriff asked aloud.

The question caught Hagen off guard. "How what?"

"How do you know that's what happened?" Trammel pushed. "You were in your office at the Pot of Gold. Your office doesn't have a window. You weren't there when Ben killed Bookman. You said so yourself. So how do you know that's what happened?"

"It's obvious, isn't it?" Hagen said. "You saw the scene yourself, or are you drunker than you're letting on?"

Lilly said, "Buck, I think you're making a lot out of nothing here."

Emily clearly didn't think so. "How did you know what happened during the fight he had with Bookman? He didn't roll over on the torch and just catch fire. He couldn't have, because his neck was already broken. We found the torch on his back, not at his side. It didn't just land there." She looked at Ben. "You set him on fire, didn't you?"

Lilly and Hagen were about to defend him when Ben began to motion with his hands again, much to the annoyance of Dr. Moore.

Lilly translated. "He said Bookman already had the torch lit when Ben tried to stop him. He tried to set Ben on fire. He hit Bookman hard in the jaw and collapsed. Ben doesn't remember what happened after that. The next thing he remembers is being shot by Buck in front of the saloon."

Dr. Moore added as he continued his stitching, "He may be in a state of shock. It's been known to happen after an especially violent event. I saw it in soldiers after the war, when I was a young medic. It's often temporary and, in a day or so, I'm sure Ben will have a complete and clear recollection of what happened."

Trammel was not so sure. "Well, if he didn't before, he will now, thanks to Hagen."

The dandy's eyes narrowed. "I don't appreciate the insinuation, Sheriff."

"And I don't appreciate the interference," Trammel said. He could still feel the whiskey in his system. He knew how it worked on him, and allowed his temper to run more freely, so he fought hard to keep hold of it. "You were awfully eager to take the side of a bouncer you hardly know. And you knew just enough facts to make Bookman getting burned to death sound like an accident. Why? And don't tell me I'm imagining things because I'm drunk, because we both know I'm not." He turned to face Hagen. "How did you —"

Hints and fragments began to rush together in Trammel's mind. Whiskey did not only serve to grease the rails of his temper, but in the right measure, it also helped him think clearer.

Adam Hagen had summoned Dr. Moore from New Orleans.

Adam Hagen had spent time in New

Orleans before he went to Wichita.

Dr. Moore was about to say something earlier when a look from Hagen shut him up.

This might not have been the first gunshot wound Moore had fixed. Trammel's mind made the leap. This was not the first time he had sewn up Ben either.

Adam Hagen, Dr. Jacob Moore, and Ben London had all been in New Orleans together.

Ben had not been working for Lilly by accident. Hagen had sent him there. And he had brought him here with Lilly for a reason. Just like he had brought Dr. Moore here for a reason.

By the time he heard himself say the words, Trammel already knew the truth. "Ben's working for you, isn't he?"

Hagen blanched as he began to slowly back away. "Now, Buck. Just calm down for a moment. Take a breath and remember yourself."

Trammel did not move and he did not lose hold of his temper. "You understand those hand signals he does, don't you? Maybe you even taught them to him when you two worked together in New Orleans. That's Indian sign, isn't it? You'd have picked that up when you were in the cavalry."

Hagen moved farther back as his left hand moved closer to his pistol. Ben moved off the doctor's table and stood next to Hagen. Dr. Moore set his scissors aside and looked down.

Hagen held out his hand to Trammel. "There's no reason to get angry, Buck. I can explain everything."

"Explain!" Lilly yelled. "You mean you and Ben have been working together this entire time? I thought he was working for me."

Ben made some hand movements, but Hagen spoke for him. "Ben was working for you, Lilly. He was loyal to you, and only you. When I wrote you upon arriving here at Blackstone, you told me you were having trouble finding someone to replace Trammel. Ben happened to be looking for work and I sent him to see you. From what you have said and from what I have seen, the arrangement has worked out to everyone's advantage."

But that was not enough for Lilly. "Then why didn't you tell me you were sending him?" She looked at Ben. "Or why didn't you tell me you knew Adam? Even when I told you we were coming to Blackstone. Or since?" She placed her hands on her hips. "Or did you just talk me into coming to Blackstone and make it seem like it was my idea?"

Hagen tried to laugh it off, but Trammel saw something different in his eyes. "You're all making this sound far more sinister than it is."

But the more Trammel thought about it, the more it all made sense. Since the day they had ridden into Blackstone together, Adam Hagen had a reason for every single thing he did. The saloons. The laudanum den. The partnership with Lucien Clay. Buying up the mines. Bringing Dr. Moore, Lilly, and Ben to town. Every action designed with only one goal in mind. To pull King Charles Hagen down from his throne.

Trammel decided it was time for some answers. "I've got four men dead and a hell of a lot of angry people asking a lot of questions. And if they don't like the answers, they're liable to burn this town to the ground. What are you up to, Hagen? No more dancing around. You'd better tell me, and right now."

Lilly cursed as she pulled her shawl tightly around her shoulders and stormed out of the doctor's office. Trammel turned to watch her head back toward her saloon and saw no one had followed her. He did not go after her, for he knew she would be safe at the Gilded Lily.

Hagen nodded toward the door. "If the crowd out there is as nasty as you claim it is, you ought to see her home, Sheriff. Wouldn't want her getting mixed up in all of this, now would we?"

"She was mixed up in this the second you talked her into coming here." He gestured toward Ben. "But she was just the side bet, wasn't she? Ben's the real reason why you wanted her here. What is he? Your muscle? A hired hand you can use instead of relying on Clay's boys from Laramie?" Yes, Trammel decided. It all made sense now. "Ben didn't just happen to notice a bunch of riders coming into town. He was keeping an eye out, wasn't he? On your orders. Lilly was just part of the bargain, wasn't she?"

Hagen grinned. "A bargain of which you seem to be the beneficiary most nights, wouldn't you say?"

Trammel started toward Hagen and Ben got in the way.

Emily got there first and headed Trammel off. "It's been a long, bad night, Buck, and Hawkeye needs you. We can pick this up in the morning, after I take a look at Bookman's body before the burial. The time to think will do us all good." She placed a hand on his shoulder but did not lead him. "What do you say?"

Emily always had a way of knowing how to calm him down, and she still did. He pointed at Hagen and Ben. "Neither of you leave town, understand? No trips to Laramie and no walking around in public. If someone kills one of you before I write up my final report, I won't be held responsible."

"We will all follow your wishes to the letter, Sheriff," Hagen said. "But let's not forget that I'm the aggrieved party here, Buck. Bookman was attacking my establishments and planned to kill my customers, probably on orders from my father. I never claimed to be innocent in all of this, but I'm not the only guilty one wrapped up in it."

Trammel did not want to allow Hagen to have the last word, but Emily urged him to leave with her, which he did.

CHAPTER 18

As they walked along Main Street, Trammel was glad to see the crowd in front of the Pot of Gold had thinned out a bit, thanks to Hawkeye on horseback, ordering the people to keep moving.

Emily had noticed it, too. "Hawkeye has really grown into the job, hasn't he?"

Trammel was happy to talk about anything other than death, if only for a little while. "I think the job has grown around him," Trammel said. "He's still got a lot to learn, but he's off to a good start."

"That's thanks to you," she said. "He still idolizes you, you know."

"He's learning by my mistakes lately," Trammel said. "Doesn't seem like I can do anything right anymore."

"Don't say that."

"It's true. The streets are full of men in laudanum stupors. Mike Albertson's got a big crowd coming to town on Saturday to march against them. King Charles tried to burn down Adam's laudanum den tonight, and I've got four dead men on my hands. Hell, even the mayor hates me now. If this was happening to someone else, I might think it's funny, but it's not. It's happening to me."

Emily walked quietly beside him. "These things blow over, Buck. And somehow you always find a way to make it right. Don't ask me how, but you do."

"I did when I had you. Now, I'm not so sure."

"You have Lilly," Emily said. "You two seem happy."

Trammel did not want to talk about her now. Not with Emily. "That's different. We're different. She's not you."

"I certainly hope we're different," Emily remarked. "She's a saloon keeper and I'm a medical woman. We don't even look the same."

"You know what I mean," Trammel said, wondering if this might not be the whiskey talking. "I was different when I was with you. Better, maybe. Sharper." He was beginning to think he sounded like a fool. "I don't know. I'm just not the same without you and I don't like it. That's nothing against Lilly, it's just the way it is."

The crowd was getting louder the closer they got to the Pot of Gold, so Emily stopped and made Trammel stop, too. "Listen to me, Buck, and listen good. You didn't call it off between us. I did. And it's not because of anything you did, but of who you are. It's because of what you are that made me end things, and that's not because you're bad. It's because you're good. You're strong and brave, and not just because of your size. You could have this whole town eating out of the palm of your hand, paying off to you instead of to Hagen, but you don't. You use that strength to help people, and to stop men from hurting this town. I didn't break it off because of what you did or because you killed people. I know why you did all that. I broke it off because I'm selfish. I don't want to share you with anyone else. Not this town, not your past, no one. I broke it off because I'm scared that one day, you're going to be up against something you can't beat. Something that's bigger even than you. And if that day came while we were still together, I'd be a widow again."

She reached up and touched his cheek, sending a calm, familiar warmth through him. "I didn't break things off because I didn't love you anymore. I broke them off because I love you too much. More than I've ever loved anyone else, including my husband. He was a good man, but he wasn't you. And because his death almost killed me, I can't imagine what yours would do to me. And that's the only reason why we're not together right now, Steve. It's because I love you too much, I'm too scared to let you love me."

Trammel felt dizzy from her touch and he lost his grip on his control. He allowed the feeling that had been building up inside him all these months spill out. "They're smarter than me, Emily. Adam. Charles. Lucien Clay. Even Mike Albertson. They're all smarter than me, and all I ever do is clean up their messes. They're all angling for a piece of this town and I can't get ahead of them. All I can do is clean up after them and write up the reports and hope like hell I get there in time to keep more people from getting killed."

Emily caressed his cheek a final time before lowering her hand. "You're not stupid, Steve. You might not be as smart as them, but you're smart enough. You put together Adam's plan back there in the office before I did. Even before Lilly did, and Ben has been working for her for over a year. Maybe you're not as smart as them, but you don't have to be."

Trammel had not thought of it that way. "Why not?"

"Because all of their plans, all of their schemes, no matter how fancy they are, run right through the middle of this town." She poked him in the chest. "And that means they have to get through you if they want to win. And that's why they'll lose."

She turned him around before he could say something he would probably regret, linked her arm through his, and pulled him toward where her wagon was parked at the Pot of Gold.

"Come on, Sheriff. Walk me to my wagon so I can get a few hours of sleep before we head up to the ranch tomorrow."

Trammel gladly walked with her. "Think you'll get much sleep after all of this?"

"No," she admitted, "but it's nice to think I will. I have to try anyway. Though I don't relish the idea of seeing Bookman again. I know he was a horrible man, but no one deserves to die like that."

Trammel could still feel the cold steel of the pistol Bookman had placed against his neck several months before. He would not be shedding any tears over his passing. He decided to talk about something else. "What do you think of Dr. Moore? He do a good job on Ben's wound."

"He did," she allowed. "Not as good as me, of course."

For the first time in a while, Trammel laughed.

Chapter 19

The next morning Charles Hagen sipped whiskey as he listened to Dr. Downs sitting across from him as she offered her professional opinion on how John Bookman had died.

He had never noticed before how pretty she was. Graceful and intelligent, too. She was still young, perhaps thirty-five or so, and could become quite remarkable given the right support. He regretted not paying more attention to her before now, but vowed to remedy that in the future. He also reminded himself that he was mildly drunk, though it was not yet eight in the morning.

Sheriff Trammel's presence served to ruin the effect. He loomed behind her like a dark cloud.

"I've completed a thorough examination of John Bookman's remains," Dr. Downs told him.

"A mere formality, I suppose," Hagen

said. "We all know how he died."

"Looks can be deceiving," the doctor told him. "This may come as cold comfort to you, but Mr. Bookman did not die from being burned to death."

Hagen's jaw tightened. "I know. He died when I shot him to put him out of his misery."

"He did," Emily allowed, "but although he was close to death, it wasn't only due to the burns he received from the torch. He was going to die because his neck had been broken long before that."

Charles Hagen set his glass on the desk before he spilled it. "What?"

"His neck was broken here," she explained, showing the impacted area on her own neck. "It wasn't caused from a fall or by being struck by a blunt instrument like a club or a piece of iron, but separated and crushed. The damage was similar to what happens during a hanging, though in Mr. Bookman's case, he did not die right away. That has been known to happen in hangings, too, especially when the knot is not tied properly."

But Charles Hagen did not care about other cases or other men, only John Bookman. "You mean he was alive when he was being burned?"

"Yes," Emily said, "but I don't think he was able to feel it. It was still a horrible experience and scarred his lungs, but you can rest assured he did not feel it. If he had, I doubt he would have lived long enough to speak to you."

Recovering from the shock of the nature of Bookman's death, Charles Hagen regained his composure and finished the rest of his whiskey. "Yes, that is cold comfort indeed, Doctor, but I'm glad his suffering was minimal."

He looked up at Trammel. Good Lord, he was a big man! "As for you, Sheriff, you undoubtedly remembered that John spoke to me before . . . before I did what had to be done."

"Yes, sir, I do."

Hagen liked that the sheriff still called him "sir" despite all their past disagreements. "But what you don't know is that he told me the name of the man who killed him. At the time I thought it was the man who had set fire to him, but now I know his assault was far more brutal than that." Charles Hagen jutted out his jaw and aimed it at the sheriff. "I know the man's name, Trammel. I sincerely hope you know it, for if you don't, I will have to take matters into my own hands per our agreement."

Trammel did not hesitate. "Ben London broke his neck and set him on fire."

Hagen was surprised and pleased by the sheriff's honesty. "That's the same name John gave me. Now the only question is whether or not you've already arrested him."

"He's been confined to town," Trammel told him. "He's recovering from a bullet wound, so he won't be going anywhere for a while. I'm still looking into a few things."

"Things?" Hagen roared. "What things? The man is guilty, sir. You said so yourself. You also have John Bookman's dying declaration, which is a mighty powerful bit of evidence in any court of law in the land. I'm no attorney, but even I know that much."

"That's my understanding, too, sir," Trammel admitted. "And if I need to arrest him, you can rest assured I will."

"If?" Hagen repeated. "There's no 'ifs,' 'ands,' or 'buts' about it, sir. Ben London is guilty. You'll arrest him, by God, or if you're afraid of him, I'll do it for you. I'll hang him from the nearest tree and he'll be a long time dying."

"You do anything to that man or any other in Blackstone, you'll find yourself in the cell next to him," Trammel said. "Or with him, if you force the issue."

Hagen wagged a crooked finger at him. "I know what this is. You've worked out a deal with Adam, haven't you?"

"No one's worked out anything with anyone," Trammel told him. "Including me. I'm still trying to work out a few things myself, such as why Bookman took three men into Blackstone to attack the laudanum den in the first place."

In all the blood and horror that had filled his thoughts those past dreadful hours, Charles Hagen had allowed himself to forget how it had all started. It seemed as if it had happened years ago, but less than twenty-four hours had passed since he had given Bookman the orders that had ultimately cost him his life.

He sat in his chair as though he had been struck by lightning.

Trammel seized on the great man's silence. "See, the real problem here isn't who killed your men, Mr. Hagen. In fact, that's just about the only clear thing about this whole mess. Ben London killed them. The bigger question is what they were doing in town." The big man leaned on Hagen's desk. "And on whose orders."

The proximity of Trammel served to bring King Charles back to his senses. "You don't imagine I had anything to do with it, do you?"

Trammel remained leaning on his desk. "Bookman was your right-hand man. The men he brought to town with him worked for you. They were ready to kill people in Adam Hagen's laudanum den. You and Adam hate each other. So, yeah, the thought of you ordering them to do it had crossed my mind."

The sheriff brought down a thick hand on his desk, causing Charles to jump. "What's the matter, Mr. Hagen? I thought you were all fired up about getting some answers. How about giving some of your own? You ordered Bookman and the others to attack the laudanum den last night, didn't you?"

Charles Hagen froze. He had always done so in the opening moments of a crisis. Bad news from his lawyer, Montague, or a financial problem he had not anticipated. An acquisition gone wrong or learning of a devastating business problem from one of his sons. One of his real sons anyway.

This usually was done in the privacy of his den. Despite his reputation to the contrary, he had never been the kind of man who thought well on his feet. He had discovered during childhood that he could not lie worth a damn, but he knew the truth could be a terrible weapon if used too soon. That was why he had taught himself to be a cunning man instead. To plan everything out in advance so that when disaster did eventually strike — which, inevitably, it would — he had a plan in place to respond appropriately to buy time until he decided upon the right course of action.

Planning in advance had become more than second nature to him. It had become as much a part of him as his own limbs and organs. He did it without thinking and, as the initial shock of Trammel's accusation began to subside, he remembered he had also planned for this without realizing it.

He took a piece of paper from his desk and handed it to Trammel. "I'm afraid this may have had something to do with it, Sheriff."

Trammel took the paper and held it so that the doctor could read it, too.

"That's the notice about the march Mike Albertson is planning for this Saturday," she said. "Mrs. Higgins was handing them out yesterday."

Trammel looked at Hagen. "What's this got to do with Bookman and the others being in town last night?"

The story Charles Hagen had concocted even before he had summoned Bookman into his study came to his mind. "I'll admit that I was not in a good way when I came back to the ranch last night. Seeing John like that and being forced to do what I did threw me. Despite what Adam may have told you, I do have feelings, Sheriff. I don't care about many people, but I counted John Bookman among them. I was angry and confused about all that had happened. I didn't understand why such a good man had died in such a horrible manner. I was too upset to speak to any of my men, and they were still reeling from the loss of Bookman and not much help anyway, so I turned to the one place I thought I could find answers. The small home John has on the spread."

"He didn't live in the bunkhouse with the other men?" Trammel asked.

"No," Hagen told them. "It's difficult to maintain authority over men when they all sleep in the same place, so I always allowed John to live separately from them. To maintain the right amount of distance from the men in our employ. It was an indulgence, I suppose, but one he never abused." Hagen pointed at the handbill Trammel now held. "I found that among his things, along with a small journal he had begun to keep. I know it was an invasion of his privacy, but the dead have no dignity to offend, so I sat on his bunk and began to read it. The words he wrote down surprised me, Sheriff. Their depth of thought confounded me. I had known John Bookman for decades and never knew him capable of such feeling."

"What did it say?" Emily asked.

"Ramblings about the evils of laudanum," Hagen lied. "He had lost a sister to the dreaded stuff, a fact he had managed to keep from me all these years. It's a strange thing, Trammel, to see a man I thought I knew spill out his mind on paper like that. And with such hatred. I suppose the animosity that exists between me and Adam had breathed new life into that hatred. Perhaps he even felt it had given him license to act against the place that reminded him of his sister's unfortunate passing. I don't know."

Hagen rubbed his hand across his mouth for effect. "And now I suppose we'll never know."

Trammel placed the handbill on Hagen's desk. "I'll need to take a look at that notebook you're talking about."

As part of his natural course of thought, Charles Hagen had already taken that into account, too. "You can't."

Trammel's jaw clenched. "This is no time

for games, Hagen."

"You can't because I don't have it anymore," Charles admitted. "I was so horrified and disgusted by what I had read that I tossed it into the fireplace. A foolish thing to do, I know, but as I said, I was not in my right mind. I know that makes your investigation more difficult, Sheriff, and for that I apologize, but in the fog of war, things happen that we don't intend to happen."

" 'Fog of war,' " Trammel repeated as he walked to the windows that looked out on the width and breadth of the Blackstone Ranch. It was a view Charles Hagen had spent countless hours admiring and had designed his house around. Whenever pain or turmoil about the ranch reached his desk, he took comfort in being able to look up from his troubles and see the very thing he was fighting to preserve. That which he had built with his own iron will, and he would be damned if Adam, or his puppet Trammel, took it from him.

Hagen watched the sheriff linger by the windows, as if something had caught his eye. Even Dr. Downs began to look uncomfortable.

Hagen did not like the silence. "I know I've upset you, Sheriff, especially after our unpleasant conversation last night, but —"

"What fireplace?" Trammel interrupted him.

Hagen had not been expecting that. "I'm afraid I don't understand what you're talking about."

Trammel pointed at a wooden cabin in the near distance. "I take it that's where Bookman lived, isn't it?"

Hagen did not have to look at what Trammel was pointing at to know what it was. "Yes, that's the foreman's house where he lived. Why?"

Trammel turned away from the window. "What fireplace? That one doesn't have a chimney. Just a bunch of piping sticking out of the roof."

"Yes," Hagen said, trying to hide his annoyance. "It's a potbellied stove. You don't expect me to allow the man to freeze to death in the winter, do you?"

"No," Trammel said. "But you just told us that you sat on his bunk and was so taken by Bookman's words that you threw the notebook into the fireplace." He poked a thumb over his left shoulder. "There's no fireplace in there, Mr. Hagen. Just a potbellied stove. You said so yourself. So you couldn't have thrown it in the fireplace, could you?"

Hagen cursed himself for telling too

elaborate a lie, but quickly recovered. "Of course not. I flipped through the book in there and saw there was a great deal to read, so I brought it back here to the main house, where the light was better." He pointed to the fireplace at the other end of the study. "I sat there where the light was better and, upon finding the more troubling parts, threw the book in the flames in disgust."

Trammel looked around the room, and Hagen noticed the doctor was following the path of his eyes. "Those oil lamps on your desk look like they'd throw off a hell of a lot more light than that cozy spot by the fire would."

A cold sweat broke out on Hagen's back as the sheriff slowly walked from the desk to the fireplace. "It's an awfully long way to throw a book from where you're sitting. Pages would probably fly open, even if you did manage to chuck it pretty good."

Trammel crouched beside the still-burning embers and took a closer look at the fire. He grabbed a poker and began moving some of the logs.

"You must've had one hell of a fire going here," Trammel said, "because I don't see a scrap of it left. Not even in the ashes. Something like that usually leaves some kind of trace, especially if it was a notebook, like you said. Usually a scrap of the cover would still be in there."

Hagen was as panicked as he was annoyed. "I wasn't in the right state of mind to judge the quality of the binding, sir. It was a notebook. I threw it in the fire. It burned. That's all I know. I was wrong for doing it, but I wasn't thinking properly. I don't think any of us were after what we witnessed last night."

Trammel stood up and replaced the poker in the stand. "Well, I've got to tell you, Mr. Hagen, you've got a stronger constitution than I do and I'm not afraid to admit it."

The sheriff was playing coy and it was beginning to concern him. "How's that?"

Trammel clapped his hands clean of the dust from the fire. "Because after what we saw last night, I didn't want any part of a fire. Sounds like you didn't mind it, though. Like I said, you've got a stronger constitution than me."

Hagen could see the effect his words were having on Dr. Downs and knew he needed to draw this meeting to a close before he dug himself into a deeper hole. "I doubt anyone has a stronger constitution than you do, Sheriff Trammel, but I'm afraid I have important business to attend to. We lost four men last night, and we'll be burying them within the hour. I've also lost my foreman and three good men only days before I'm supposed to bring horses and cattle down to the railroad in Laramie. I'm quite busy, so I hope you'll excuse me. Just let Mr. Montague know when you want my official statement and he'll be glad to provide it."

He shook hands with Dr. Downs as she got up to leave. Trammel opened the study door for her and held it open as she passed, but not before taking a final, long look at the fireplace. He looked at Hagen and smiled. "Yes, sir. A hell of a fire. Good day to you."

He tipped his hat and left, softly closing the door behind him.

King Charles Hagen snatched the whiskey from the desk and filled his glass to the brim and drank it down hard.

He had intended to drive Trammel away. Now he had only served to make him curious. And dullards were at their most dangerous when they were curious.

CHAPTER 20

Dr. Emily Downs struggled to keep up with Trammel's long strides as they walked back to her wagon. "Well, what do you think?"

He grabbed hold of her by the waist and hoisted her into the wagon box without asking her first. She normally would have taken offense at him handling her like she was a child but knew there was no malice behind it. He was so troubled by their conversation with Charles Hagen that he probably had not even realized he had done it.

During their short time together, Emily Downs had learned that there was a time and place to talk to Buck Trammel and this was not it.

He climbed atop the horse he had borrowed from Elias's livery as she snapped the reins and got her horse to begin pulling the wagon back down the hill toward Blackstone.

As cumbersome as it may be at times, Emily Downs had grown fond of using her wagon instead of a single horse. She had always found riding sidesaddle almost as uncomfortable as a regular saddle. And the wagon afforded her more room to haul things if and when she needed it. In her line of work, she never knew when she might need the extra room, especially given what was happening in Blackstone these days.

She watched Buck grind his teeth as he rode his own horse beside her. She knew he normally rode much faster than this but was riding slower for her sake. She could tell he was upset by their conversation with King Hagen. He always ground his teeth when he was annoyed.

She waited until they were well out of earshot of the ranch house before saying, "Enough brooding, Buck. What did you think of our talk with King Charles?"

"I think there's more horse poop in that den than there is on this road," Trammel said. "Bookman didn't keep a diary, nor that handbill neither. Bookman and the others didn't ride into town on some crusade. He did it on Hagen's orders just so he could hit Adam where it hurt most. And do you want to know the worst part? I'm kind of sorry Bookman didn't get his way."

"You don't mean that," Emily said. "Think

of all the people who would have died."

"Most of them are already dead," Trammel said. "Their bodies just haven't figured it out yet. As for the Celestials, it would've taken Hagen a while to replace them and the laudanum, too. Would've made Blackstone a livable town again. There's no denying that."

Trammel spat off to the side of his horse and wiped his mouth with the back of his hand. "Now all we've got is a big mess brewing with that damned march of Albertson's only a few days away."

Emily hoped her services would not be needed during the march, but she was also a realist. "I wonder where Mr. Hagen got that handbill for the march. I agree it wasn't in Bookman's place."

"Probably got that with the rest of his mail or found it someplace."

She waited for him to say something more, but saw the sheriff sit upright in the saddle. "Or maybe things are a lot simpler than that. Maybe he had it printed himself."

Emily quickly followed his line of thinking and did not like where it led. "You think Mr. Hagen could be behind all of the trouble Mike Albertson is stirring up?"

She could tell the idea was as new to Buck as it was to her and he was still piecing it together in his mind. She knew he had a habit of speaking before thinking sometimes, but not in a way that caused trouble to himself or insult to others. He only did it among people he genuinely trusted, and she was always honored when he did it around her. She liked to see the way his mind pieced things together. She liked it when he surprised himself by showing he was smarter than he thought.

"Charles Hagen backing Albertson would answer a lot of questions," Trammel said. "I never bought his retired-freighter-turned-crusader bit. He just rode in here one day and started raising hell the next. It didn't ring true to me. It feels like somebody's backing him, and King Hagen's as good a choice as any. It's certainly not Adam."

Emily had not thought about it that way. "Albertson did seem to drop from the sky one day, didn't he?"

If Trammel had heard her, he did not show it. His mind was on the scent of something and she watched him follow it as he rode. "He's renting a room from Mrs. Higgins but doesn't seem to spend a lot of time there."

"How do you know?" she asked.

Trammel looked guilty, and she knew he had been up to no good. "I kind of talked my way into his room. The place looked like no one even lived there at all. There wasn't anything in the room that showed he spent a lot of time there. Not even a bag to pack his stuff in. I know freighters are used to traveling light, but there should've been something personal about the place. The room looked like it had never been touched. Found a lot of newspapers from Laramie, though. And not the *Laramie Daily* either. I only found the *Laramie Ledger,* which you can't find in Blackstone."

"That is strange," Emily agreed. "If he's so dedicated to changing the town, why not live here full-time? And why does he spend so much time in Laramie?"

"All good questions," Trammel said. "And I think I had the answer until I lost it."

"What do you mean?" she asked.

"I found a notebook tucked under Albertson's mattress," Trammel admitted. "A real notebook, too, not like the one Hagen lied about. I hid it in the back of my pants when Mrs. Higgins came up the stairs but lost it at some point last night. I think it fell out when I ducked to avoid Ben shooting at me, but I'm not certain."

Emily was disappointed, but she understood why it happened. "Did you go back and check later?"

"Yeah." Trammel frowned. "I had forgotten all about it until I got back to the jail. I went outside and looked all over for it, but it was too dark. It could've happened anywhere, I guess. I don't care that it's lost, but I'm worried about the wrong person finding it."

"What do you mean?"

"If some stranger finds it and throws it away, or uses it for themselves, great," Trammel explained. "But if they give it to the wrong person, like Adam, it might cause trouble. I didn't have the chance to read it, so I don't know what it says. Either way, Albertson is going to come looking for it when he finds it's missing, and Mrs. Higgins will tell him I searched his room. I knew that would happen when I took the book. I was just hoping to be able to confront him with what was in the book when he did."

Emily was glad to be able to provide a solution. "I'll look for it for you. Today, when we get back to town. It would look silly for the sheriff to be looking around for something like that in broad daylight. Might tip off too many people and raise more questions than answers. If I do it, it'll be much easier. I'll probably get a few kindly gentlemen to help me look for it, too. I'll start at the spot where you fell when Ben shot at you and work my way around there. I'll even check at Dr. Moore's office. Even if you lost it there, he might not have read it or given it to Adam."

Trammel smiled at her. "You're quite resourceful, Dr. Downs."

She smiled, too. "I have my moments."

As they approached the Stone Gate, Trammel reined in his horse and allowed Emily's wagon to ride through first. She thought about the men Buck had taken on alone at that dreaded place only a few months before. The bravery he had shown and the wounds he had suffered. He had fully recovered since then, thank goodness, but their love had not. The Battle of Stone Gate, as Mr. Rhoades had taken to calling it in the *Bugle*, had shown the world who Buck Trammel really was. And it had shown her that she loved him too much to be able to endure losing him. She'd had to let him go or risk losing herself again in grief.

She was almost thirty-five years old and still found the complexities of life fascinating.

Emily looked back and saw Buck had ridden through the break in the stone wall to catch up with her. "I think they should have the decency to put a sign or something up there to commemorate what happened. You deserve it."

But Trammel clearly did not agree. "Rhoades made it out to be a hell of a lot more than it really was. Just a dustup between a sheriff and a couple of hired guns, is all. I'm just glad the right people died. Sorry you got caught up in it in town. Sorry about a lot of things that happened that day. And afterward."

They had reached the part of the road that revealed the town of Blackstone in its entirety. It had changed so much since she and her husband had first found it years before. It had been a miner's bank, a general store, and a couple of rundown hotels back then. It had since grown a bit to accommodate more people and more services, like lawyers and other shops for thc miners and ranchers to frequent. Now, with Adam Hagen's influence, New Main Street had served to almost double the length of the main thoroughfare of the tiny town, and the new buildings, despite their purpose, made the town look more modern. More finished. She hoped the houses Adam was building would attract good people to this good place and make Blackstone an even better town than it already was.

She also hoped that the conflict between Buck and Adam would find a way to resolve itself. She hoped each man would give enough to cast their differences aside and resume their friendship. Each man was formidable in his own right, but together, they could help make Blackstone the kind of town she had always dreamed it could be.

But while she remained hopeful, she was not naïve and doubted that either man would budge an inch from their position. Adam wanted enough money and power to fight King Charles, and laudanum was the way to get it.

Buck wanted law and order in Blackstone, and one of the best ways to get it was to cut down on the laudanum Adam and his Celestials sold.

Agreeable men would find a way to sort out their differences. To compromise. But Adam and Buck were not the compromising sort. Agreeable men did not survive long in the Wyoming Territory.

She decided to try to pull Buck out of his own thoughts by talking about something cheerful as they rode together back to town. "You have to admit the town looks awfully pretty from up here."

"Enjoy it while it lasts," Trammel said. "Adam wants to build a mill off Main Street. Those new houses he's building are supposed to be for all the workers he plans on hiring."

"I've heard that. Sounds like a nice way to bring some new people to town."

"Bet they won't be allowed in his laudanum den," Trammel said. "He's weakened the town enough with that poison to take it over. He'll probably make them pack up and move up into the hills to serve the miners."

Emily had not thought of that. "I bet you're right. It's almost ingenious."

"That's Adam for you," Trammel said. "If he'd just put that big head of his to doing some good, why, I bet he could be —"

Both of them turned when they heard a single gunshot ring out from the edge of town. It was quickly followed by a woman's shriek. They were close enough to Main Street by then to be able to tell where it had come from.

"That sounds like it came from the bank," Emily said.

"Great," Trammel said as he pulled his Henry from the scabbard on his saddle. "Just what we need. A bank robbery on top of everything else. Ride in slow, Emily, and keep a sharp eye out. I don't want you riding into the middle of anything."

He put his heels to his horse and galloped down the road toward the sound of the gunfire and scream.

Because that was who Buck Trammel was. It was the reason why she loved him and could never be with him.

She offered up a silent prayer as she watched him ride into danger.

CHAPTER 21

Trammel rounded the corner past Elias's livery at the edge of Main Street. Elias was out front, looking in the direction of the bank, his old Henry rifle in his hands.

"Shot came from the bank," the old black man yelled up at him as he passed. "Don't think it's a robbery, though. Didn't see anyone running out."

Trammel was thankful for that little bit of information as he sped by. He saw a small group of people crouching on the boardwalk on either side of the bank. They were too curious to run away, but too scared to get any closer.

The doorway of every saloon on Main Street was jammed with people looking out, but no one dared to venture outside. Not yet anyway. He knew a fair number of them were armed, and if the bank was being robbed, they stood to lose their life savings. The robbers would have more holes in them than a screen door if they stepped outside now.

Trammel was not surprised to see Adam Hagen had taken cover behind a horse trough directly across the thoroughfare from the bank. His pistol was in his left hand. Adam was a lot of things, but he was not a coward. Trammel had never known the man to shy away from the action if there was action to be had.

Trammel brought his horse up shy of the bank and yelled at Hagen, "You see what happened?"

"Just heard the shot and the woman's scream," Hagen yelled back. "No one's come out or gone in since. If it's a robbery, it's not going well."

Trammel did not take that as a good sign. If no one had come out, someone might be holding them in there against their will.

He climbed down from the saddle and began to slowly approach the bank from the side, eyeing the door the entire time. The horse ambled back toward the livery where it lived.

"Hello in the bank!" he called out. "This is Sheriff Trammel. Come out with your hands up and empty. You will not be harmed."

A bald clerk Trammel recognized as Barney Kroft came out of the bank with his hands raised. "Sheriff! Come quick. There's been a terrible accident. Mr. Montague is dead!"

Trammel ran into the bank.

Adam Hagen was close on his heels.

Trammel had to dodge his way around the cluster of weeping tellers and customers who had already gone into the office to see Montague for themselves.

When he reached Montague's office, he saw the reason for their tears.

At first, the bank president and lawyer looked like he had simply fallen asleep at his desk. His head was back and his mouth hung open, slack. But the blood that soaked the front of his shirt from the bullet hole under his chin and the pistol in his right hand on the desk told a different story. The bullet hole in the ceiling and the gore behind him said it all.

Fred Montague had committed suicide.

Trammel sagged against the door. On top of everything else facing Blackstone right now, the head of the bank had just killed himself. "Damn."

Adam Hagen wheeled into the office after him and took a step back from the terrible sight. "Good God. Fred."

Hagen began to move farther into the office, but Trammel grabbed his arm. "Outside, Adam. Let me take a look at the place first."

"Don't be silly," Hagen said. "Half the bank has already walked through the place. I was just going to look to see if he left a note, is all."

"That's my business, not yours," Trammel said. "It's best for all involved if I do the searching."

Hagen threw up his hands and remained standing against the doorway while Trammel began searching the desk for some kind of note. The desk was full of papers, so it was no easy task. He gently lifted the dead man's right hand, careful of the pistol it still held, and removed the papers beneath it. They were notes and telegrams and bank statements. The numbers meant nothing to him, but there was nothing in the papers to indicate why Fred Montague had chosen that moment to take his life.

Trammel noticed Adam was paying close attention to him as he began to open the desk drawers. He would go through all of it in detail later, but there was no obvious suicide note in any of them.

He went to the large safe at the side of the room and checked it, but it was locked. So was the back door that led to the alley outside. The key was still in the lock, and the only odd thing about it was that it looked new.

"That's strange," Trammel said. "The lock's been changed recently."

"Oh?" Hagen said. "How do you know?"

Trammel noted the scrapes around the wood where it had been fitted. "It just looks new. And those scrapes are fresh. Wonder why he did that."

"I haven't the slightest idea," Hagen offered.

Trammel looked at him. "I wasn't asking you." A nasty thought crept into the sheriff's mind. "Or should I be asking you?"

Hagen closed his eyes and shook his head. "Jesus, Buck. You can't possibly think I had anything to do with this. Why, a blind man could see he killed himself. What reason would I have for wanting old Fred dead?"

"Because he worked for the ranch," Trammel said. "Maybe it's retaliation for what Bookman tried to do last night?"

Hagen crossed his arms over his chest. "I swear. Satan doesn't get as much blame for things as I do."

"Satan's not as cunning as you," Trammel answered. The more he thought of it, the more he became sure that Montague's suicide the morning after the attempt on Hagen's laudanum den was too much of a coincidence. "Why would Montague pick today to kill himself?"

"You're the sheriff!" Hagen exclaimed. "How should I know? I had no reason to wish him dead. In fact, just the opposite. His death causes me more trouble than I had planned for."

Trammel did not like the sound of that. Voicing a concern was one thing. Having it confirmed was another matter entirely. "How so?"

Hagen looked at him as if he was the poorest soul alive. "He was predictable as the turning of the earth. To paraphrase something the Bard once said so eloquently so long ago, 'For when lenity and cruelty play for a kingdom the gentler gamester is the soonest winner.' "

Trammel did not know who this Bard was and did not care to know him either. Montague marked the fifth death in Blackstone in the past day. Things were spiraling out of hand and showed no signs of slowing up any time soon.

He turned when he heard a commotion outside and was glad to see it was only Hawkeye, leading Emily through the crowd and into Montague's office.

The deputy paled but did not turn away or get sick.

Emily set her medical bag on the desk and began examining the wound under Montague's chin and at the top of his head. She sniffed the air as she held the back of her hand near the gun barrel. "Poor Fred. Looks like a suicide to me."

"You've put Buck's mind at ease," Hagen said. "He was beginning to think it was Apache who made it look like a suicide."

Emily looked confused, but Trammel said, "Don't listen to him. Mayor Welch will be after me about a cause of death and so will Rhoades. Are you willing to go on record that it was a suicide?"

"I will," she said. "I'll finish my examination soon and have a formal cause of death by the end of the day. You'll have the certificate then."

Hagen cleared his throat. Trammel knew that sound and that nothing good ever came after it. "What now?"

Instead, Hagen went to the office door. "Deputy, would you keep the crowd out there in order for us? I need to speak to Miss Emily and the sheriff alone for a while."

Hawkeye looked past Hagen and asked

Trammel, "What do you want me to do, boss?"

"Best go outside and keep an eye on the crowd," Trammel told him. "Tell them there's no danger and we'll let them know what happened in a bit."

Hawkeye went off as Trammel had asked him to and Hagen shut the door.

"Why do I have a feeling this isn't good news?" Trammel said.

"You're always so glum," Hagen chastised him. "This is excellent news, at least for Dr. Downs."

Emily said, "Can this wait? I'd like to finish my examination of Fred's injuries and get him out of here as soon as possible."

"That's why we need to have this conversation now," Hagen said. "For you see, Emily, I've taken the liberty of removing the ugly task of town coroner away from you and placed it in the capable hands of Dr. Moore."

Trammel felt a surge of anger, but knew he had no right to be angry. He remembered not every fight was his and this one happened to belong to Emily.

He judged her reaction to be more curious than angry. "So that's why you brought him to town."

"No," Hagen assured her. "I brought him

to town because he has a method of curing laudanum addicts that works. I saw it for myself in New Orleans and I want him to do the same here in Blackstone. That will keep him busy, but given that I'm already paying him handsomely for his services, those treatments won't be nearly enough to justify the cost. I've arranged for him to be the official coroner for the town for now and, in a pinch, can assist with matters in Laramie, too. That will give you more time to complete your studies."

"Studies?" she repeated. "What studies?"

"Why, your studies to become a doctor of course," Hagen said. "At least an official one, complete with a diploma and all. Oh, I know you learned quite a bit from your late husband, and I can personally attest to your skill." He held out his right arm, and the hand was surprisingly steady. He even flexed it several times before tremors caused him to lower it.

"I would have lost that arm if it were not for you," Hagen continued, "and I'd like to pay you back for your efforts by making it official. I want you to be able to practice medicine officially anywhere in the country, or to continue to do so right here in Blackstone should you choose. With all of the new people my mill will bring to town, I expect we'll need more than one doctor pretty soon. I'd love it if you and Dr. Moore could even go into practice together one day."

Trammel leaned on a filing cabinet. "Why the sudden generosity?"

"Gratitude," Hagen said, "and these marches Albertson has held have had something of an effect on me. The suffragettes most of all. I believe women should be encouraged to enter the medical field, and not just as nurses. You deserve that chance and I would be honored if you would allow me to pay your way through medical school. I've already made arrangements with the Clearview Medical College in Colorado. They're willing to take your experience into account and allow you to take a four-month course. Assuming you pass their exams, which I believe you will, you'll be awarded a formal medical degree that will allow you to practice medicine anywhere you wish. You won't only be called doctor by default, but by fact." He finished the offer with his best smile. "So, what do you say?"

Trammel had a lot to say but knew it was not his place to say it. This was a decision for Emily to make, not him.

"This is all highly irregular, Adam," she said. "One minute I'm examining Fred and the next you're talking about medical school. Your timing is suspect at best."

"Couldn't have said it better myself," Trammel added.

Hagen's smile did not fade as he looked at both of them. "I brought it up only because the matter of determining cause of death came up. It need not take effect immediately. You still retain the right to issue a determination in Montague's case, and in Bookman's case, too. But afterward, Jacob Moore will be assuming those duties. Any certificate you issue will ultimately be signed by him. The territory officials have already signed off on the matter."

Trammel could tell Emily was slightly overwhelmed by all that had just happened, which was probably his game. He was not one to allow a good crisis to go to waste. "Emily's got a lot of work to do. Let her do her job and she can talk to you about it later."

"Of course," Hagen said, and he joined Trammel as they walked toward the back door of Montague's office. "But if you think of it, say a prayer for poor Charles. He's lost two lapdogs in less than a day. It's a great loss, even for a king."

Trammel traded looks with Emily as he followed Hagen out into the alley. He was usually able to read her emotions pretty well, but just then, he was not able to do so. Leaving her alone to do her job was the best thing under the circumstances.

Trammel shut the door behind him and found Hagen was already a good distance away from him.

"Remember what I said about the laying on of hands," Hagen reminded him.

Trammel was glad the threat of violence still held power over him. "Now you're the one who's suspicious."

"Careful, is all," Hagen said. "I know how you get when you're angry, particularly where your women are involved."

"Emily's not mine," Trammel said as he led them onto Main Street. They turned right and avoided the crowd that had gathered outside the bank. "She's made that perfectly clear."

"I was afraid of that," Hagen said. "It's not your fault, you know. Or Emily's. People can't change who they are, Buck. Not really."

But Trammel did not want to talk about Emily. Not with Hagen or anyone else. He had more important things on his mind. "I'm going to ask this once. Not as a lawman. Not as a sheriff. Not even as your former friend, but as someone who might wind up in the middle of something if you and Charles go at it. I want the truth, and you have my word I won't arrest you no matter what you say. Do you believe me?"

Hagen let out a heavy sigh. "Your word means more to me than any man's I've ever known. I hope you believe that. So yes, I believe you, and I'll tell you the truth."

"Did you kill Montague and make it look like a suicide? Did you have someone do it for you?"

"No," Hagen said immediately. "I'm not sorry he's dead, but I didn't kill him or have him killed." He seemed to struggle with this next bit. "But I can't say in all good conscience that I might not have contributed to the reason he did it."

Trammel wanted to ask more but doubted Hagen would tell him that. He was already pushing the bounds of the man's honesty. "What about Albertson? Did you bring him here?"

"I most certainly did not," Hagen declared. "I always thought Father — I mean, my uncle — had something to do with that. I never met a freighter who didn't like women and whiskey or money. That crooked-backed snake can't be bought with any currency at hand. That tells me he's not what he appears to be. I've even asked Lucien to look into the matter for me, but I haven't had much luck on that score."

In the midst of all this chaos, he had forgotten all about Lucien Clay. "Any word from him on how he's doing?"

"After the beating you gave him?" Hagen laughed. "I doubt I'll hear from him for a while, if at all. No matter. I control our partnership, so he'll do as I say. Assuming he's still alive of course."

"And what about Ben?" Trammel pushed. "He been working for you this entire time he was with Lilly?"

"Everything I said about that last night was true," Hagen said. "He's been loyal to her all this time and played no part in her decision to come to Blackstone. Now, did I bring her here knowing he'd come with her? Yes, but my interests never conflicted with her own. Now that he's here, he's keeping an eye on things for me, too. So you could say he worked as my agent when Bookman tried to burn down the den last night."

"And killed three men from the Blackstone Ranch," Trammel reminded him.

"In matters of violence, he's equal only to you," Hagen said. "I hope I never have to find out which one of you is better, for I fear neither of you will walk away unscathed."

Trammel stopped walking and allowed a

couple of townspeople to pass by before he told Hagen, "I know there's trouble coming, Hagen. I can smell it on the wind. I know you're going to have a hand in it, and this big march on Saturday doesn't help matters much. I don't know how you're planning to go after Charles, and I don't want to know. I don't care which one of you wins either. But whatever you do, keep it off Main Street. If there's killing to be done, do it up there. However it turns out, you've got my word that I'll follow the law and go wherever the facts take me. Understand?"

"Only a fool would expect anything less, Sheriff Trammel. And you may rest assured I am not a fool."

Trammel looked around when he heard his name called out and saw Mayor Welch and Rick Rhoades from the *Bugle* crossing the thoroughfare toward him.

The sheriff closed his eyes. "Just what I need."

Hagen tipped his hat. "I'll leave you to tend to the affairs of state. And thank you."

"For what?"

"For giving me your word," Hagen said. "I know it's not given lightly, and I appreciate the effort."

He went on his way as the mayor and the reporter closed in on Trammel, firing questions as they drew closer.

Damn Hagen, Trammel thought. He always had a way of turning the tables on him.

CHAPTER 22

Albert Micklewhite flinched when Lucien Clay threw his glass against the wall. Even the slightest movement caused a searing pain to course through Clay's head and jaw before cutting through the rest of him.

He had not remembered much about the ride back from Blackstone. He had come to in the carriage, only to pass out immediately from the pain. He woke up in his own bed with one of the town doctors attending to him.

"Lie still," Dr. Cullen had told him when he woke up. "I'm wrapping you in bandages to prevent you from moving your jaw too much. You'll need to use it sparingly for the next month or so until it heals. You can only eat soft foods and broths that won't require chewing. You can drink liquids through the side of your mouth, but do so sparingly. I'm going to administer morphine to help with the pain, which will leave you out of sorts for the foreseeable future."

Clay knew he looked ridiculous sitting in bed like this, his head wrapped in bandages like a kid with a toothache. The damned doctor had even tied the bandages in a bow atop his head, making him look even more foolish than he already did. The right side of his face was swollen to the point of straining the bandages and had turned black.

He was constantly hungry, and the broth his whores served to him gave him no nourishment. He had tried to get out of bed, but the concussion and the morphine made him sick to his stomach. He did not sleep or wake, but rather drifted into and out of consciousness. His whores injected him with the morphine as per Dr. Cullen's orders, but always saved enough for themselves. God only knew what diseases they had passed on to him.

But he would worry about that later. Other thoughts occupied his mind now.

Thoughts of revenge. Against Trammel for doing this to him. And against Hagen and his damnable machinations against his father for making everything more complicated than it needed to be.

The morphine had made it difficult for him to remember all the details of Hagen's plan. That was enough to change his thinking about their partnership entirely. Yes, he stood to make a fortune if all his plans fell into place, and Hagen was a man who enjoyed making plans.

But just like the game of chess that Micklewhite had tried to teach him, sometimes it was easier to just swipe all the pieces off the board and play a different game.

"I'm sorry you're feeling unwell," Micklewhite said while seated at his bedside. "And I know you miss your whiskey. Perhaps I could find a funnel so you could enjoy your whiskey that way?"

"No," he said through his tied jaw. At least he could still speak, and moving his lips did not cause him too much pain. "Go get Pete. Bring him here."

Micklewhite left the hotel room they had moved him into to fetch his chief bouncer. Pete Stride had proven himself to be a most indispensable man in the year since he had come to work for him. The big man had started out as one of the men who collected payment from the numerous people who owed Clay debts throughout the town. He managed to be more effective and less violent than anyone else on Clay's payroll. His dark features and cruel eyes made people less likely to hold out on him or lie to him about the reasons why they might not be able to pay. The result had been fewer complaints to Sheriff Rob Moran, which had made life easier for Clay. Unlike Hagen, he preferred to operate in the shadows whenever possible.

And on those rare occasions when force was required, Stride had proven himself equally skillful. He never went too far unless ordered to do so, and when he did, always knew how to handle the result so as few questions as possible were asked.

Clay had rewarded him by putting him in charge of his newest saloon, the Rose of Tralee. The place had bloomed under his guidance, and Stride had proven himself capable of more than just the rough stuff Clay required to maintain his interests.

He had often thought about promoting him to serve as his right-hand man as Hagen's schemes came to pass. But life had not always worked out the way Clay intended, and his current circumstances had forced him to move up his plans by quite a bit.

When Micklewhite returned, he had the good sense to allow Stride to enter the room first. The big man with the heavy dark beard and deep-set, black eyes was not known to show much emotion, but he winced at the sight of Lucien Clay's current state.

"Jesus, boss," Stride said from the doorway, as if hesitant to go any farther. "I'd heard you had a bad fall, but I didn't expect anything like this."

Clay had thought Micklewhite's story about him being injured in a coach accident was ridiculous, but at the time he had been in no position to prevent him from spreading it. The story had served to keep his competitors at bay, at least for now. He knew it would only be a matter of time before the other saloon owners, pimps, and dope peddlers started testing his resolve to see if his weakness might prove to be their benefit.

He would worry about that later. Through his clenched jaw, he said, "Pull up a chair. You, too, Albert."

The two men did as they were told, with Micklewhite adding, "You'll find Mr. Clay has difficulty talking due to the damage to his jaw during the fall."

"Shut up." Clay looked at Pete. "This wasn't an accident."

Pete looked him over with black eyes. He was not as big as Trammel or the Negro who worked for the Gilded Lily. In fact, he was only an inch or two taller than Clay. But he was a stocky, powerfully built man, with a thick neck and a glare strong enough to put a man in his grave. "No need to tell me that, boss. Just tell me who did it and I'll make sure they get worse."

"Forget that." A sharp pain spread through Clay's face and he thought he might pass out. He willed himself to stay awake long enough to say what he needed to say. "Your name isn't Pete Stride. It's Pedro Escola, and you had your own gang in the badlands."

Pete looked away from him. "Should've figured on you finding out eventually. I guess you're mad I didn't tell you on my own. I left that all behind when I came north. I hope you don't hold that against me, but a man has a right to a new life, don't he?"

For once, Clay was glad Micklewhite decided to speak for him. "I don't think Mr. Clay asked me to bring you up here to fire you, Pete. I think he has bigger plans for you than that." The hunchback looked to Clay for encouragement as he kept speaking. "I think he's counting on your past to help him with the problems he's facing in the present. Particularly up in Blackstone. Am I correct, Mr. Clay?"

It hurt for him to nod, so Clay said, "Keep talking."

Micklewhite seemed glad for the confidence. "I think he'd like to know about your old gang and if you know where they are."

Pete shrugged his heavy shoulders. "Not much to tell, come to think of it. We were about thirty when we broke up. Had more than that at one point, but men in that kind of work ain't always dependable. Some left. Some got killed. Some are locked up."

"Why'd you leave?" Clay struggled to ask.

"Army put a lot of pressure on us," Pete said. "They were stepping up patrols and came close to nabbing us a couple of times. I figured it was best to cut our losses and go our separate ways. I had enough to get me this far and a little left over when I came to work for you. And I've been real happy here, Mr. Clay. You know that."

"He knows that," Micklewhite said. "Now tell us about your gang. Could you get in touch with them? Maybe bring them here?"

Pete hesitated. "I'll do whatever you tell me to do, Mr. Clay, but I don't think that's a good idea. Even if I could track them all, they'd be more trouble than they're worth. These boys aren't exactly used to town life and would probably raise more hell than you'd like. But if it's hard cases you're after, there's no shortage of men to choose from right here in Laramie."

Clay knew just about every crook and

tough within town limits. He knew that the kind of men he needed for his plan would have to be better than most of them. Trouble was, he did not have a long time to plan it out the way he wanted. He had thought he would have more time, but there was nothing he could do to change that now.

He said, "Not any men. Your kind of men. Killers."

Pete sat back in his chair. "We've got a few of those about, Mr. Clay. Some nearby, too. I can send some telegrams to see where they might be. When do you want them here by?"

"Saturday." Micklewhite spoke for him. "Saturday would be the ideal day, don't you think, Mr. Clay?"

Clay blinked in agreement. To do anything more would have been too painful.

"Sounds like I've got some work ahead of me," Pete said as he got up from his chair. "I'll pull together what I can and let you know who I find. They'll be killers, Mr. Clay. Every one of them. Can't say how many I'll get, but I'll get the best available under the circumstances."

"Not me." Clay pointed at Micklewhite. "Tell him."

Micklewhite added, "Mr. Clay isn't always up to talking, so everything can go through me. All decisions on what to do will continue to be made by Mr. Clay of course. If you doubt that, you can always wait and ask him personally. I don't want anyone knowing how bad he's hurt, and no one should question that he is still in charge, not me. Is that clear?"

Clay watched Pete regard the hunchback anew. "Glad to hear that, Albert. Some men in your position might look to take advantage of the situation."

Micklewhite shunned the praise and showed Pete to the door, then came back to Clay's bedside.

Clay withdrew the pistol he kept beside him from under the covers and aimed it at Micklewhite. "You lie, I'll kill you."

The hunchback was unfazed. "I wouldn't dream of it, Lucien. After all, my investment is at stake here, too. Now, let me get you a pencil and some paper so that you can begin to write down what you want done."

Clay slipped the pistol back under the blankets. Micklewhite just might prove useful after all.

CHAPTER 23

"Sorry for bringing my problems to your doorstep," Trammel told Moran, "but I just didn't have enough room in my jail to hold those hopheads anymore. Thanks for letting me use your prison wagon to haul them down here."

"No trouble at all," the sheriff of the City of Laramie told him. "My boys have already loaded them onto the train. A cattle car isn't exactly first-class accommodations, but they're too dope sick to notice. The railroad wasn't happy about it, but they don't have to be. They'll be someone else's problem now."

"Amen," Trammel said. "Where do you think they'll wind up?"

"Most of them will probably jump the train in Utah," Moran said. "But they'll find the Mormons a whole lot less hospitable than us. But they won't come here again. We'll make them regret it if they do."

Moran poured coffee into a mug and handed it to Trammel. "But from what I hear, dope fiends are the least of your troubles these days."

Trammel took that as his cue to tell the sheriff everything that had happened in Blackstone that past week as the sheriff settled down behind his desk with a mug full of coffee for himself.

When Trammel was finished, Moran said, "Quite frankly, everything you've just told me is a hell of a lot worse than what I heard."

At just over six feet and a few years over thirty, Moran was one of those lawmen who had not yet hit his prime and would be a formidable presence in town for decades. Trammel knew he had been brought to town from Abilene by the Laramie Businessmen's Association a few years before to replace the previous sheriff, who had been openly in Lucien Clay's pocket.

But Moran was his own man and had a reputation for being as fair with the law as he was in handling a gun. He was the kind of sheriff every town wanted, but few had.

He was the kind of lawman Trammel wished he could be, but doubted he ever would.

"Sorry for not bringing better news,"

Trammel said. "But I figured if anyone could understand, it would be you. I don't have too many people I can talk to about things like this up in Blackstone. At least no one who's not wrapped up in this in some way. Hawkeye's a good kid, but he's just a kid."

"I'm glad you thought to come to me," Moran said. "I thought having one Hagen in the territory was enough. But two is even worse. And the notion that they're going after each other doesn't help matters any."

He settled into his chair with his coffee. "Bookman and Fred Montague dead in the same week. And you're sure Fred killed himself?"

"Yeah, I'm sure," Trammel said. "I would've bet anything that Hagen did it, but he didn't. And neither did Big Ben either. Witnesses saw them both in their respective saloons at the time."

"Hagen could've hired someone else to do it," Moran observed.

But Trammel did not think so. "He played a role in driving Montague to kill himself. I'm sure of that. But I've seen plenty of suicides in my time, and that's how this one played out. What Hagen did to drive him to it is anyone's guess."

Moran gave that some thought. "Maybe

he felt like he was caught in the middle between Charles and Adam. Maybe one of them had something on him. You know how fond Montague was of his nieces. Hell, Queen Victoria doesn't even have as many nieces as that old fox claimed to have."

Trammel laughed. "True. But I don't have much time to think about why he did it. Doesn't much matter anyway. No suicide note, so I'll probably never know."

"Especially with the trouble you've got coming your way." Moran sipped his coffee. "Every hotel in town is buzzing about the crowd they're expecting for that big march this Albertson fella is cooking up for Saturday. Could be nearer to a hundred people or more."

Trammel set his mug on Moran's desk. He did not feel like coffee just then. He was awake enough as it was. "I can tell something's going to happen, Rob. Don't ask me why, but I know."

Moran grinned. "That's the copper in you. And the sheriff, too. It's funny the way you can sense these things after a while. It's like smelling a storm on the wind on a clear day with blue skies. At least King Charles had the good sense to move his drive ahead."

This was the first Trammel had heard

about it. "What do you mean? I saw him yesterday and he didn't mention anything about it. I thought he was bringing them down next week."

"So did I." Moran found a notice from the railroad on his desk and handed it to him. "Got word last night that he's decided to move them down here today. The railroad's got room for them and he's taking every car they've got available."

Trammel read the notice, and it confirmed what Moran had just told him. "Why would he do something like that? Why today?"

"Never been much of a cattleman myself," the sheriff admitted. "Horse wrangler either. But King Charles is a deliberate man, and if he does something, it's for a reason. I've got an idea on what his reasons might be, but it's nothing you're going to like to hear." He looked at Trammel's coffee mug. "Want something stronger than that?"

"I'd prefer to hear it sober, thanks."

Moran did not argue. "I think he's moving his stock now because he'll want his place clear of it as soon as possible. He probably thinks Adam is coming for him in a big way now that Bookman and Montague are out of the way. He probably figures Adam might do something to them, so the sooner those hooves are at market, the less his losses are liable to be. That's the only explanation I can see for it."

Trammel dropped his head into his hands and ran them over his hair. He had not thought of that. He had not thought Adam would stoop so low as to poison animals, particularly horses, considering he used to be a cavalryman.

But he also knew Adam's hatred for Charles knew no depths and he was more than capable of doing something like that, especially if it meant ruining his uncle. "I hate to say it, but you're probably right."

"It gets worse," Moran said. "That means he'll have more available hands at the ready come Saturday, when those hundred marchers descend on your town. I wouldn't put it past him to mix in his boys with the marchers to raise some hell. You've been around more of those things than I have. It doesn't take much to get them set off. I was at a Granger march once where Quakers set to beating some folks."

Trammel could believe it. He had seen how quickly a mob could turn ugly. He had seen it in New York, when he had been a policeman there, and in Chicago, when he had been with the Pinkertons. A group of individuals could turn into an angry mob in a hurry, leaving a lot of death and destruction in their wake.

Buck Trammel had always hated asking for help in any situation, but given what he was facing now, he saw no choice. "You think you could spare some men to help me out this Saturday?"

"Not a chance," Moran said, "and it hurts me to have to say that. I'm going to have my hands full with them here in town, not to mention keeping an eye on all the other things that happen here every day of the week. Robberies. Beatings. Drunks. I'd offer to send a couple of my men along with the marchers to help you out, but I can't spare a single one. You know I would if I could."

Trammel had expected that answer but was still disappointed by it. He let out a heavy breath and decided to drink that coffee after all. Maybe it would help clear his mind some. "Think I could pay some of the miners to set off some of that dynamite they use and blow up the tracks?"

Moran laughed. "I'd be inclined to chip in if I thought it would do any good." But then the sheriff stopped laughing. "But you might be on to something there."

Trammel saw he was thinking of something.

And a moment later, the same thought came to him.

Both men set their mugs on the sheriff's desk and went to the map on the wall that showed the southern part of the territory. It included Laramie and Blackstone at the top.

Moran traced the route between the two towns with his finger. Trammel spoke before Moran had a chance to do so. "There's only one passable road between here and Blackstone."

"That's right," Moran said. "And most of those marchers are going to be riding up there on wagons. Every hauler from three towns around will be here, waiting to bring them up there. Some will be on horseback, but most will be sitting on haystacks and traveling by buckboard, singing hymns and battle songs the whole way up."

Trammel pointed at the placc on the map where the City of Laramie ended and the town of Blackstone began. "That's the narrowest part of the road. Got a fair amount of marshland on either side of it. Be tough to get a wagon across it, should something block the road, like a tree."

"Several trees," Moran suggested. "These aren't city folk coming to this thing. They're not afraid of hard work and will clear a tree quicker than you can blink. The more the better. Should an unfortunate event like that happen of course."

"Of course." Trammel had come to Laramie hoping a talk with Moran would help him see things in a better light. He was glad he had gotten the answers he needed.

Moran continued. "There's no way of telling when something like fallen trees might happen, but it can't happen too early. If it happened on Friday morning, there might be enough time for us to get some people out there with axes and workhorses to clear the way."

Trammel caught on to his way of thinking. "But if it were to happen on Friday afternoon, just before dark . . ."

Moran finished the thought for him. "Then we'll have a whole passel of unhappy pilgrims on our hands who'd have to turn back. Probably have the march here in town, which is fine by us. My men and I can handle that."

Trammel patted the spot on the map with renewed happiness. "Would be a shame to disappoint all those folks. But there's no arguing with nature."

"The Good Lord above works in mysterious ways." Moran patted him on the back. "Come on. I'll walk you out."

Trammel had always been amazed by how busy the streets of Laramie seemed to be.

He knew the place was three times the size or more of Blackstone, but there always seemed to be something going on in the bustling railroad town. Tradesmen going to and from work. Travelers from the railroad browsing the town's shops, and their saloons. Drovers selling everything from barber supplies to ladies' fashions to snake oil flitting about the various businesses and homes as they plied their trade.

He had been a lawman in Manhattan and Chicago, so he was accustomed to crowds, but those cities were larger. The buildings taller and the throngs of people spread out over a wider area. Laramie seemed to have as much activity as those cities, if not more, crammed into a much smaller area.

Upon first arriving in Blackstone, Trammel wondered if he could get used to working in a town so small. Now, he wondered if Laramie might be too much of a challenge for him. He was glad the place was in such capable hands as those of Rob Moran and his deputies.

As the sheriff walked Trammel to where his horse was tied up, Moran said, "I was waiting for you to bring it up, but because you haven't, I will. I heard about your run-in with Lucien Clay the other day."

Trammel had wanted to mention it, but

his more recent troubles had pushed it out of his mind. "What did you hear?"

"The story is that one of his horses threw a shoe on the ride back from Blackstone and he got thrown about his carriage. He's supposed to be fine but is recuperating in his own set of rooms in the Laramie Grand."

Trammel was content to let the story stand if Moran allowed it. "Treacherous road between here and Blackstone."

"I happened to be in front of the Grand when they pulled him out of there," Moran went on. "He looked like he got hit by a train. From what I hear, he's got a busted head and a broken jaw, but those are just rumors his people are working mighty hard to tamp down. They insist he's still running the show."

Trammel understood the ruse. If people thought he was weak, every crook in town would try nibbling at his hide. "What do you think?"

"As sheriff of Laramie, I'm glad he's laid up for a while," Moran admitted. "But he's still alive, which ain't exactly good. Not for me, and not for you either. See, I think he did get hit by a train. A great big one that stands about six-seven and weighs about two hundred pounds."

Trammel knew when he was caught. "I'm

two-thirty and he had it coming."

"He's had it coming and worse since the day he was born," Moran said. "But I've never seen anyone throw him a beating before, much less one that bad. So on top of all your other problems, I'd keep an eye out for strangers in town. Watch the shadows especially close. He's not the kind of man who'll come at you straight on, but when he does, he'll send someone who tries to kill you. And they'll be good at it, too."

Trammel figured as much. He would have cursed his own luck if he thought it would do any good. It was getting as though he could hardly scratch his backside without causing some kind of bad blood between him and someone else. "Anyone I ought to watch out for in particular?"

Without turning around, Moran said, "Look over my right shoulder at the front porch of the Molly Malone."

Trammel glanced in that direction and saw a large, swarthy-looking man glaring at him from across the bustling thoroughfare. "You mean that mean-looking half breed who's trying to stare me to death?"

"Name's Pete Stride," Moran told him, "but I hear he used to run with his own gang in Indian Territory. Gave it up and crawled in here about a year ago. He's worked his way up from one of Clay's thugs to the topman in his outfit. I haven't seen much of him since Clay's been laid up, so I have a feeling whatever revenge Clay's plotting against you will come from old Pete over there."

Trammel chanced a second glance at him and saw all he needed to see. "He's not much. I've gone up against worse."

"This one's a little different," Moran warned him. "He's not a mindless thug like the rest of the men who work for Clay. This one's a thinker. You won't lure him into any ambush like you did with the last bunch Clay sent up your way. And he won't let you corner him at a place like Stone Gate like the Pinkertons did. He'll come at you from the back, so make sure Hawkeye lives up to his nickname. I'd like to see you aboveground a might longer."

"So would I." Trammel held out his hand to Moran, who gladly shook it. "Thanks for listening to my bellyaching in there, Rob. It meant a lot. More than you know."

"Think nothing of it," the sheriff said. "I'll do my part down here. You just handle your end of things and maybe we can pull this thing off."

Trammel untied his horse from the hitching post and climbed into the saddle. The old mare Elias had given him shifted a bit under his weight, but did not offer any serious protest.

Trammel was surprised when Moran stopped him before he turned the horse toward Blackstone and beckoned him to come closer. "Say, Buck. A city boy like you knows how to handle an ax, don't you?"

Trammel laughed in spite of himself. "Can't say as I do, but I'm a quick learner."

Moran scratched his head. "Nothing goes easy for you, does it?"

"Never has," Trammel said as he backed the mare away from the jail. "Why should it start now?"

As he turned the horse toward the road to Blackstone, he could feel Pete's eyes on his back. He was glad they weren't bullets or he would most surely be dead.

Chapter 24

King Charles Hagen was already in the saddle when the first hint of daybreak began to spread across the eastern sky. He had already been up more than half the night by then, helping his men prepare to bring his horses and cattle to meet the train at Laramie. It was the first drive without John Bookman's steady hand to ensure everything ran smoothly. It took two men to fill his foreman's shoes. King Charles had thought about leading them to market himself, but his days of wrangling cattle were long past and best done by younger men.

But Hagen did not trouble himself with the past. There were enough troubles in the present to keep him occupied. And more than enough to watch out for in the days and weeks to come. Love and hate, Charles decided as he watched his men prepare his animals to go to their pens down in Laramie before boarding the train. Love and hate made the world go around the sun. Love raised the cattle and horses and tended to the land they fed from. Hate had forced Hagen's hand to bring them to market a week sooner than he had expected. He imagined Adam and his henchmen were planning to move against the herding, so he'd moved it up a week and spoiled their plans. Yes, his own men griped about the rush to market, but their objections did not last long. They knew all that Hagen had lost and deferred to his judgment. If he said the horses and cattle were to be brought to market, to market they would go.

And as he watched the pen open up and saw the first of his animals bolt toward freedom only to go where his men led them, he felt a glimmer of that old love he had once felt for this place, this life. A love of raising things and helping them grow so they could be sold and benefit his family. And hating the knowledge that they had been born only to be slaughtered for his family's fortune.

He watched the last of the cattle leave the pen and, as was his custom, he rode over to the gate himself. He was not a man who allowed himself to indulge in many customs, but being the last man to close the gate on a cattle drive was one of the few he believed in.

He had done the same thing an hour earlier when his men set out to bring the horses to Laramie. Each of them had been saddle broken and would make ideal mounts for the army. They moved faster than cattle and could see better in the dark.

Driving horses and cattle to Laramie was far from the difficult task of driving them thousands of miles from Texas to Montana, but it certainly was not a task for a greenhorn. Care needed to be taken to make sure none of the animals lost their way, especially in the marshy area Hagen had taken to calling Midpoint, where the road narrowed considerably and had bog on either side. Over the years, there had been several ideas floated by various people to drain the marsh and make it suitable for development. Perhaps even a railroad spur that led straight to Blackstone.

But King Charles had always blocked such efforts. A spur would only encourage more people to come to Blackstone, and he felt they already had too many as it was. Too many of the bad sort anyway. He had intended to always keep Blackstone small. A place where his men could find women and whiskey and his miners could spend their wages. The sleepy little town had served its purpose well for a long time until Adam showed up. Madam Pinochet, as despicable as she was, was manageable and kept things in town to a dull roar.

But Adam had no intention of keeping things quiet. Just the opposite. He was a locomotive barreling forward with his horn blaring the entire way.

Charles had indulged his nephew long enough. Any spark of paternal feeling he may have felt for him had died when he packed the boy off to boarding school and then West Point all those years ago. His love for his sister had faded as he began to forget what she even looked like. She was just a far-distant memory to him now and nothing more.

His nephew may be barreling toward him now, belching the black smoke of rage and blaring a horn of fury, but he was still, at his heart, only a train.

And just like all trains, it needed a track to ride on lest it derailed. A single gap anywhere along its route could spell disaster for the train and all the passengers it carried.

Charles Hagen drew in a deep breath of crisp, early morning air. He had lost John Bookman and he had lost Fred Montague.

He knew Adam was responsible for both deaths and he intended on making him pay.

He had invested in Adam and Bartholomew and Caleb as he handled all his investments. With an eye toward the future. Bart was in Denver, managing the company's interests there. Caleb was working for a prominent banking house and learning the game of high finance. He had already been quite successful in expanding the company's holdings in various industries and Charles always looked forward to his letters, telling of one new venture or another.

He had invested his daughters wisely as well. Deborah had married into the powerful Forrester family of Colorado, and Elena's beau in Philadelphia was well on his way to a partnership at one of the finest law firms in town.

Pondering the great expanse of his life while he watched another herd go to market had done his old heart a great deal of good. He was sixty now, and although he had the drive of a man half his age, his body had a habit of reminding him of his years.

He brought his horse about and looked at all he had built. The rolling grazing fields. The tree line he had helped clear with his own hands. A ranch that would take a day or more to ride if one were to attempt to do so.

And as the first rays of sunshine began to spread across the eastern horizon, King Charles Hagen felt like a man renewed. He may have lost his two best men, but by God, he had his sons and his daughters' men. He would summon them home at once and give them new charges to expand his empire once and for all.

And this weekend, when his men had returned from the market, he would use the chaos of the Albertson march to wreak havoc on Adam's saloons. Bookman may have failed in his task, but King Charles Hagen's new men would not. Their actions would turn a peaceful march into a full-blown riot that would result in every building Adam owned being put to the torch, including that blasted laudanum den he prized so much.

He listened to the wind as he trotted back toward the ranch house. The place was deserted for the first time in as long as he could remember. Oh, there still were a handful of men tending to the animals grazing in the far-off fields, but the empty bunkhouses and the area around his home would allow him some solitude. He planned to put his time alone to good use.

He tied his horse to the hitching rail instead of bringing her into the barn because he might want to go for a ride later.

But the old mare fussed when he wrapped the leather rein around the post. He stroked her muzzle and told her to steady down, but she would not be placated.

Hagen had always known her to be an animal of quiet temperament and easy disposition. She never fussed like this unless she had caught the scent of something on the wind.

He did not bother going for his guns yet, as it might just be the coming of a storm. He smelled the air himself, but it did not feel like rain to him.

That was when he saw what the mare had sensed. A flash of movement in the tree line. It was hard to make out at first, especially in the weak light of dawn, but it was there. Men on horseback riding through the pines, hoping the shadows of the trees would keep them hidden.

It had, but not for long.

He was not able to get a close enough look at them to see how many of them had come onto his property, but it did not matter, for one trespasser was one too many.

No one came on his land without permission. He would see to it that every single one paid for the infraction with their lives.

He was about to turn back to get his horse when he felt an incredible tightness envelop his arms and chest. The pain was excruciating, and he found it impossible to move. He had seen his father die of a heart attack and wondered if he might be facing the same fate. Perhaps it was just easier to give into it, not fight it. Dying alone on the ranch he loved was a better fate than he probably deserved.

He would pitch forward and allow nature to take its course.

But when he tried to fall forward, he found that he couldn't. He overcame his initial shock about the paralyzing pain to see that he was being gripped tightly about the chest by two large, black arms holding him in place. He struggled to get free, but it was no use. He was not going anywhere, no matter how hard he fought.

Being unable to take a full breath was bad enough, but the applause that followed his failed attempts to break free chilled him to his core.

"Well done, Uncle." Adam Hagen clapped as he came out of the ranch house. "Never let it be said that King Charles went down peacefully."

His nephew took his time walking around

to face his uncle. He even had the audacity to be smoking one of his cigars.

"Enjoying yourself, mister?" Charles managed to say before the arms tightened around him once more.

"Can't say that I am," Adam admitted. "While we were waiting for you inside, I looked around the old place, tried to drum up some kind of memory from days long past that would've tugged at my heartstrings and made me call the whole thing off. Finding no good memories in the house, I even went upstairs to look out the window at the land I once thought of as mine. No luck there either. Everywhere I looked, I found another spot where you yelled at me, berated me, told me I wasn't good enough. That I'd never be as good as Bartholomew or Caleb at anything. I remembered wanting to be sad to leave this place the day you packed me off to boarding school, but I couldn't.

"I was glad to be rid of you."

Charles was finding it harder to get a decent breath and saved what he could as he said, "I gave you money. My name."

"Money," Adam repeated. "The one thing that matters less to you than I ever did is money. You used it like you used everything else you valued in your life. As a weapon. As a tool to keep inconveniences at bay.

Inconveniences like me." Adam peered into Charles's eyes. "I might not have been your son, but I was your sister's boy. Your blood. Didn't that count for anything?"

"I tested you," Charles rasped. "I pushed you to be straight and good. Not crooked and rotten."

"As straight and good as you turned out to be," Adam said. "Like having Bookman try to smother me when I was hurt. That's what finally turned me from being a nuisance to a nemesis. That's the day I decided I wasn't just content with being a thorn in your side. I wanted to pull you down off your throne. Off all this."

"I'm bored." Charles struggled for more breath. "Are you going to talk me to death or just kill me?"

"Killing you would be a waste of all my time and effort, Uncle. I don't want you to die until I can show you how I've finally managed to defeat you. Bookman died because of you. Montague died because of us. But you will die because of what I have done."

Charles fought to remain conscious as his breathing became more restricted. God, this man was strong!

"Don't let him pass out yet, Ben," Adam said. "Let him breathe a little so he can see the next part for himself."

King Charles opened his eyes and saw Adam holding a document before his eyes. He had seen it before and recognized it immediately. "That's my will. How in the devil did you get hold of it?"

"Montague gave it to me." Adam beamed. "And before you protest, you can rest assured his betrayal didn't come easily. I used his fondness for young girls against him and forced him into doing it. I think that's why he killed himself. He knew I would be moving against you, and soon, so he did not want to be around when the bad news reached you. A cowardly way to go out, but I can understand it."

The big man's hold on him may have loosened, but he still found it hard to get a decent breath. "You'll never get this ranch. Bart and Caleb will fight you every step of the way."

"They won't have much to fight with," Adam told him. "Those men you saw in the pines are associates of mine. They're in the process of adding something extra to all your troughs and grain, something that will wipe out your remaining herds within a matter of days. A fever, or a fungus of some kind. The Celestials are a secretive bunch, but they assured me you'll be wiped out in a week."

Charles summoned up all his remaining strength and tried to lunge at Adam, but the brute's grip held firm.

Adam held the will in front of him like a shield. "I got Fred to show me your old will, and needless to say, I didn't like what I read at all. I wasn't mentioned anywhere in the entire document. Had it been drawn up since our falling out, I could hardly blame you, but you had it drawn up ten years ago. So, I had Fred make some minor revisions."

Adam flipped the pages for him as Charles continued to struggle in vain to get free. "I'll get the mines and the ranch and the steel and the shares in the railroads and everything else you own. Bart and Caleb can continue on as salaried employees and the girls will still get their stipends. I'm not a total monster."

"It'll never hold up in court. A judge will —"

Adam flipped to the last page, which bore Fred Montague's stamp over Charles Hagen's signature. It was a perfect match for his own.

"It'll hold up, Uncle. I had Montague date it to the week I returned to town, back when you and I were somewhat civil to each other. The boys will find this among your personal effects and in Montague's office."

He folded the last will and testament of Charles Hagen and slipped it into his inside coat pocket. "I did it, Charles. I finally used one of your biggest weapons against you. The late Fred Montague and the law. I ended you the same way you've ended so many others."

Charles Hagen was leaning quite forward now. The black man's hold on him had slacked, but he still could not breathe. The pain in his chest grew worse with each thud of his heart.

"Set him down easy, Ben," he heard Adam order. "We don't want to make Moore or Emily's job too hard, now do we? Any blemishes on his face might raise suspicion. It would also ruin the funeral. And we want our fallen king to look regal for those who come to see him, don't we?"

Charles felt himself being softly lowered to the ground. He tried to get back up or even crawl away, but his limbs refused to cooperate, and his mind was beginning to dim as the darkness fast approached. The sort of darkness not even the sun could chase away.

It took all his strength and will to force his right hand to grab a handful of dirt and grip it tightly. "Mine," he whispered. "Always . . . mine."

The last thing he saw before his mighty heart failed him was the sight of his nephew looking down at him, smoking a cigar and flicking an ash his way.

Fortunately, the darkness took him before the ash hit.

Adam Hagen tucked his cigar in the corner of his mouth and squatted to check the old man's pulse. He felt the wrist first, then placed two fingers on the side of his neck. Neither place revealed a pulse. He held his hand beneath the nose to see if he could detect a breath but could not.

The vacant eyes half-open told him the whole story.

King Charles Hagen was dead.

Adam rose to his full height and dusted off his hands atop his uncle's corpse. He looked at Ben. "Well done, my friend. Well done indeed. But our day is not over yet. We still have much to do."

He looked down at his uncle's body and searched his own soul for some remorse. Some pang of guilt that might have caused him to feel sorry for what he had done to this man. Some regret over their relationship souring. Some memory from days long past of some kindness he had shown him in his life.

But he felt nothing.

No remorse. No guilt. No joy.

All he saw was an obstacle that had fallen. Something that had been blocking his path to power had now been removed. He was not King Charles Hagen any longer. He was just a dead old man holding a handful of dirt.

He stepped over the body and went back into the ranch house to finish his purpose and bring an end to his torment.

Chapter 25

The following afternoon, Trammel turned into a gust of wind as Dr. Moore and Emily examined the corpse of Charles Hagen.

Trammel and Hawkeye kept the cowhands at bay. "Let them work, boys," Trammel told them. "No one's cheating you on seeing him. There'll be time enough for that when they're done."

Some of the men kept their distance, leaning on the corral as they hid their tears. He wondered which one of them had been the first to find Hagen when they returned from the drive. It must not have been a pretty sight. The birds had already been at him, and, given the number of feathers scattered all over the area, the cattle baron had been the last meal for one of them.

"Sheriff Trammel," Dr. Moore said. "Come take a look at this."

But Trammel did not dare move. The men of the Blackstone Ranch were not happy at seeing their former boss being picked at in the open like this. Not by birds or by doctors.

"I think it's time to let these boys place Mr. Hagen's remains on Miss Emily's wagon, Doc. They want to make sure their boss is tended to as soon as possible."

He began to protest, but a soft word from Emily quelled it in time. Trammel could tell the men were anxious and scared, and he could not blame them. Charles Hagen was the kind of man who seemed to be indestructible. To find him dead would have been bad enough. But to see his remains defiled by nature was too much to take.

Hawkeye turned and said to the doctors, "They're getting restless."

Emily and Moore stood up together and took their medical bags with them. She said, "Could some of you men be so kind as to help me bring Mr. Hagen to my buckboard?"

Twelve men stepped forward with long pieces of burlap to cover the body and wrapped it tightly. One of them said, "Burlap ought to keep the birds away when we ride with you into town, ma'am."

With six men on each side, they picked him up as gently as if he was simply sleeping and carried him over to Emily's buckboard and placed him inside. The men stood back in a ragged line and removed their hats.

The man named Mackey felt compelled to remove his, too. Hawkeye followed his lead.

One of the men said, "We'd like to ride into town with you and stay there while you tend to him, ma'am. We won't be a bother, I promise. We just don't think it's fitting to leave him alone, him not having any blood kin to tend to him and all."

She glanced at Trammel for approval. "If it's fine by the sheriff, it's fine by me."

The men scattered to grab their mounts for the ride back to town, but stopped when Trammel said, "Wait."

The men stopped where they were and turned to face him. It was clear to him they were all itching for a fight. Any excuse to unburden themselves of the pain they were feeling, as if hitting someone else could help rid them of it.

Hawkeye tensed beside Trammel, but Trammel made a point of looking each man in the eye as he spoke. "Anyone who wants to go into town with Mr. Hagen is welcome to do so as long as they agree to one thing. No trouble of any kind from any of you. I've heard all the same rumors you boys have, and I'm looking into them. You've got my word on that. Adam Hagen accepted my word, and he'd expect all of you to do the same thing. If you want to tend to Mr. Hagen, tend to him. But no drinking. No fighting, and no acts of vengeance. I'll give you boys all the leeway I can, but not if you cause trouble. Keep your guns in their holsters and no hell-raising. I don't want to put any of you boys in jail at a time like this, but I will if you force it."

He looked each of them in the eye in turn again as he said, "Any questions about that?"

They all silently shook their heads.

Trammel did not believe them, but he did not have enough men to stop them. "Go ahead, then. Mount up."

The men went for their horses and Hawkeye relaxed some. "That could've gone either way, boss. I don't know how you do it."

"Neither do I," Trammel admitted. "Mount up and lead them into town. I'll bring up the rear and grab any stragglers who might think about going after Adam."

As Hawkeye went to get his horse, one of the older ranch hands approached him. He had a thick gray mustache, but no beard. His skin was as weathered and worn as an old saddle. The skin around his eyes was wrinkled and sat in a permanent squint. The slouch hat he wore had seen countless winters and summers.

The people back East had an image of a cowboy as a square-jawed Adonis with two guns on his hip and a beautiful lady to protect. But Trammel knew that the man who was walking toward him now was what a real cowboy looked like.

"Afternoon, Lonnie," Trammel said and offered his hand. "I'm sorry about Mr. Hagen."

Lonnie shook his hand. "Thanks for allowing some of the boys to ride in with him. The rest of us'll tend to the herd while they're in town. When we're done here, we'd like to ride in with them, but the others will ride out peacefully. That's a promise. I just don't want you or your deputy getting jumpy, thinking we're riding in for any other purpose."

Trammel appreciated the thought. "You've only got about twenty men or so left?"

"Twenty-four," Lonnie told him.

"Then I'd appreciate it if you only sent in four at a time after this first bunch is done," Trammel said. "You can send as many as six at a time if you want, but no more than that. I know you boys are hurting, but I don't want any trouble. You understand my reasons."

Lonnie nodded. "Six it is, then. No more, only less. I promise."

Trammel was glad to hear it. "You in charge of this place for the time being?"

"I guess so," Lonnie said. "I'm here the longest and I'm the oldest, so that's how it usually works. What do we do now, Sheriff? What about our wages?"

Trammel wished he knew. "I don't know. The Hagens are scattered to hell and gone, but I imagine they'll get here in a couple of days. They'll decide on things after that. Until then, best if you try and keep the peace."

Lonnie scowled as he said, "There's one Hagen that's closer than them all, but if he steps foot on this land, I —"

Trammel cut him off before he said too much. "I won't let that happen. I'll make sure he stays out of here. You won't be seeing him any time soon. But you have to promise not to go looking for him while he's in town. And don't pay attention to any gossip either. If you don't hear it from me, it's a lie. Deal?"

The two men shook on it and the matter was settled, but Lonnie clearly still had something on his mind.

"What is it?" Trammel prodded.

"It's just that a bunch of us rode out to check the stock when we found Mr. Hagen as he was," Lonnie said. "The cows we left behind are all still here, but the horses are gone. All of our best breeding stock. Some of the boys tracked them and it doesn't look like anybody stole them. They just cut the fence and let them scatter. Why would anyone do that? Why not just take them?"

Trammel had not known about the animals, but now that he did, he understood why. "Do your best to bring them back, Lonnie. The family will want to know how many head they have to work with. I'll let you know as soon as I hear more."

Trammel climbed into the saddle and brought around the horse Elias had given him from the livery.

The men were lined up six aside of Emily's buckboard when she released the brake and set her horses moving. Hawkeye kept a somber but steady pace as he led the long, sad procession down the hill from the ranch into town.

Trammel brought up the rear, keeping a good distance back from the group. This was their moment and he did not want them to feel like he was crowding them.

He doubted he would have much to worry

about until they hit Main Street. He would have to keep an eye out for any of them who might break free and take a run at Adam Hagen.

Trammel only hoped the damned fool had the good sense to stay out of sight for a while.

Blackstone had seen enough death for one week. He did not want to add to it if he did not have to.

Trammel was surprised by the reception that awaited them as they turned on to Main Street. The boardwalks on both sides of the thoroughfare were packed with men, women, and children to watch the procession as it passed by. The men took off their hats. The women bowed their heads. Children followed the lead of their parents and looked somber.

The saloons, all of them controlled by Adam Hagen, sported black silk bunting across their signs. Lilly was out in front of the Gilded Lily clad in a black dress and veil. There was no sign of Ben London anywhere.

It was the silence of it all that struck Trammel the most. The only sounds he heard were the creak of Emily's buckboard wheels as it rolled through town, and the jangle of the bits from the horses that rode beside it. A slight wind caused the signs to rock back and forth and squeak as they did so. But beyond that, only silence.

Trammel kept a close eye on the ranch hands as they slowly approached the Clifford Hotel. His gut ran cold when he saw Adam Hagen on his second-floor porch, wearing a black suit. He held a black hat over his heart as he stood at attention and slowly offered a salute as Emily's wagon rolled by.

Trammel moved his hand toward the Colt in the holster under his left arm. He did not pull it but was ready to do so if any of the ranch hands took offense to Adam's presence.

The men put great effort into looking the other way as they passed the hotel, which made Trammel feel a bit better about things.

The crowd began to disperse when the buckboard made the turn off Main Street toward the barn where she prepared the dead for burial.

Trammel lingered in front of the hotel, eyeing Hagen the entire time. He remained at attention, his ruined arm quivering from the effort of holding his salute until the men climbed off their horses and carried Charles Hagen's body into the barn.

Only then did he break off the salute and place his hat back on his head.

He looked down at Trammel, puzzled. “What’s that look for?”

The town was still relatively quiet, so Trammel kept his voice down. “You’ve got one hell of a nerve.”

“For what? Standing at attention as my father’s remains passed by? We may have had our differences, but I’m still his son.”

Trammel had no affection for Charles Hagen either. His anger was stirred by the danger Hagen’s presence presented. “Those boys are blaming you for this. Every man on that ranch thinks you killed him. You’d do well to stay inside until after the funeral.”

“I’ll do no such thing. My father —”

“Quit calling him that!” Trammel said, much louder than he had intended. “I’ve got six dead men in the past week because of you, and I don’t want you to be the seventh. I gave those boys my word I’d keep you in line and, damnit, that’s what I’m going to do, even if I have to lock you up to do it.”

“Why, Steve.” Hagen smiled as he leaned on the railing. “I didn’t know you cared.”

Trammel was in no mood for Hagen’s mouth. “Don’t push me, Hagen. I’m going to be taking a long, hard look at that man’s death, and if I even have the slightest shred of proof that you're involved, I'll see to it that you swing for it. Nothing your boy Moore does will be able to stop me either."

Two Chinese men appeared on the porch behind Hagen, both of them carrying Winchesters. They had long knives tucked in their sashes.

"While your concern for my well-being is touching, you have no cause for concern. As you can see, I'm quite well protected. As for my . . . relative's passing, what makes you or anyone else think I could've possibly been involved?"

Trammel remembered something Lonnie had said to him back at the ranch and decided to push it a little further. "Those boys up at the ranch didn't exactly curl up in a ball and cry themselves to sleep when they found Mr. Hagen dead. They went to check on the stock and found a lot of peculiar tracks around the area."

"That so?" Trammel noticed Hagen had stiffened a little. Not enough for someone who did not know him to notice, but enough for Trammel to catch. "What kind of tracks?"

"All over the place," Trammel hedged. He did not know the facts, so he did not want to corner himself with a lie that was too elaborate. "Tracks that don't add up. And the horses are missing, but not the cows. Imagine that. Any ideas on why that is?"

Hagen made a great show of thinking about it, casting his eyes to the sky as if waiting for some word from above. "No, can't say I do. Could be some renegades, though. Blackfeet or Cheyenne maybe. Could account for the odd tracks because they don't shoe their ponies."

"It's a thought," Trammel lied. "I'll make sure Lonnie looks into it. He'll be running things until the family gets here. I'd stay particularly far away from him. He's not exactly fond of you."

"Duly noted." He gestured to the two Chinese behind him. "But as I said, I'm well protected. Still, poor Lonnie. He must be taking the loss particularly hard. Tell me, did Dr. Moore or Emily say when he died?"

"Not when or how," Trammel told him. "They'll let me know later, and I'll be sure to put it in the report when they do. But who am I kidding? Moore will tell you everything long before he gets around to telling me."

"Nonsense," Hagen said. "You'll find Jacob is a consummate professional who will carry out his duties to the letter, sir." He looked out toward Emily's barn. The ranch hands were gathered around in a loose circle outside, smoking cigarettes and talking.

"I only hope he didn't suffer. His death will sting for them for a long time. I hope the animals didn't do too much damage. That would make Emily's job that much harder."

Trammel grinned. "Who said he was found outside? I didn't say that."

Hagen kept looking out toward the barn. "It only stands to reason that he would die outside. God would not be so cruel as to take him in his sleep. He would've wanted the last thing he saw in this world to be his beloved ranch."

"Careful, Adam," Trammel said as he rode toward the barn. "You just made your first mistake."

He found Hawkeye standing around in front of the barn, away from the ranch hands. He was looking awfully green, and Trammel wondered if he might get sick. "You all right?"

The young man raised his head and breathed in deep. "I didn't get a good look at him at the ranch, but when they pulled that burlap off him, I saw plenty then." His stomach rumbled and he let out a muted belch. "I've seen what birds can do to a cow, but never a man."

It was times like these that Trammel was reminded that Hawkeye was barely out of boyhood himself. "Think you're up for another ride back to the ranch?"

The thought of being away from the barn seemed to brighten his spirits. "Sure, if you can spare me."

Trammel was glad to hear it. "Ride up there and find Lonnie. Tell him to keep an eye on the cattle."

"Sure, boss," he said as he went to his horse and pulled himself up into the saddle. "What do you want me to tell him to look for?"

That was the problem. Trammel did not know for sure. He just had a feeling. "He'll know what to look for better than I could. I've just got a feeling someone may have left the cows for the same reason they let the horses go. I know that's not much, but it's just a feeling I have. He'll know whether or not it's a dumb idea."

"I'll tell it to him just like that," Hawkeye assured him. "I'll be back as soon as I can. I think it's best if we're both here after nightfall. I've got a feeling those boys from the Blackstone Ranch are cooking up something and I don't want to leave you here on your own when they make their move."

Trammel would be happy to have him around. He'd proven himself to be mighty handy in tight situations.

He watched his deputy ride off and saw Lilly walking along Main Street toward the jail. She was still wearing the black dress and veil he had seen her wearing as he rode by on his way into town. Black was never her best color; it made her look pale and small. And even from this distance, he could tell she had been crying.

He dug his heels into the Appaloosa's flanks and brought the horse to a full gallop. He reached her in time to cut off her view of Hagen at his porch.

"Lilly," he called out to her as he reined in the horse and climbed down from the saddle. "What's wrong?"

She held a black silk handkerchief to her nose and turned away from him. He knew she was not one for tears, so if she was crying, there was a reason. "What happened? I promise I won't get angry."

She buried her face in his chest as she sobbed. She was saying something, but between the crying and her voice muffled by his shirt, he didn't know what she was saying.

He eased her away from him and saw her

veil was sopping wet. "What brought all this on?"

"Everything," she cried. "Hagen's dead. Montague's dead. Bookman's dead. Who's next? Me? You? Ben?"

Trammel unlocked the jailhouse door and ushered her inside. Now that it was just the two of them, he hoped he could get her to make sense. "Did anyone make any threats against Ben?"

"Not directly, no," she admitted. "But you know how people are. They talk about things they claim they've overheard. How they're going to lynch him come this Saturday. How they're going to see justice done come this Saturday, by hell or high water." She stopped another round of tears before they got started. "They don't say anything while Ben's around, but I can hear them when they think I don't. It's such ugly talk, Buck. We didn't have this in Kansas."

Trammel was saddened, but not surprised. He had heard this kind of talk in Kansas and Chicago and New York, too. Usually there was nothing behind it. The more they talked, the less they did.

But Blackstone was a different town today than it was yesterday. King Charles was dead. Adam Hagen held sway over Blackstone for now, at least until the rest of the

Hagen kids got to town.

Trammel had known how to handle Adam. He had the pressure of King Charles to keep him in line. But now there was no one standing between Adam and the top of the mountain, and Blackstone was caught in the middle. Adam would not let anything happen to Ben if he could avoid it. But whether or not he could avoid it was the big question. There was a great big hole in this town where King Charles used to sit, and it would take a lot of fancy steps from Hagen to fill it.

"You see anyone hanging around the saloon you don't like, you throw them out," Trammel told her. "Don't try to do it yourself, and don't have Ben do it if you're worried about him. Have the barman do it, or send someone to get me. Better yet, come fetch me yourself. That way I'll know you're safe."

She stopped sobbing when she noticed the door to the cells was open. "The jail's empty. Where'd all the dopers go?"

"Bundled them up and brought them down to Laramie," Trammel said. "Sheriff Moran and his boys are going to load them onto the next boxcar out of here and send them on their way. The railroad's not happy about it and neither is Hagen, but I couldn't care less. They're out of our hair and won't be coming back."

"I thought things were a bit quieter in town the last couple of days." She looked up at him over her shoulder. "I thought it was because I was missing you. You haven't been around much, Buck. Not since that business with Ben and Bookman."

"I guess I haven't," he admitted. "It's been a rough few days around here, Lilly. A lot of reports to write, so the truth has a chance to get out there. This town will go up like a tinderbox if the wrong rumor catches the wind. Rhoades and me have been doing all we can to keep people from getting damn-fool notions about what's happening and why. So far we've been able to keep everyone in line, but that all could change in the blink of an eye."

"I know," Lilly said as she dried the last of her tears. "That's what has me so worried. For my saloon. For us, too."

He had heard that tone from her before and knew what it meant, but he had to be sure. "What does that mean?"

She sat at the edge of a chair and said, "It means I'm tired, Steve. I'm tired of the mess I walked into the day I stepped off the train. I didn't know it was going to be this bad. I didn't know about Adam hating his father, and the laudanum den and the trouble. All I knew was that you were here, and Ben would be with me, and that together, maybe the three of us could make a good life here. Ben at the saloon, and you for everything else that went into making life good."

Trammel had been afraid of this. She always had an eye on the door, looking for a reason to run. A reason that never came, but always left him wondering what she would do if it did. He had a feeling he was about to find out, for that reason had finally come. "And you don't think we can have a good life here? You and me?"

"You chose to sleep in here for the last couple of nights instead of my bed," Lilly said. "Or at your room in the Oakwood Arms. You never once swung by unless you happened to be in that part of town to check on me or see how I was. I've never been a woman who needed a lot of coddling, but every woman needs to be held once in a while."

"Men, too," Trammel said. "Someone's lit a fire under this town, Lilly, and it feels like it's going to boil over any minute. And this march coming on Saturday is going to bring a lot of trouble with it. I just know it. I can't just spend time with you while the rest of the town is on edge. Not with this march looming over us." He hated to say what he was thinking, but he would hate himself more later if he did not say it now. "Maybe you should think about closing up the saloon for a couple of days. Or at least Saturday, until the whole thing blows over. Things are liable to be more civil after that."

She looked up at him. Hopeful. "Why do you think so?"

"Because whatever tension has built up around here is liable to be gone by then. And when it is, I'll have to pick up the pieces. But one way or another, it'll be over. If you're at the saloon, you'll be in danger. But if you're in here with me, you'll be safe."

"I was thinking of another way," she said. "You remember Delilah from Wichita? Used to work at the Pot O Gold Saloon?"

He remembered her being popular on account of not being particular about the men she allowed into her bed. "What about her?"

"Well, she's respectable now," Lilly told him with renewed enthusiasm. "She runs the girls in this new place that opened up in Laramie called the Rose of Tralee. We were such great friends back then, and she's already said she wouldn't mind it a bit if I came to stay with her for a couple of days."

Trammel could think of ten reasons why that was a bad idea. One was worse than the other. "I was just down in Laramie the other day, and Sheriff Moran expects a lot of trouble in town on account of the marchers. And that saloon is owned by Lucien Clay."

"I know Mr. Clay," she said. "He was there to greet me when I stepped off the train in Laramie. He was awfully nice to me and Ben. Gave us lunch and everything without any charge."

You'll pay for it eventually, Trammel thought but did not say. Clay never gave anything away without getting more in return. "Laramie's liable to be just as dangerous as here. And I'd like to think you'd prefer to be with me than staying in a whore's room in town."

He saw Lilly's eyes harden the way they did when she got angry. "Lots of people do all sorts of things for money, Steve. Selling themselves cheap is nothing new. Look at what you do for a living."

Trammel could see she was getting angry, which made her unpredictable, so he did his best to calm her down. "I'm not against her for what she does, Lilly. I just don't think a whorehouse is the best place for you to be right now, that's all."

She got up and stood as tall as a woman of five feet could manage. She had iron in her spine now and was every bit the prairie countess she had been when they had first met in Kansas. "I thank you for your concern, Sheriff, and I'll certainly take it under advisement. The Gilded Lily will remain open during the march, whether I'm there or not. I have no intention of missing out on a big payday like that and I have every confidence that Ben can keep people in order."

"Lilly," Trammel said. "Don't be like this."

But he had no luck in melting the ice that had formed between them. "I know how busy you must be, so I'll allow you to go about your business, sir, and bid you a good day."

Before she got to the door, Trammel said, "I'm going to need Ben's help tomorrow. It's hard work, but I figure he's up to it."

She placed her hand on the knob but did not turn around. "Mr. London is my employee, not my servant. He can decide whether or not he helps you. Good day, sir."

Formality suited some women, but not Lilly. She had never been able to pull it off. She looked like someone impersonating a grand lady rather than being a grand lady herself.

But he had no intention of telling her that and did not have the inclination to argue with her. It was best to let her go off on her own and cool down for a while than waste time arguing with her.

She opened the door and went outside, not bothering to close it behind her.

And Trammel did not shut it either. He figured the place could use some fresh air.

Chapter 26

With Montague dead, the only legitimate business owners left in town were Mr. Robertson at the general store and Elias, who ran the town livery. The rest were the saloon keepers from the Pot of Gold, the Vic, the Brand, and the Gilded Lily. The man from the claims office had already left town, as had the two lawyers who lived off the business that the Blackstone Bank fed them.

The rest of the people gathered in front of the jail that afternoon were just ordinary citizens who had come to hear why the sheriff and the mayor had called a quick meeting.

Fortunately, Adam Hagen chose to attend from the security of his second-floor balcony, though he had sent two of his Chinese guards down to watch the front of the Clifford Hotel. Emily and Dr. Moore stood off to the side. Hawkeye stood next to Trammel.

Mayor Welch cleared his throat as he stood on the boardwalk next to Trammel and began his speech. "I know a lot of you are wondering why the sheriff and I have asked you to gather like this. Our reasons are simple. All of you know that there is a march planned on Main Street this Saturday. That's only a day or so away. We expect a hundred people or more to flow into town between now and then. Some estimates are as high as two hundred, depending on who you talk to."

Trammel watched the saloon keepers lick their lips like hungry alley cats. Lilly held her shawl tightly around herself as she refused to look his way.

"Everyone here stands to make a decent amount of money from this march. We know that no one likes a drink better than a pious crusader."

A ripple of laughter went through the men Hagen paid to run his saloons. Lilly did not laugh.

"You're going to have plenty of strangers mixed in with your regulars from tomorrow night until most of Sunday. The sheriff and I want to remind you of a few things, especially given all that has transpired in our town over the past few days. Sheriff Trammel?"

Trammel did not need to step forward. He knew he was big enough to be seen and loud enough to be heard by everyone around. He hoped his voice carried over to the six men who had resumed standing watch over Mr. Hagen's body. Lonnie had promised to stay all night to keep some of the ranch hands in check.

Trammel began. "I know all of you people are here to make money. No one's begrudging you that. But we all need to work together if we're going to keep order in this town while our guests are here. I know a lot of your customers are still mourning the loss of Bookman and Mr. Hagen. Montague was a lawyer, but I'm sure there are at least one or two people who were sorry to learn of his demise, too."

Another ripple of laughter. He noticed even Lilly laughed, despite herself.

"I'm not expecting any of you to act like deputies," Trammel went on. "Leave the law up to me and Hawkeye. But I want you to watch out for any and all prairie rats. Not everyone who comes to march will be peaceful. There's likely to be a few looking to start fights and for any excuse to break things. We already had one bunch try to burn down the laudanum den this week, and I wouldn't be surprised if some well-meaning crusader tried to do it again."

Some of the townspeople cheered at that, none louder than Mrs. Higgins. "It's the Lord's will," she shouted. "He will smite the wretches the way he smote Sodom and Gomorrah. His will be done!"

Those with her shouted "Amen" while the saloon keepers shouted oaths of a more vulgar variety.

Trammel talked over all of them. "If you hear someone getting loud or getting rowdy, throw them out of your saloon. If they won't go or there's too many of them, come get me or Hawkeye, here, at the jail and we'll take care of it."

He made sure to look each saloon keeper in the eye for the next part. "I know you all work for Adam Hagen. These are his saloons and he's liable to tell you to ignore what I'm telling you right now. Normally I wouldn't go against what he tells you, but this time I am. If I hear about you letting trouble slide on account of making a buck, I'll clear out your place and lock it up tight for the next month."

The keepers grumbled. Lilly looked elsewhere.

"If you think I'm fooling, just try me,"

Trammel said. "If you think you've got enough squirreled away to keep you fed and housed for the next thirty days, then try me. But seeing as how none of you fine folk strike me as having much money in the bank, I'd advise you to do what I say."

He decided to leave them with the simplest message he could manage. "Don't cause any trouble. Don't let any trouble start. Tell us if there's a problem and we'll handle it. Anyone curses at you, ignore it. Some of these marchers are going to try to goad you into doing something. Don't fall for it. They're just words. Don't turn them into deeds. And don't turn them into martyrs either. Any questions?"

The keepers all looked up to where Hagen stood on his balcony. Trammel followed their gaze and found Hagen standing there, still in a black suit and hat, looking down on the proceedings. He spoke loud enough for everyone to hear him with a clarity that surprised Trammel.

"Any man who disobeys Sheriff Trammel's orders will be fired. Any man whose negligence causes one of my saloons to be closed will be shot. Do as they say and you'll all receive a reward for your efforts. Defy them and you'll get a bullet from me."

He bowed toward the sheriff. "I yield the

remainder of my time to Sheriff Trammel."

Trammel had to hand it to him. He certainly knew how to make a speech. "Go on about your business. We'll tell you if anything changes."

The men were all too happy to go back to their respective saloons. When Lilly lagged behind them, Trammel hoped that she was waiting to talk to him. But she made no effort to even look at him, much less talk to him. He had seen her angry before, but never like this. It would take her a long time to calm down, if ever.

Mayor Welch bid him a good evening and headed back to the Oakwood Arms. Mrs. Higgins and her gaggle of reformers flocked around him and dogged his steps back home.

Emily and Dr. Moore moved through the thinning crowd and stepped up to the boardwalk.

"Well said, Sheriff," Moore complimented him. "Short and to the point. Anything that happens now is on their heads."

His compliment was cold comfort. "The only thing I want on their heads is their hats, Doc. I don't want trouble any more than they do."

"But trouble may come anyway," Moore went on, "and if it does, you'll need all the help you can get. I'd like you to deputize me, if only in a temporary capacity. I know you have your reservations about me, considering my association with Adam Hagen. But don't let the spectacles fool you, sir. I know how to fight and handle a gun. I'd be honored if you'd allow me to pitch in while the marchers are here. My medical duties would come first of course, but these marchers will bring more trouble than any two men can handle, even for you and Mr. Hauk, here."

Trammel looked at Emily, whose expression encouraged him to accept Moore's offer.

And from his balcony, Hagen called down, "Take the man up on his offer, Buck. You'll also have my help to maintain order, too, if you want it."

Trammel pointed up to where Hagen stood. "You're going to stay locked up in your room until this march is over. There are too many people who want you dead, so the less we see of you, the better."

"You're no fun at all," Hagen sulked.

Trammel judged the doctor. He was younger than he appeared, maybe thirty or so. And fitter, too. His full, clean-shaven face made him look softer than he was. Perhaps there was more grit to this man than he knew. He might come in useful after all. "Let me see your hands."

Hawkeye looked at Trammel, puzzled, while Dr. Moore complied. Trammel examined them and, just as he had expected, they were soft and free of calluses. He let the hands go. "You have any experience chopping down trees?"

Moore clearly took it as an odd question. "I was never a lumberjack, but I've cut down a fair share in my time. My father believed in his sons knowing the benefit of hard labor. Why?"

The march was less than two days away. He hated telling anyone about his plans so soon, but he saw that he had no choice. "Because unless we want this town overrun by outsiders on Saturday, we're going to have to make some fast work of some trees tomorrow afternoon." Trammel spoke to Hawkeye. "You and the doctor, here, should head over to Robertson's and see how many axes he has in stock. We'll need to borrow them if he lets us, or buy them if he makes us. Don't argue with him. Just tell him I sent you and we need them for the safety of the town. Come back and tell me what he says. In the meantime I've got to go see a man about a horse."

Trammel began to walk across toward

Emily's barn, where Mr. Hagen's body was being kept. Lonnie and five other men were sitting around a campfire they had built out front. The ranch hands had pitched some tents near the barn in case it began to rain while they kept vigil over Hagen's remains.

Emily trailed behind him. "What are you up to, Buck?"

He slowed his pace to accommodate her. He was not accustomed to sharing his plans with anyone, but Emily had always been an exception. "We're going to block those marchers from coming into town. We're going to block the road tomorrow afternoon with chopped-down trees."

Emily looked like she was going to raise an objection, then stopped herself. "That's actually not a bad idea if you do it at the right place."

"We'll place them at the narrowest part of the road, where there's swamp on all sides," Trammel told her. "We'll tell them the trees fell down during the night and blocked the road, which they won't believe, but it'll make a fair number of them turn back, especially the wagonloads of people. They'll never clear the muck of the swamp. Those on horses might chance it, but most of them won't."

"How many trees will you chop down?"

she asked.

"Depends on how many men I get. Three or four big ones ought to do it. I just need a draft horse to pull them into place. I'm hoping Lonnie's got some on the ranch."

"It'll definitely discourage them," Emily said. "I hope you're not too proud to ask Ben to help."

"I'd be desperate enough to ask Adam to help if that right arm of his was any good. So yes, I'll be asking Ben."

Emily looked like she had something else on her mind. "I saw that you and Lilly seem to have had some kind of falling-out. I'm sorry about that, Buck. I really am."

Trammel could tell by her tone that she was. "Her reasons are the same as yours. She just got there a different way, is all." He desperately wanted to talk about something else. "I hear you're using some new way to keep Hagen preserved until his family arrives. How'd you manage that?"

"With formaldehyde the undertaker in Laramie gave me," she said. "I noticed he had a constant cough, and my husband had a book that warned how dangerous formaldehyde can be. I made the amount last by adding cheap wine and salt to the mix. It cuts down on the odor and slows the decomposition process."

He smiled despite the gory subject. "You're an enterprising woman, Dr. Downs. Always was. You'll do well in that school Hagen's going to send you to. Hell, you'll probably teach those men a trick or two they haven't thought of yet."

"I've decided not to go," she said. "At least not until I can pay my own way."

Trammel was surprised. "It was a generous offer. Don't look a gift horse in the mouth, Emily."

"I don't eat apples snakes tell me to eat either."

He could not argue with her there.

By then they had reached the barn. Emily went in to tend to the body while the men all stood up when they saw Trammel. Only Lonnie stepped forward to greet him. "Evening, Sheriff. Quite a gathering you had over there. Heard what you told them. I only hope they're wise enough to listen to you."

Trammel nodded toward the ranch hands standing around the campfire. "Sounds like you've found a way to keep these boys in hand."

"Don't go thanking me too much," Lonnie said. "I've been having a hell of a time keeping them from taking a shot at that piece of dirt on his balcony up there."

Trammel looked back and saw Hagen sitting outside, despite his orders. He even tipped his hat when he saw the men looking at him.

"It'd be a tough shot from this distance," Trammel said.

"Maybe for you, but not for my boys," Lonnie told him. "But they've listened to me this far, so I'm hoping they keep doing it. What's on your mind?"

"Do you have a draft horse or two up at the ranch you could spare and a man to handle them?"

"We've got four and any one of my men can handle them," Lonnie answered. "What are you looking to do?"

He laid out his plan to block the road the following afternoon.

Lonnie took in the entire plan without a single interruption, then said, "No one will believe they just fell there, but I have a feeling you don't care about that."

"I want to keep them out of town," Trammel said. "And I don't care how I do it. I figure that spot is the best to keep them from getting here."

"You figure right," Lonnie said. "We'll do more than help, Sheriff. My men and I have cleared more trees than you've ever seen. We'll do all the work and block that road good and strong. And we'll open it up again when you tell us we can. That's the deal."

Trammel had always been wary of offers that sounded too good to be true. This case was no different. "What's the catch?"

"No catch at all," Lonnie said. "We don't want those people up here either. They're liable to start something that my boys could be blamed for. We'll block it off for you and clear it so the Hagen family can get through once they get here. I think Caleb is supposed to be the first. On Monday."

That was more than Trammel had known and he did not bother asking Lonnie how he did. "The road needs to be blocked by tomorrow night so no one has time to warn Laramie about it. There are other ways up here, but —"

"None a wagon can use. Leave it to us, Sheriff. It's the least we can do after you've been fair to us. That word you gave us about the cattle saved the ranch. Their drinking water was tainted. We managed to cut the sick ones from the herd before it spread. They'd all be dead or dying by now if it hadn't been for you."

The two men shook hands and Trammel walked back to the jail. He still was not sure if he could trust Lonnie. He'd been too quick to agree to everything he had asked and more.

But he also did not have much of a choice. The men from the Blackstone Ranch knew how to clear an area quicker than he did. He knew they would probably ask a favor of him. He only hoped he could grant it when they did.

Chapter 27

The headline of the *Laramie Daily* said it all:

King Charles Hagen Is Dead

He finally did it, Lucien Clay said to himself. *He finally had the guts to do the deed.*

He set the paper aside, deciding that reading the article would be a waste of time, and he had no time to waste. He needed to set his plan in motion and the hour was growing late.

Micklewhite knocked on his hotel door and paused for a few seconds before opening it. When he did, he poked his head in first, before coming in. He was back in his Michael Albertson garb: a brown suit and a shabby hat. He was completely unrecognizable save for the permanent stoop he bore. Pete Stride entered the room after him.

"It's time, Mr. Clay," Micklewhite said.

"Time for you to review the troops, as it were."

"I think you're going to like the men I picked, Mr. Clay," Pete added. "They're stone-cold killers, every one of them."

If Clay had a dollar for every time a man had boasted of his skills with a gun or a knife, he would not need to take on Adam Hagen like this. He could easily buy him out and still have more than enough left over to buy England.

Boasts meant nothing to him. Results were the only thing that held any currency with him.

He ignored Micklewhite's offer to help him get out of bed and did so on his own. The pain in his head was still there, but the dizziness had subsided, and he walked around his room several times a day on his own. Yes, he was defying the orders of his doctor, but Lucien Clay had never been one to follow the rules.

He gestured toward the lamp by the window and told Micklewhite, "Move that."

He did not want his new employees to see him bandaged up.

Micklewhite did as he was told as Pete parted the drapes for him and pointed down at the street below.

Clay saw the streetlamps had already been

lit and realized it was much later than he had thought. Spending most of his day in bed had robbed him of all sense of time.

Pete had arranged for the ten men he had hired to attack Blackstone to stand across the street so Clay could get a decent look at them.

He steadied himself against the window and saw several familiar faces among the men Pete had hired. Most were local toughs who rolled drunks with the aid of a knife or a gun. A few were strangers to him but bore the grizzled look a man tends to acquire from years spent sleeping out of doors.

All of them had the same look about them that Lucien saw himself whenever he shaved each morning.

"Some of them are pond scum," Clay said as he sat in a chair by the window.

"They'll serve a purpose when the time comes," Pete said as he let the drapes fall closed. "They'll stop bullets meant for me and the others. Maybe even do some damage before someone kills them. The roughest of the bunch will be with me when we go after Hagen."

Clay pointed at Micklewhite. "Go down and scatter them. Moran will get suspicious."

He paused for a moment before he realized Clay wanted to talk to Pete in private. He went off to carry out his task.

Once Micklewhite was gone, Clay asked, "When will you leave?"

"Figured Saturday morning would be time enough," Pete said. "Get up there before the crowds and blend in with them once they get there. Pick out a couple of choice spots to hit and wait for the fun to begin."

Clay had assumed as much, which was why he had wanted to talk to him alone. "You go with Albert. Tonight. The others can go up on Saturday morning early."

"Consider it done," Pete said without hesitation. "I'm not questioning you, Mr. Clay, but can I ask why?"

Normally Clay would not have minded. Questions like that proved a man had common sense. But with it being hard for him to talk through a broken jaw, he had to be economical with his words. "Trammel is busy tomorrow. Hagen may be exposed. Kill both if you can. Hagen first."

"Smart, sir. Real smart." He got up to leave. "I'll put Andy in charge of the others while I'm gone. He'll make sure they get up there in time."

Clay was glad Pete Stride was not a complicated man like Micklewhite. Albert's role in plunging Blackstone into chaos was almost over. After hell broke loose in Blackstone this weekend, Micklewhite would be more of a hindrance than a help. He expected to have 20 percent of the town once Clay was in charge. Clay intended for him to get 100 percent of the blame. The county would be looking for someone to swing for the death and destruction caused by the march, and Clay would see to it that man would be Micklewhite. A known rabble-rouser and charlatan from back East with designs of his own to take over the town. Once Hagen was dead, all his holdings would fall to Clay, both legally and illegally. Blackstone and the ranch would be his for the taking. The rest of Hagen's plan would fall into place and he would expand from the Wyoming Territory into other parts of the country. The Celestials would help secure his holdings wherever they went, for a healthy sum of course.

It would be a reasonable price to pay, for the Chinese only cared about money. Clay wanted power and knew how to keep it.

But he needed to get it first. And by this time Saturday night, he would be holding the entire territory in the palm of his hand.

He glanced over at the *Laramie Daily* and reread the headline announcing Charles Hagen's death. The old world had died away. A new world was just being born. "The king is dead," he said to the empty room. "Long live King Clay."

Lonnie got the five ranch hands who were getting ready to ride back up to the Blackstone that night to gather around. These men were different from the new hires who would be filtering into town to watch Hagen's body. They had all been with the ranch for several years. Lonnie knew he could trust these men because he had trusted them with his life several times over.

"None of us will be here tomorrow afternoon," Lonnie told them. "The others will have to split their time to cover us while we do a favor for the sheriff."

"What kind of favor?" Will asked. He had been with the outfit almost as long as Lonnie. "What's he ever done for us anyway, except keep us from killing Adam?"

Lonnie could not argue with him on that score. "Look at it as a favor for the sheriff that benefits us more. Tomorrow afternoon we're going to cut some trees and brush and use them to block the road for the marchers on Saturday. Send most of them back to Laramie, where they belong."

"How's that help us?" Josiah asked. "I thought we wanted the marchers here to keep Trammel busy while we took care of Adam."

Lonnie did not need Josiah to tell him about the plan. He had been the one who had come up with it in the first place.

"This is what you might call a change of plans," Lonnie explained. "But we plan to use it to our advantage. We're going to cut down five big trees tomorrow and stack them up good, where the road cuts through the marsh. I heard most of the people are coming up on wagons, so that'll be enough to turn most of them back."

Will did not look happy. Neither did the others. "I still don't see how that helps our plan any."

Lonnie was all too happy to tell him. "Because it'll not only keep people out, it'll also keep people in."

The men seemed close to understanding what he was saying, but they were not there yet. He had to remind himself that these men were not thinkers. They were used to being told what to do. Thinking, like any skill, got rusty if you did not use it enough, so he spelled it out for them.

"Caleb's telegram said that he wanted everything cleaned up before he or the rest of his family got here next week. Now it takes a little time to read between the lines, but all of us know there's no love lost between Bartholomew, Caleb, and Adam. He couldn't say it outright in the message, but I understand it loud and clear. He wants Adam cleaned up and cleared out of here by Monday. The best shot we're going to have at him is Saturday. Some of those marchers are bound to get through, especially those on horseback. But even if they don't, we've got enough well meaning fatheads in town to create enough of a distraction for us. We'll find out where Hagen's holed up, we'll hit it hard, and bring him out alive."

Will tilted his head toward the Clifford Hotel and the balcony that was now empty. "Hagen's got the Celestials guarding him. They won't give up easy."

"It won't make much of a difference," Lonnie told him. "Wherever he is, there'll be more of us. We grab him, alive if possible, and drag his miserable carcass all the way up to the ranch. If he's still alive by then, which I doubt, we'll do our best to keep him alive until Caleb gets here, so he can have the honor of finishing him off. If not, he and Bart will just have to be satisfied with desecrating his remains. Sound good?"

All of the men voiced their agreement

except for Josiah. Lonnie knew Josiah had always been the most thoughtful of the group, not that anyone would ever confuse him for a philosopher.

"We were counting on that march keeping Trammel so distracted that he wouldn't know what we were doing," Josiah reminded them. "Fewer marchers will put us up against Trammel, won't it?"

"Maybe," Lonnie allowed. "But Caleb's orders were plain enough. Trammel and Hawkeye aren't our concern."

"He's a pretty big concern of mine," Oleg said. He was the biggest of the old group and did not often express concern or fear. "We've all seen what Trammel can do to people. He's even managed to make something out of Hawkeye. We were hoping we'd have a hundred or so marchers between us and Trammel when we took Hagen, but these odds —"

"Don't change a thing," Lonnie finished the sentence for him, "just like Hagen's Celestials don't change anything. We'll hit this town with twenty-five men. Not even Trammel can beat those odds."

He was troubled when the men did not look so sure.

Lonnie decided to try another tactic. "Look, you boys know how I feel about

Trammel. He's a good man, and I'm not itching to fight him. We won't if we don't have to. And we won't have to if we play it smart and stick together. You five are going to be the cornerstones of all this. For it to work, I need you boys to be steady so the new boys are steady, too. Once we have Hagen up at the ranch, dead or alive, we can fend off any attack Trammel and Hawkeye try. We can keep them at bay and reason with them. Or hold them off until Caleb gets here and let him handle it."

Lonnie looked each man in the eye and liked what he saw. Their concerns had faded. They would do their duty. They would represent the Blackstone brand.

"Get a good night's sleep, because we've got a lot of work ahead of us tomorrow."

"And a lot of good work on Saturday," Will said.

The other men grumbled their agreement. It was music to Lonnie's ears. "Amen."

CHAPTER 28

"Well?" Emily said as she removed the sheet to reveal her handiwork. "What do you think?"

As Trammel looked at Charles Hagen's corpse in the casket she had ordered to be built, he decided it would be best for him to say nothing at all.

Dr. Moore spoke for him. "Remarkable, Emily. Simply remarkable. He looks like he's lying down for a nap. His color is perfect. Not waxen at all. How did you do it?"

Trammel thought of other things while she went through the specifics. He thought the whole idea of dressing the dead was a ridiculous waste of money. The dead were dead, and no amount of powder or fancy chemicals could change that. But more and more folks wanted to look at their departed loved ones for a while before planting them in the ground.

But there was no arguing Emily's skill. Charles Hagen certainly looked lifelike enough. He looked like he might open his eyes and pop out of the coffin at any moment, something Trammel sincerely hoped would not happen.

"Buck?" she said, breaking his train of thought. "What do you think?"

He played it safe. "Doc Moore said it all. He looks fine, Emily. You'd never know the birds had been at him. How long do you plan on keeping him here?"

She seemed disappointed. "What difference does that make?"

"Because the sooner he's out of town, the fewer ranch hands Hawkeye and I have to worry about hanging around here."

Doc Moore's hand went to the Colt he had taken to wearing on his hip since their last conversation. "Have they made any threats or stepped out of line?"

"No," Trammel admitted. "And that's what worries me." He shrugged it off. "Maybe I've just got the jitters after everything that's happened."

But Moore did not seem so eager to write it off as a case of nerves. "A man in your line of work must listen to his instincts, Sheriff. If you feel something is happening here, you might be right."

Trammel grinned. "Is that your professional medical opinion, Doc?"

"Hardly. Just the observation of a man who has spent more than his fair share of time in troubled towns like Blackstone."

Trammel had tried hard not to like Jacob Moore. He was Adam Hagen's man, and Emily's competition. But the more he spoke to him, the more he realized that the good doctor was a tough man to dislike.

Knowing Emily would not be happy until he said something original, he said, "The only thing that bothers me is the smell."

"That's the diluted formaldehyde I used," she said. "I dilute it with wine and salt and spices. Once we load him on the wagon and bring him up to the ranch, it should dissipate quickly. It's poisonous in its raw state."

"And given the state of unfortunates in town," Moore said, "I'd keep it under lock and key. Men have been known to use it as a drug."

Trammel looked at him. "You're kidding."

"I wish I was," Moore said. "Its effect is said to be even greater than laudanum, and it kills the user after only a few doses. The mind is a mysterious thing, Sheriff. Its cravings often destroy the body that gives it life."

Trammel was in no mood for a philosophical discussion. It was already past dark, and he wanted to get in one last patrol with Hawkeye before he let the young man get some sleep.

"You two have a good night," he said as he picked up the Henry that was leaning against the wall. "If you need me, I'll be on patrol for a while, then at the jail for the rest of the night."

"I trust it'll be a quiet night, Sheriff," Moore said. "I understand you have fewer guests these days. At least those suffering from the effects of laudanum."

Trammel had to give him credit there. "I don't know what you're giving them, but it's working. I haven't picked up a doper from the alleys in days. Thank you for that."

But Moore rejected the praise. "No need to thank me, Sheriff. I'm just doing what I was brought here to do."

Once again, Trammel kept his opinion to himself. He imagined Adam Hagen had not brought Moore to Blackstone just to treat laudanum addicts. But he figured he would find out the real reason soon enough. There was no need to start a debate now.

He bid them a good evening and was almost out of the barn when Emily said, "You'll be in the jail tonight, Buck?"

He turned when he reached the door.

"Yep. Seeing as how I'm the sheriff, that's usually where you'll find me. Why?"

"No reason," she said as she fiddled with the sheet that had covered Charles Hagen's corpse. "I just thought you worked days now, and Hawkeye worked nights."

Trammel grinned. She had figured out there was trouble between him and Lilly. "Things change, Dr. Downs." He touched the brim of his hat. "See you around."

He walked out into the cool night air that had settled over Blackstone. He acknowledged Lonnie and the other men, who were eating supper around the campfire they had going near the barn.

He knew some of the people in town thought it strange that he preferred to walk everywhere instead of ride. But he had grown up in Manhattan and worked a significant time in Chicago, so walking was his preferred way of getting around. He found that he saw more from a slower pace, which was an asset in his line of work. It might take him longer to get from place to place, but speed was not everything. Taking his time had served him well up until now and he had no intention of changing any time soon.

He looked up at the balcony of the Clifford Hotel and was glad to see it was empty.

The lights inside the room were on, but at least Adam had the good sense to make himself less conspicuous. He only hoped he did the same on Saturday. Because despite what he had told the townspeople earlier that day, Trammel knew there was absolutely nothing he could do to save him if the marchers stormed the hotel and went after him. Hagen and his Celestials would kill a lot of them, but probably not all. Having two dead Hagens on his hands would be a nightmare.

He found Hawkeye standing outside the jail, his rifle at his side as he leaned against the porch post. He was surprised when he saw the young man's breath, because although it was a chilly night, it was not cold enough to turn a man's breath into vapor. When he got closer, he saw that Hawkeye had a cigarette tucked between his lips.

"Evening," Trammel said as he stood next to his deputy.

Hawkeye looked down at him, squinting. "Evening, boss."

"Mind telling me what you're doing?"

"Smoking," Hawkeye said as a thin cloud of smoke escaped his mouth. "It relaxes me."

Trammel was sorry the boy was in such a hurry to grow up. "I can see that. You mind telling me why? I've never seen you smoke before."

"Mr. Hagen gave one to me." Hawkeye was clearly trying not to cough. "Said it came from a package of cigarettes. Makes me feel fancy."

Trammel thought otherwise. "You look like you're going to be sick. Take that damned thing out of your mouth and let's go."

Hawkeye barely managed to toss the cigarette into the thoroughfare without burning himself. He coughed heavily as they began their patrol. "Sorry, boss. I didn't really like it anyway."

"Keep it that way," Trammel told him. "Nobody likes it at first, but like everything else in life, you get used to it after a while. Besides, you don't get paid enough to afford cigarettes."

"I know. It's just that Mr. Hagen told me it was time for me to grow up a little."

"I wish he'd take his own advice," Trammel said. "When did he give it to you?"

Hawkeye coughed again. "As he passed by on his way to the Gilded Lily. I thought he was just being nice."

"That's the trouble with him. He seems to be doing one thing while he's really doing something else."

Hawkeye looked confused. "I don't understand that one, boss."

"Neither do I." Trammel noticed there were more people on the street than usual for a Thursday night. A lot of new faces and more horses along Main Street. "When did all of these people show up?"

"Just after sunset," Hawkeye told him. "A wagon came through Main Street and dropped them off at the Clifford. I counted about thirty or so, but none of them looked dangerous. Older women, mostly, with men I took for their husbands."

Trammel judged Hawkeye to be correct. All of them were out taking a stroll either before or after supper. They were taking in Blackstone at its bleakest, when the lights came on and the rodents came out. The sound of several tinny pianos and bawdy singing echoed throughout the thoroughfare like a fever dream. If these pious folks came to town early for wholesome entertainment, they were in for a bitter disappointment.

"Kind of funny, isn't it?" Hawkeye asked as they walked along the boardwalk. "All of these people here to march against Mr. Hagen, yet they're staying at his hotel and eating at his places."

"Nothing funny about it," Trammel observed. "People tend to resent the people who give them the things they most enjoy. And I'd wager we'll be seeing a few of those prayerful people staggering along here in a few hours as they go back to their rooms."

They had just begun to cross onto New Main Street when Trammel saw two riders turn off the road to Laramie. It was too dark and they were too far away to see their faces, but there was no mistaking that one of the riders had a crooked back.

They stopped their horses in the middle of Main Street for a moment before urging their horses toward Bainbridge.

Hawkeye had seen them, too. "One of those men looked like Mike Albertson."

Trammel had thought the same thing. "Wonder who he rode into town with. Looks like they're heading over to Mrs. Higgins's place. Let's go ask them. We'll pick up our patrol later."

They dodged a couple of wagons bringing more people into town as they crossed Main Street and reached Bainbridge Avenue. They came to Mrs. Higgins's house just as Albertson and his friend climbed down from their horses. Neither of them had seen the lawmen approaching.

Trammel gripped the Henry a little tighter and saw Hawkeye had done the same.

"Evening, gents," Trammel called out to

them from the darkness. "Welcome back, Albertson. Looks like you've been gone a while."

Something in the way the second man moved told Trammel he was raising a gun. Trammel pushed Hawkeye to the left as he dove right.

Three shots cut through the night air as Trammel hit the ground.

He could see the man wheeling his horse away from the house as he tried to get away.

Trammel sat up and aimed as straight as he could manage at the dark, fleeing figure and got off three shots of his own. He had no idea if any of them had struck their target, but he had not heard anything hit the ground either.

"Don't shoot!" Albertson called out as he held his hands in the air. "I'm unarmed!"

Trammel aimed the rifle at him. "Hawkeye, you all right?"

"I've got him covered, boss," the young man said from the darkness nearby. "He's not going anywhere."

Trammel struggled to get to his feet. He had felt ridiculous, sitting flat on his ass in the dirt while someone had been trying to kill him, but he had not been given much of a choice.

He soothed his bruised ego by snatching

Albertson by the collar and throwing him against Mrs. Higgins's door, where the light was better. He pressed the barrel of the Henry against the back of the rabble-rouser's head. "You keep your hands on the wall until I say otherwise. You move, I'll kill you."

Albertson placed his hands against the wall, just as Trammel had ordered.

The front door opened, and Mrs. Higgins appeared, clutching a bathrobe at her chest. "What's all this ruckus about?" She squinted at the men in the darkness. "Is that you, Sheriff? Mr. Albertson?"

While Trammel leaned his gun against the wall and patted Albertson down, Albertson said, "Go back to bed, Mrs. Higgins. It's all a grave misunderstanding. I'll explain everything in a moment. I promise." Mrs. Higgins did what Albertson had told her to do and shut the door.

Trammel patted down Albertson's pants and heard the unmistakable clink of gold coins in his pocket. He dug in and pulled out a velvet bag roughly the size of his hand. He weighed it and realized it was indeed gold.

He continued to pat down Albertson and found a knife in his boot, which he threw aside and out of Albertson's reach.

Trammel grabbed him by the shoulder and turned him around, keeping him pinned against the wall with a heavy hand to the chest. "You've got one chance to explain yourself before I lose my temper."

Albertson asked, "Can I lower my hands now, Sheriff?"

"Slowly."

Albertson lowered his hands slowly and said, "Like I told Mrs. Higgins, this is all a horrible misunderstanding, Sheriff."

"Getting shot at is pretty clear to me," Trammel told him. "Why, and who is he?"

"I'm afraid my cousin Abraham is still a dangerous man, Sheriff," Albertson explained. "He's a sinner, same as me, and has only recently begun to reform his ways. When you approached us in the dark like that, it seems his old instincts got the better of him and he shot at you before riding away. Please don't take it personally."

Hawkeye was at Trammel's side now. His rifle was still aimed at Albertson. "Kind of hard to take getting shot at any other way but personally."

Trammel was not done questioning him. "What's he doing here with you? And why'd you two ride up from Laramie so late?"

"Like I told you," Albertson said, "my cousin is seeking to reform his ways and has been helping me organize the march in Laramie. I'd have thought you would be happy about that, Sheriff. Everyone knows you're as unhappy with the laudanum dens as we are. You'll find yourself in good company on Saturday."

Trammel pulled him off the wall, then pushed him back hard against it. "And you're going to find yourself in jail if any trouble starts. I'm going to hold you personally responsible for anything that happens."

Albertson frowned. "I am not my brother's keeper. Or, in the case of what happened here tonight, my cousin's keeper."

Trammel held the bag of gold coins in front of his face. "And where'd you get all of this money? The collection plate?"

"Our cause has support from many quarters, Sheriff Trammel. There is no shortage of people who applaud our efforts to call people to be better and renounce sin. What you hold in your hand is the sum of the donations we have received from concerned citizens who wish us well."

Trammel did not believe it. "Who's your donor?"

"Someone who wishes to remain anonymous," Albertson said. "And will remain so."

Trammel began to put things together as

he kept Albertson pinned against the wall. The two men had ridden up from Laramie after dark, probably to keep from being seen. One of them took a shot at him and rode off, leaving Albertson behind with a pocketful of money. That did not sound like a reformed man to him.

The whole march suddenly took on a different look to him.

"This anonymous contributor of yours wouldn't happen to be Lucien Clay, would it?"

Albertson did not so much as flinch. "I know of Mr. Clay, but I don't know him personally as we find ourselves on opposing sides, sir."

"Do you?" Trammel pressed the crooked man harder against the wall. The wood began to crack behind him. "Or maybe it only looks that way?"

Trammel watched an element of iron appear in Albertson's eyes. "You may think whatever you like, Sheriff, but what you can prove is another matter entirely. So, are you going to return my gold and let me go, or are you going to push me through poor Mrs. Higgins's wall? I don't think she'd be too happy about that, and you know how difficult she can be when she puts her mind to it."

Trammel let the man go and stepped away from him. Albertson rolled his crooked shoulders as he tried to get some feeling back in them. "I'm going to forget any of this ever happened as a gesture of goodwill between us. Now, as for my gold —"

Trammel stuck the sack in his pocket. "You'll get it on Monday, when the bank is open."

Albertson flinched. "That's not legal, Sheriff. Some might even go so far as to call it robbery."

"I call it prudent," Trammel said. "If it's a donation, like you say, then you won't be needing it until after the march is over. But if it's to be used as a payoff for some thugs you've hired to cause trouble, then you're going to find yourself in one hell of a spot when you don't have their money." Trammel patted the coins in his pocket. "You sure you want to stick to your story about it being a donation?"

Albertson licked his lips. "I'll want a receipt for that. I know exactly how much is there, so if any of it is missing, I'll make a formal complaint in Laramie about it. That much I promise you, Sheriff."

"We'll push the receipt under the door before morning," Trammel told him. "Don't worry about that. You just worry about what you're going to say to the men expecting this money. We've had a lot of deaths around here this week while you were away. I wouldn't want yours to be one of them."

Albertson picked up his hat from the ground. "Your concern overwhelms me, Sheriff. It truly does." He gestured with the hat as he said, "A good evening to you and your deputy."

He hobbled inside the house and shut the door behind him.

Trammel considered hanging around in front of the house, listening at the door to hear how Albertson explained himself to Mrs. Higgins, but thought better of it. He and Hawkeye were awfully good targets in the light of the old woman's house and he had been shot at enough for one night. No sense in pressing his luck.

He finally turned his attention to his deputy. "You sure you're all right?"

The deputy nodded but was still looking at the closed door. "I don't like this, boss. I don't like it one bit."

"Neither do I. Come on. We've got a patrol to finish."

Pete Stride pulled his horse up short when he felt something warm and wet flowing down his leg. He had not felt the impact of a bullet, but he had been in enough scrapes to know you did not always feel it at first. The pain only started after the moment had passed.

He cursed the darkness as he got down from the saddle. He kept a tight grip on the horse's reins as he felt his body for holes or blood. He had to go by feel because he was in the middle of nowhere on a moonless night. The lights of the town were small in the distance.

He felt around as best he could and realized he had not been shot, but his right leg was damp. He smelled it in the darkness, and the metallic tinge to it told him it was blood.

He rubbed the right flank of his horse and felt the bullet wound. His hand came up slick as the horse shied away from the pain.

Pete cursed loudly in the darkness. He had no idea where he was, except a good distance away from town. He had no idea if Micklewhite had stuck with his Albertson story or had given him up to Trammel. He had gotten a good look at the lawman in Laramie and could not blame a man like Micklewhite for folding if he did. The sheriff looked like he knew a lot of ways to hurt a man and would not mind using any of them.

But Pete had more pressing concerns at

the moment. His horse had been shot just above the right hip. It was bleeding and the bullet was still in there, though he had no way of knowing how deep. It did not appear to have hit anything vital, but Pete knew it was only a matter of time before it began to affect the way he walked. Infection would probably set in over the next day or so. He would need to find another horse, and soon.

He swore again, this time at his own foolishness for rushing the shot at Trammel the way he had. He had recognized the big man immediately when he stepped from the darkness but had been taken by surprise. He had let down his guard and now he was stuck in the middle of nowhere with a lame horse in the pitch darkness of unfamiliar country. He had not been prepared to spend the night outdoors and knew it would grow colder still. And if he took the saddle off the horse and bedded down where he was, he could find himself out in the open and exposed come morning. Trammel would probably come looking for him and he needed to put as much distance between him and the sheriff as possible. Besides, if he took the saddle off the horse, he might not get it back on again. If the bullet wound was as bad as it looked, the animal would be in more pain the longer it stayed still.

He climbed back into the saddle and decided to keep moving, but at a much slower pace. No one seemed to be coming after him, so there was no reason to hurry.

He knew that the horse could see in the dark and that the Blackstone Ranch was somewhere nearby. He remembered Micklewhite's babbling on the ride up here from Laramie, and his tales about the horses and cattle on the Blackstone Ranch. He knew Hagen had poisoned the cattle, but not the horses. Maybe he would get lucky and find one at the ranch.

He remembered Micklewhite had told him the ranch overlooked the town, so he rode in that direction. He picked out a single star from the countless ones overhead and headed in that direction. It was not much of a plan, but it was all he had.

He had been riding in that same direction for what he judged to be about half an hour when his horse faltered a bit and tossed its head. It had caught the scent of something on the wind. Something Pete hoped was another horse, and not a wolf or a coyote. Those predators usually stayed away from humans during the day, but the night was their world and they knew it.

He urged his horse onward up the gradual incline until he caught the smell, too. Coffee and campfire. The cowboy's friend. And, on that night, Pete Stride's friend, too.

His days in the badlands had taught him how to ride quietly by cattlemen. He brought his horse down to a lope, but urged it to keep riding around the low flame that was now visible. He knew one jangle from his rig could put the men on edge and send them into the darkness to investigate. He dared not risk it.

The wounded animal did not make a sound as they rode past the five men around the campfire. Pete Stride watched them pass a jug among themselves as he and the horse crept by at a fair distance.

He could smell cattle were nearby, and if Micklewhite's rambling was any indication, there should be horses close, too. But he could not catch their scent on the wind and his mount's steps were beginning to falter. That wounded right leg was failing. It would only be a matter of time before it gave way, and Pete could not risk being pinned beneath the animal until Trammel or one of the ranch hands found him the next morning.

There was only one thing left for him to do: find the Blackstone Ranch's stable, which Micklewhite had mentioned on the ride up to Blackstone. He could steal a horse from there and sneak back into town.

But going near the stable was also the most dangerous thing he could do, because someone was likely to hear him while he was there. But it was a chance he had to take.

Again he rode wide of the campfire and toward the general direction of where he thought the ranch house might be. The house would be deserted, so he knew there would be no candles or oil lamps to reveal it in the darkness.

But in the near distance he could see a series of buildings that blocked out the stars behind them. He used his nose to guide him toward the stable and found a small lamp burning when he got there.

It was just in time, too, for his horse was beginning to limp noticeably now, and that right leg would give out any minute.

Pete climbed down from the horse and pulled his horse along with him. He might lose his rig if the horse fell now, but at least he would not have his leg crushed by the large animal.

He continued to walk toward the lamp burning outside the stable and stopped.

It did not feel right. Why would they leave a lamp burning at the stable unless someone was around to keep an eye on it?

He got his answer when he was about to enter the stable. The feeling of gunmetal against the back of his neck was cold enough to make Pete freeze where he stood.

"You mind telling me what the hell you're doing out here this time of night?"

The voice was unfamiliar and could belong to anyone. Trammel. His deputy. A ranch hand. "I was looking for someone who could help my horse. He's hurt real bad."

"So I noticed," the man said. "Been trailing blood all over the ranch. A blind man could follow it, if he had a nose for blood."

Pete kept his arm straight, only moving it at the elbow to grab the knife he always kept tucked in his belt. This damned fool was too close to him. Hc was already dead. The trick was to get his gun before he fired it. "If you could help me with my horse, mister, I'd be obliged to you."

The gunman pushed him forward with his firearm. It felt like it probably was a rifle, not a pistol. That was very good. Pete saw that as very good news indeed.

"Get moving into the stable where I can get a better look at you."

Pete led his wounded horse toward the stable and the man with the gun prodded him. When Pete felt the angle of the barrel against his neck change as the man reached for the lamp, the old outlaw pulled his knife as he spun around. His left hand knocked the rifle aside as his right slashed across the ranch hand's belly. The man dropped to his knees, cradling his belly, as Pete took hold of the rifle. He realized it was a shotgun and he tossed it away. He did not have much use for shotguns at present.

The man dropped the lamp and used both hands to try to stop the bleeding. Some of the dry straw on the stable floor began to burn beside him, which only made Pete's selection of a horse that much more urgent. He found a chestnut mare that looked strong enough and decided he'd take her. His horse, along with all the rest of the animals in the barn, was growing anxious as the flames from the lamp started to spread. The wounded rancher, now flat on his back, did his best to stamp out the flames with his arm. All he got for his trouble was his shirt catching fire.

Pete tied his horse to the nearest post and hefted off her saddle. The mare in the stall fussed a little, but did not kick him. He threw his saddle atop her and buckled the straps under her barrel. He pulled the mare out of the stall and was about to ride off when the dying man with the burning arm said, "Don't leave the horses to die, mister. They don't deserve that."

Pete realized he was right. He urged his horse back into the stable, where he reached down and opened all the stalls. Each horse bolted from the building and away from the rapidly spreading flames. He looked toward the campfire and saw the dark outlines of men closing in on the barn.

The last horse to escape was Pete's wounded one. He untied her reins from the post and watched her ride away with the others. He gave his new mare her head and let her follow the fleeing horses. Her hoof-prints would blend in with the others until he was far enough away from the ranch to turn back toward town.

He looked back at the stable as the horse ran away. No one was following him, and several men were attempting to put out the fire. It had not spread very far, and Pete figured they had saved the stable. If they got the ranch hand a doctor in time, they might be able to save him as well.

Pete continued to allow his horse to blindly follow the other horses through the darkness. It was going to be a long night for him, and a lot of other people in Blackstone, too.

CHAPTER 29

A warm oven and a quiet jail were a dangerous combination for a lawman, even Buck Trammel. He had his feet on the desk and his chair at just the right angle to make himself cozy enough to fall asleep. He would pay for it later with a sore back and tight shoulders, but at that moment the price was worth it. And he needed sleep.

Trammel did not think he had been asleep long when he was jolted awake by someone pounding on the jailhouse door. He got up and went to the rifle rack as he called out, "Who's there?"

"It's Bobby from the Clifford," said a young boy's voice through the door. "You'd better come quick. There's cowboys coming."

Trammel recognized the voice as belonging to the little orphan boy who did odd jobs around the Clifford.

He took down his Henry from the rack

and listened at the front door before opening it. He did not want to walk into a trap. Hearing and seeing nothing of concern, he went outside, shut the door behind him, and walked next door to the Clifford. He had no idea what time it was, but it was late enough for the streets to be empty. He could not even hear the tinny pianos or the bawdy singing coming from the saloons along Main Street. What could possibly be so urgent at such a time of the morning?

He glanced over at the barn where the ranch hands were holding vigil over Mr. Hagen's remains. Lonnie had agreed to keep the number down to around six. But now there were about twenty men near the barn. And all of them were mounted.

"Evening, Buck," Adam said as he stepped out of the hotel and onto the boardwalk. "Looks like the natives are getting restless."

Trammel saw the man was in a fresh suit, and his Colt was back on his right hip, but his eyes were red and puffy. "You just wake up?"

Hagen kept looking at the men by the barn. "Figured I ought to grab as much sleep as I can while I can. The night clerk heard a bunch of men ride into town and sent Bobby to wake us. Looks like he had a good reason, too. I'll have to remember to raise his salary."

Trammel saw the men looking over at the hotel and knew they were making the decision to ride over. "You do anything to antagonize them? And don't give me one of your cute answers. This looks serious."

"I've done what you said," Hagen told him. "I know going on the porch bothers them, but I can't look like I'm afraid in my own town, Buck. I still have an image to uphold and a town to run." He nodded toward the men. "But I haven't done anything to warrant this."

Trammel found there was always the trace of the truth in any lie Hagen told. He rarely answered a question directly when sarcasm would do. He was in the habit of avoiding the truth even when he did not have to.

But Trammel found himself believing him when he said he had no idea why the men of the Blackstone Ranch were gathering nearby. Lonnie had given him his word and Trammel intended to hold him to it.

"I'm going over to see what's going on."

Hagen surprised him by grabbing his arm. "Don't. Not yet. Stay here and wait it out."

Trammel looked at the right hand on his arm until Hagen realized his mistake and removed it. "Give me one good reason why I should."

"Because you don't know what you're walking into, for one," Hagen said. "And this might not have anything to do with us. It might be a ranch problem. Or they might be taking their time changing the guard. Or they might have been planning this from the beginning and think now is the best time to betray you and come after me. No matter how you look at it, watching this from afar is the wisest thing to do. Please."

Trammel decided to stay in front of the hotel. He had lived through enough fights with this man at his side to know he understood situations like this. Maybe better than Trammel understood them. His size and grit often made up for his lack of insight, but not even he would stand much of a chance against twenty mounted men in open ground.

"Where are your Celestials?" Trammel asked as he kept watching the scene.

Hagen was watching the men, too. "They're close. Don't worry about that. These boys will regret it if they start any trouble now."

Trammel watched Lonnie climb up on his horse and hoped they turned left and headed out of town along the back road that led up to the ranch.

Instead, they rode straight for the Clifford Hotel.

"Damn," the sheriff said out loud.

"And here comes our answer." He pulled his Colt and held it flat against the holster.

Trammel kept his pistol tucked under his arm but held the Henry tighter. He walked toward the approaching riders, intentionally putting himself between them and Hagen. Trammel rested his rifle butt on his belt. The barrel pointed up at an angle.

When the men were only a few yards away, Lonnie raised his right hand and brought the men to a stop. He slowed down his horse and approached the sheriff at a slower pace.

"Me and my boys have had enough, Trammel." Lonnie looked over at Hagen. "We're here to give that low-down skunk what he deserves. I'm asking you to get out of our way and let us do what needs doing."

"I'm not going anywhere, and neither is Hagen," Trammel said. "Not until you tell me what all of this is about."

"Someone rode out to the ranch tonight, cut open poor Ray, and set the stable on fire." Lonnie pointed at Hagen. "Someone working for him."

"Whoever did it wasn't working for me," Hagen said.

"Liar!" one of the ranch hands called out, and the rest agreed.

Trammel did not know which one was Ray but figured he would probably recognize him by sight. "Is Ray still alive?"

"Barely," Lonnie said. "They tell me the dirty dog sliced open his belly and he's barely hanging on."

Trammel turned to tell Bobby to go fetch Dr. Moore, but saw the little boy was already running toward the doctor's office at Hagen's direction.

"What about the stable?" Trammel asked. "Any stock hurt?"

"My boys got there in time to keep the fire from spreading, but Ray's arm is burned pretty bad. It's a miracle he's still alive." Lonnie pointed at Hagen again. "But fire's his way of doing things, ain't it? So it was either him or that colored guy up the street who did it like he did it to Bookman."

Trammel held up his hand before the men got any more worked up than they already were. "Did Ray tell you what the man who did this looked like?"

One of the riders behind Lonnie said, "That's all he kept saying when I left him. Big guy, black beard, had a knife and was damned fast."

Hagen said, "No one who works for me

looks like that."

"So he says," Lonnie said to Trammel. "He could've hired it done. Brought someone up from Laramie to do it."

Trammel remembered his dustup with Albertson and the man he claimed as his cousin earlier that night. The only time he had a decent look at the man was when they stopped at the head of Main Street before riding away. The man he saw had the same build the ranch hand described.

And Lonnie's mention of Laramie gave him a pretty good idea of who the attacker might be.

"Hagen's right," Trammel told them. "I know most of the men who work for him and none of them look like the one Ray described. But Hawkeye and I had a run-in with a man earlier tonight that matches that description to the letter."

Lonnie did not look impressed. "I care less about who did it than who he was working for." He glared at Hagen. "And I'm pretty sure I'm looking at the man who hired him."

Trammel spoke over Hagen as he said, "The man I'm looking for doesn't work for Hagen, but someone else who's been causing trouble in this town. I'm asking you boys to wait until sunup to see if we can track this man in the daytime. I think you'll see that I'm right."

Lonnie stiffened in the saddle. "You taking Hagen's part in this, Trammel?"

"I'm saying Hagen doesn't have a part in this," the sheriff responded. "And I'm not going to let you boys lynch him without proof. If this man is working for Hagen, I'll arrest him. He'll stand trial for it."

"You said that about Mr. Hagen, too," one of the ranchers called out. "And you haven't done squat about it."

"I'm still looking into that," Trammel said. "Me and Doc Emily, too. We're waiting for the family to get here before we tell them what we found."

Lonnie sneered. "Still protecting your friend, eh, Trammel?"

"I'm enforcing the law." He sensed a shift in the men and knew they were getting ready to do something. He kept the rifle butt on his hip but moved it slowly, until it was pointing at Lonnie's head. "I'm done trying to reason with you boys. Now I'm telling you to wait until morning before you jump to any conclusions. And that's exactly what you're going to do."

The men flinched when ten Chinese men stepped out of the shadows behind the riders. Every one of them had a rifle. Every one of them was pointed up at the ranchers.

Lonnie looked back at the Celestials and realized he and his men were surrounded. "Never thought you'd be the kind of man to take up with heathens, Trammel."

"Oh, they're mine," Hagen said. "Well, a few of mine anyway. I think I have a couple more in the shadows."

Trammel lowered his rifle and said, "Damnit, Lonnie. I'm not looking for a fight here. Come back at dawn and you, me, and Hawkeye will take you to where all of this started. We'll track the wolf together and I promise you, we'll get to the bottom of this."

Lonnie was chewing it over when Dr. Moore rode up to them and pulled his horse up short. "I came as fast as I could. Where's the wounded man?"

Lonnie snapped out of it and said, "Up at the ranch, at the stable."

"I don't know where that is, but if you men can bring me to him, I can try to save his life. But hurry. We haven't a moment to lose."

Lonnie looked back at his men. "Six of you stay here with Mr. Hagen. The rest of you take the doc up to the ranch."

If the men disagreed with him, they did not show it. Six men at the back turned and rode past the Chinese riflemen to the barn. The rest rode out along Main Street with Dr. Moore in the middle of them.

That left Lonnie alone with Trammel and Hagen.

Trammel could finally allow himself to breathe. "You made the right choice, Lonnie. We'll start the search in the morning. You've got my word."

"And you've got mine," the topman said. "Because if I find out Hagen had anything to do with this, not even you will be able to keep me from him."

Lonnie brought his horse around roughly and galloped after the others along Main Street.

Hagen holstered his pistol. "Well, that was invigorating, wasn't it?"

But Trammel was in no mood for his mouth. "Are you sure none of your men had anything to do with this? Maybe struck out after them on their own, hoping to please you?"

"Not a chance." Hagen grinned. "None of my men would have left Ray alive."

Chapter 30

Lonnie hated being wrong, but he had no choice but to admit it. Right after sunrise, he had ridden to the jailhouse only to find Trammel and Hawkeye ready to go. They led him to old Mrs. Higgins's house, where he saw what had happened, as Trammel had described. The marks in the compact dirt in front of the place pointed to a squabble. He found the spent bullets Trammel had ejected from his Henry. Even the crack in the front wall of the house was there, just where Trammel told him it would be.

The two lawmen had hung back to let Lonnie follow the track of the fleeing man. He had never considered himself much of a hand at tracking, but he could read the signs as well as the next man. Certainly better than a city slicker like Trammel ever could.

He followed the tracks up the incline and spotted broken blades of grass. Droppings and hoofprints continued up to the ranch and around the bunkhouse, before doubling back on themselves toward the stable. The wood bore scorch marks from the fire. The ground was still stained with Ray's blood. All the stalls were empty, and he had sent out some of his men to round the horses up and bring them back.

He leaned over and spat over the side, careful not to hit Trammel or Hawkeye when he did so.

"Looks like I owe you an apology, Sheriff," he said. "I can admit when I'm wrong."

But Trammel was not looking for that. "After all the crap Hagen has pulled in this town, I can understand why you blamed him. I'm thankful you stopped and listened to reason."

Lonnie looked down at the blood on the ground and urged them to ride back toward the bunkhouse, where Dr. Moore was tending to Ray's wounds. "Can't believe Ray lived after being cut like that and losing all that blood. The human body's a strange thing."

"Doesn't hurt that Doc Moore's a good doctor," Hawkeye observed. "He's the reason why Ray's still aboveground and not in it."

"He's alive," Trammel said, cutting him short. "That's all that matters. Your men track where his attacker headed off to?"

Lonnie shook his head. "We followed it as much as we could, but they all ran in the same direction. It looks like he broke away from them after a while and headed back into town, but I told the boys not to bother following him. It's rocky as hell and hard to track someone through there. Besides, I figured him heading back into town kind of made him your problem."

"I like the way you think, Lonnie." Trammel extended a hand to him. "No hard feelings?"

Lonnie shook his hand, knowing he would be breaking his promise to him by this time tomorrow. "None whatsoever, Sheriff. And I didn't forget about taking down those trees either. A chipmunk would have a hard time getting past the tangle of trees we plan on leaving."

"Good man." Trammel pulled up short of the bunkhouse. Hawkeye followed his lead. "I imagine you and your men have plenty to do around here, so we'll head back to town and get looking for the man Ray described."

"We'll let you know when we're done blocking the road," Lonnie told him. "I think you'll like what you see."

Lonnie watched Trammel and Hawkeye

ride back down into town as Tom, one of his ranch hands, came out of the bunkhouse.

Lonnie asked him, "Ray still doing OK?"

"The doc says he'll pull through," Tom told him. "I would've bet a year's wages he was done for when we brought the doc up here. It was one time I was glad I was wrong. He'll be laid up for a few weeks, but he'll be better before we know it. The doc is just finishing up with him now. Says we have to keep the wound clean on account of inspection."

"Infection," Lonnie corrected him.

"Well, whatever it is," Tom said, "I'll be the one tending to him."

Lonnie knew he would. "Thanks for handling that for us. It'll allow me to think on other things."

Tom slid his hands into his pockets as he watched Trammel and Hawkeye ride down toward Stone Gate and the town beyond. "Guess you and the sheriff are friends again."

Lonnie shrugged. "You could say that."

"You still intend to go after Hagen tomorrow during that march?"

"Won't be much of a march," Lonnie told him, "especially after we block that road this afternoon. But yeah, we're still going after Hagen tomorrow."

"That won't make your friend the sheriff very happy."

Lonnie spat. "Friends don't always agree."

As they rode through Stone Gate, Hawkeye could not hold his silence any longer. "I hate it when you get quiet like this, boss."

Trammel had been too deep in thought to realize he was quiet. "Why?"

"Because it means something's bothering you or you're cooking up something," Hawkeye said. "And either way I don't learn anything unless you talk. That's what bothers me."

"I don't set out to bother you, Hawkeye," Trammel said. "Just working some things over in my mind. The man who shot at us and almost killed Ray is a man by the name of Pete Stride, out of Laramie. He's one of Lucien Clay's topmen."

Hawkeye let that sink in. "Then that means Lonnie was right. Mr. Clay and Mr. Hagen are partners. So, this Stride fella was working for Mr. Hagen."

"I don't think it's that simple," Trammel said. "I think Clay only has one partner in this world and that's himself. I think Clay sent Stride here to start some trouble during tomorrow's march. I don't think it's just him, but he got here early to get the lay of the land. Pick out the best places to start trouble. Maybe to go after Hagen himself."

Try as he might, Hawkeye still could not make sense of what Trammel was saying. "But if he's partners with Mr. Hagen, causing trouble in Blackstone will cost him money, too, won't it?"

"A man like Lucien Clay is willing to pay a certain price for control," Trammel explained. "Maybe he figures a hundred percent of everything is better than fifty percent of something."

It was still a lot for Hawkeye to think about. "I'd be happy with a quarter of what those two make between here and Laramie."

Trammel grinned. "You'd make a rotten crook, Hawkeye. Better stick to the law."

"I plan on it." A new thought came to him. "So, if this Pete Stride fella came back to town, where do you think he is?"

"We're going to begin at the beginning," Trammel said. "Let's pay Mrs. Higgins a visit."

CHAPTER 31

Trammel and Hawkeye watched Mrs. Higgins leave her house and paddle along Main Street. The basket she carried swayed easily on her arm, which Trammel took to mean she was going to Robertson's store to buy provisions.

He wondered if that was because she had an extra mouth to feed.

Trammel and Hawkeye tied their horses to a nearby tree and approached her house on foot.

He was glad Hawkeye was wise enough to remain quiet while Trammel figured out what to do. "I want you to head around to the back of the house, but stay low while you do it. Crawl if you have to. I don't want them seeing you out a window if they're in there. When you get to the back of the house, stay on the side. Don't stand in front of the back door. If they come running out, I don't want them running into you."

Hawkeye looked like he understood. "Anything else?"

"Shoot anyone who isn't me." He gave the deputy a good push and sent him on his way while Trammel drew his Colt from under his arm and headed for the front door. He crouched up the steps as gingerly as a man his size could manage, but a few creaks of the dry wood were unavoidable. He only hoped they had gone unheard by anyone who might be inside the house.

He was about to put his hand on the doorknob when the top part of the door exploded outward. He dove to the side. Another blast took out a good chunk of the wall to the right of the doorway.

Trammel rolled and got to his feet just as a third blast obliterated the window above him, showering him with shards of glass.

In his mind, he judged the time it would take for the shooter to lever in a new round, popped up, and fired blindly through the shattered window. He heard a man cry out and the sound of something heavy hit the floor, like a shotgun.

Trammel stole another glance through the window and looked inside the house. His height allowed him to see a man getting to his feet as he tried to get away down the hallway.

Trammel got to the hole in the door and aimed his Peacemaker through it. The fleeing man was too broad and moving too fast to be Albertson, so he knew this must be Pete Stride.

Trammel took careful aim and fired, catching the man high in the back.

The impact did not bring him down but sent him stumbling forward toward the kitchen, where he crashed through the back door and into the yard.

Trammel pulled open the ruined front door and ran down the hall to catch up with Stride as he shouted, "Hawkeye! Stay away! He's got a knife!"

No sooner had the words left his mouth than the sound of a rifle firing came from outside.

Trammel rushed through the broken back door and found Stride lying facedown in the dirt about thirty yards away.

Hawkeye was approaching him quickly, aiming his rifle down at Stride as he moved.

"I got him, boss!" Hawkeye called out as he closed in. "That last one brought him down."

Trammel jumped down the back stairs as he yelled, "Stay away from him!"

But Hawkeye closed in like a man anxious to claim his first kill.

Stride sprang like a viper, snatching the rifle barrel and pulling it toward him and Hawkeye with it.

Down toward his knife.

The young man let go of the rifle and fell awkwardly across the outlaw's middle.

Trammel stopped and tried to get a clear shot at Stride, but his deputy was still in the way, all arms and legs.

The outlaw pushed Hawkeye off him and threw the knife at Trammel.

Trammel easily dodged the spinning blade, but the distraction was just long enough for Stride to barrel into Trammel. The impact was hard enough to send his Colt tumbling from his grip.

Trammel landed hard on his back but tried to grab hold of Stride as they fell. The outlaw was too quick for him and rolled away to retrieve his knife. By the time Trammel got back to his feet, Stride had hold of the knife.

"Big man," Stride said as blood ran down the right side of his shirt. "Big talk, if you ask me."

Trammel had always hated knives. It was almost impossible to avoid being cut by one, and even the slightest nick in the wrong place could be deadly. He knew he would have to time his next strike perfectly if he had any hope of avoiding a blade to the belly.

Stride bluffed a charge, which made Trammel jump back. The outlaw smiled. "That's it, Trammel. Keep on dancing for me. Go ahead."

Another bluff made Trammel jump the other way. He kept his arms up in the classic boxing stance.

Stride made a third bluff as his blade sliced through the air, only this time, Trammel didn't move back. He moved forward as he threw a right cross that connected squarely with Stride's chin.

The heavy blow snapped his head back and sent him reeling. The outlaw landed on the ground, splayed out like a star. The knife was still in his hand.

Having no desire to go up against Stride again, he looked for his Colt and found it only a few yards away. As he went to retrieve it, he saw Hawkeye was still on his knees.

He wanted to tend to the boy but didn't dare turn his back on Stride.

"You hurt?" he called out to his deputy.

He could hear him gasping for breath and knew he was fine. "Wind knocked out," was all the boy could manage to say.

"You'll be fine," Trammel told him as he reached to pick up his Peacemaker. "Just give it time."

He had just grabbed hold of the pistol when he heard the unmistakable sound of a hammer being cocked. "Leave it."

Trammel looked over in the direction of the sound and saw Mike Albertson at the back door, aiming a rifle at him. "You touch that pistol, you die. And don't let my handicap fool you, Sheriff. I'm a hell of a shot with a rifle."

Trammel thought about testing that theory, but looking down the barrel of a rifle had a habit of changing his mind. The cripple might be bluffing, but Trammel did not know enough about him to call it.

He slowly stood up, leaving his pistol in the grass. He only hoped that all the noise had caused someone to go get help.

"A smart man." Albertson grinned as he slowly drew closer, keeping the rifle trained on him. "Big men like you are rarely smart, too."

Trammel would not give him the satisfaction of raising his hands. If he got close enough, he could make a play for that rifle. He wanted to be ready to move fast if he got the chance.

"Who are you?" Trammel said. "You're not like any old freighter I've ever come across."

"Wouldn't you like to know?" Albertson sneered. "Wouldn't you just like to have that one last bit of information before you die? Well, Sheriff Trammel, you're just going to have to go to hell without that knowledge."

"I'll save you a spot on the rock next to me." Every muscle in his body tensed as he knew he was about to take a bullet. He watched Albertson's eyes for any hint that he was about to squeeze the trigger. The slightest hint and he would charge him. Even if he got hit, he hoped momentum would carry him toward the hunchback before he got off a second shot. If he could only get his hands on him, Trammel might have a chance.

"I must admit I'm enjoying this," Albertson acknowledged as he stopped between him and the fallen Stride. "It's not every day that a man like me gets to see a man like you grovel."

Trammel felt his temper beginning to build. He hoped it would be enough to carry him through the impact of the bullet. "You going to talk all day, or are you going to get to work?"

There it was. The look of resolve to finally shoot.

Trammel had begun to lower himself into a crouch to spring at him when a neat hole appeared in Albertson's forehead. Man and rifle fell backward.

Trammel turned and found Hawkeye on the ground in the firing position, a thin trail of gunsmoke rising from the barrel of his rifle.

The young deputy smiled as he got to his feet. "Sorry, boss. I thought you were talking to me."

CHAPTER 32

Hagen leaned against the door to the cells as he looked at the unconscious prisoner on the cot. "What did you say his name was again?"

"Stride," Trammel told him for the third time. "Pete Stride. Or at least that's what Rob Moran called him down in Laramie. Said he worked for your friend Clay."

Hagen sighed heavily as he came back into the jail. "I heard you the first two times, Buck. I just needed to hear it again. Forgive me, but I don't take betrayal well."

Trammel continued working on his report. "I take it you know him because he worked for Clay?"

"You take it right," Hagen said, sitting down next to the reporter Rhoades. "Him and Albertson working together. That fits. It fits too neatly for comfort. I should have known something was amiss. I should've known."

Rhoades was frantically writing down all this in a notebook on his lap. "So, it looks like Albertson and Stride were working for Lucien Clay against you."

"Looks that way," Trammel said as he tried to concentrate on his report. Rhoades's presence in the jail was trouble he did not need at the moment. He wanted to get all the details down on paper while it was fresh in his head. The reporter's questions only distracted him.

Hagen was no better as he asked Trammel, "How much did you say you took off Albertson last night?"

"A hundred in gold coins," the sheriff told him again.

"A tidy sum," Hagen observed. "It was probably to pay off whoever they plan to send to infiltrate the march. Probably some rough types who would cause trouble." He tapped the arm of his chair as he thought it over. "Smart. Very smart, Mr. Clay."

Rhoades looked hopeful as he said, "Can I quote both of you saying you fear trouble at the march tomorrow?"

"No," Trammel and Hagen said in unison.

Trammel said, "No direct quotes from either of us. The report I'm finishing up here will give you everything you need to know for your article. Just play down the parts about violence until after the march. We don't want to give anyone ideas about causing trouble. There are probably enough men out there looking for a fight as it is."

Rhoades looked deflated. "Well, I'm going to need to have some kind of quote in my article, gentlemen. Otherwise it'll look like you are unprepared, which is just as bad as talking about the possibility of violence."

Trammel looked up from his report and glared at the reporter. "You make sure you tell them we're ready for anything."

They heard a knock at the door just before Hawkeye came in. Trammel had sent him to take a look at how the men from the Blackstone Ranch were blocking the road. He feared the young man might come in blabbering about the good work Lonnie and his men had done, but upon seeing the reporter, he only said, "Evening, everybody."

Trammel was glad the kid was growing into the job. He said to Rhoades, "You need to leave now, Richard. I'll send along the final copy of my report for your morning edition as soon as it's ready."

Rhoades stood up and put his hat back on his head. "And when will that be?"

"The quicker you leave, the sooner I'll get it to you."

That was encouragement enough to send the reporter on his way.

Hagen watched him leave. "One of us should have the decency to shoot him. Save the poor devil a lifetime of embarrassment."

Trammel did not have any time for his nonsense. "How are Lonnie and his men?"

"Got it all done in a couple of hours," Hawkeye said. "Draft horses make all the difference in that kind of work. Stacked three trees across the road and crossed two on top of them. Even threw some thorny bushes at the front to make it tougher for people to get to. Yes, sir. There'll be a lot of disappointed people tomorrow morning."

"I just hope we won't be among them," Hagen said.

Just when Trammel was beginning to see a glimmer of hope, Hagen had to come along and snuff it out. "What's that supposed to mean?"

"Nothing," the vice peddler said as he examined his nails. "It's just that by blocking the road, the men of the Blackstone Ranch have not only blocked anyone from getting in, they've also blocked most of us from being able to get out. We're at their mercy until they decide to move the roadblock, which I wager won't be until Bartholomew and Caleb tell them to do so."

Trammel was glad that was his only objection. "A man on horseback can still get out of town if he wants. It's just much tougher for a wagon, which is what we wanted, because most of the marchers are riding up here on wagons."

"I hope you're right," Hagen told him. "I sincerely do. Especially because you've put all of our lives into the hands of the same men who have threatened to kill both of us at one time or another."

Trammel had finally finished his report and was walking over to the *Bugle* to deliver it as promised. Hagen and Hawkeye followed.

Trammel watched as another wagonload of marchers arrived in town. With all the hotels being filled to capacity, tents had begun to pop up in the empty lots between Blackstone and the ranch. Some had even set up in the half-built houses Hagen had put up.

"You want me to clear them out of there?" Trammel asked Hagen. "They're trespassing."

"Let them stay," Hagen told him. "They're probably doing it to provoke me, but I won't let them. Both of you should adopt that policy for the next couple of days. Ignore any attempts at provocation from anyone.

Unless gunplay is involved, I'd advise you to grow a very thick skin and look the other way."

Trammel knew Hagen was right, which made him angry. Hagen was smart and steady in a fight. If he would have just decided to work on Trammel's side of the law instead of his own, the territory would be a much better place. Instead, he worked only for himself, and for his revenge on Charles Hagen. Now that the man was dead, Trammel wondered what angle Hagen would take to get the empire he felt he deserved.

"That should be the last of the wagons that made it through, right, Hawkeye?"

"I'd say so," the deputy told him. "Nothing came through while we were cutting. Let's just hope no one finds the pile in the night and sets to clearing it. One stick of dynamite will turn those trees into toothpicks."

"They won't have dynamite," Hagen assured them. "They're poor people, and the blockage is well situated to be far enough from town so the miners won't be tempted to help." He patted Trammel's back. "A wise plan, my friend. A wise plan indeed."

The three men stopped walking when they found themselves across from the offices of the *Blackstone Bugle.*

"Well, gentlemen," Hagen announced, "would any of you like to join me for a drink at the Gilded Lily before you give Rhoades your report?"

Trammel told Hawkeye, "Go ahead if you want to, but I'll be turning in early."

"What's the matter?" Hagen chided. "The place just isn't the same since Lilly decamped to Laramie this afternoon?"

That was exactly the reason why, but Trammel would not give him the satisfaction of admitting it. "Big day tomorrow, Adam. For you, too. A hangover will only make it worse."

"Perhaps," Hagen allowed, "but sobriety won't make it any better." He beckoned Hawkeye to follow him. "Come, my young friend, and allow me to show you wonders the likes of which you've never seen and won't soon forget."

Trammel encouraged him to go. The next day would undoubtedly be a big one, but it also might be his last. If the last couple of days had shown Trammel anything, it was that Hawkeye was well on his way to becoming quite a man. He had to trust that he would not allow himself to get too drunk with Hagen. The young man knew how important Saturday was. Experience was a better teacher than words.

"Don't go having too much fun." Trammel looked at Hagen. "And if he comes back itching, I'm going to hold you to blame."

Hagen threw his arm around the lad's shoulders and began to fill him with stories and lies of men and women he had known in his travels.

Trammel knew he should be concerned with leaving the young man alone with a vice peddler like Hagen. But he also sensed that Hagen would never allow any harm to come to him.

He stood alone on the crowded boardwalk and watched the newcomers building tents and shaking hands and making new friends. Robertson had kept the general store open late and it looked like the place was doing great business. The few dining halls on that side of Main Street were packed with people, and the smell of roasted pig wafted from the camp that had been set up just outside town. Sounds of laughter drowned out the saloon sounds of pianos and song, and Trammel wondered, even for a moment, if Blackstone could be more than what it was. If this was not a glimpse of what it could be. He certainly hoped so, for he might very well die for this place tomorrow.

He walked across the thoroughfare, glad the wagons and horses moving in both directions stopped to allow him to pass. Given his size, he knew he was tough to miss.

He opened the door of the *Bugle* only to find Emily Downs on her way out.

"This is a surprise," Trammel said as he held the door open for her to leave. "What are you doing here?"

"Answering some questions about my embalming methods on Mr. Hagen," Emily told him. "I doubt he'll be able to use any of it, but Mr. Rhoades was very insistent." She smiled. "What's your excuse?"

He held up his report. "I usually give him a copy of the official report of what we do every day. He thinks what happened at Mrs. Higgins's place today will make for a great story."

"Not for poor Mrs. Higgins," Emily said. "I had to give her a sedative. Her house is a shambles. She feels horrible that Albertson tried to kill you. She really does."

"He was a con artist," Trammel said. "He fooled a lot of people, not just her."

She reached up and touched his right cheek, which made him wince. It had not hurt until then. "That's quite a bruise you've got there."

Trammel had no intention of removing her hand. "It'll heal."

"You should have Lilly tend to it," Emily said.

Trammel forced a smile. "Kind of hard for her to do that from Laramie."

She slowly withdrew her hand. "Oh, Buck. I'm sorry to hear that. Is it because of the march tomorrow?"

"That and other things, I guess," Trammel told her. "She got a good look at the kind of work I do and I don't think she liked it. Kind of like someone else I know, not that I can blame her. Or you."

"Still a lousy thing to do to you right before tomorrow." She looked at all the new faces who passed by in town. "I was hoping word would spread about Albertson's attempt on your life. I thought it might keep some of these people away. But I guess they were already on the road, so it was too late to make much of a difference."

The size of the crowd already bothered Trammel. And the few people who were able to get to town on horseback would come angry about the roadblock. "Yeah," was all he could manage to say.

"I heard you took a prisoner away," Emily said. "How's he doing?"

"Hasn't woken up since Hawkeye and I

dragged him into the cell," Trammel said. "Guess I hit him pretty hard."

"I've seen how you hit," she reminded him. " 'Pretty hard' doesn't begin to cover it." An idea came to her. "I'll be happy to take a look at him for you if you'd like. I mean, I know I'm not as accomplished as Dr. Moore, but —"

Trammel laughed. "Let me give Rhoades this report and I'll take you over there."

"Good. And if you're hungry, maybe I could fix us some dinner."

Trammel's dark mood brightened. "Sounds like a great way to end a bad day."

Lucien Clay pounded the mattress with both fists in impotent rage. "How could Micklewhite have been so stupid?" He looked at the man who had told him the news and spoke through clenched teeth. "Are you sure he's dead?"

"I'm sure that's what I heard down in the saloon," the man called Sully said. "A couple of others heard the same thing. And Pete's in jail, too. Looks like Trammel's taken care of both of them, sir. What do you want us to do?"

Pete and Micklewhite's bungling had damaged his plans but had not entirely wrecked them. If anything, their failure might cause Trammel to let down his guard.

But he had to act quickly and not allow his anger to get the better of him.

"You've been to Blackstone before?"

"I can get there in the dark, if that's what you're asking," Sully told him. "If we leave now, we'll get there around first light."

He liked this one. He thought faster than Pete. Maybe this would not be a total loss. His jaw ached as he said, "Round up the others and ride there now. Use the back roads. Kill Hagen, then Trammel. Micklewhite had your money, but I'll pay when you come back."

Sully headed for the door. "We'll be back as soon as we can, sir."

But Clay was not done. "And Sully" — he pointed at his face — "tell anyone about this and you die."

"It's nobody's business, sir. You can count on me."

Sully left Clay alone with his own thoughts. Everything was in motion now. In fact, it had been in motion for hours. If Sully had not overheard some barroom gossip, he might not have known about it until it was too late.

He closed his eyes and hoped it was not too late already. He even would have prayed to God if he thought it would do him any good.

Chapter 33

At just before dawn the next morning Trammel was at the livery, speaking to Elias. "Pick me out a winner. I'll need a good-looking horse to impress the visitors."

"You need a good horse period," the black man scolded him. "It's not right for a man in your position to be borrowing horses all the time. What if all I've got is some broken-down old nag for you to ride? A big man like you needs a big horse."

A city man his whole life, Trammel had always figured one horse was as good as another. But Elias had spent his entire life around horses, so his words had weight. "I suppose you're right. Got any suggestions?"

"It just so happens I do. I'll set it up for you. Wait here."

Trammel did not have to wait long before Elias led out a chestnut roan that was already fitted with his saddle.

It was a fine-looking animal, even in the

early light of dawn. The animal had a bright look in its eyes and was sturdier than any of the other animals Elias had lent him recently.

"Where have you been hiding this one?" Trammel asked as he patted her muzzle.

"Haven't hid him anywhere," Elias said. "He was Mr. Montague's horse. Named him Starr with two 'r's' at the end. Don't ask me why. He's a two-year-old gelding and strong as hell. Too much horse for Mr. Montague to handle if you ask me, but because no one asked me, I kept my mouth shut. But he's the perfect animal for you."

Trammel let the horse smell his hand and was glad he did not try to take a bite out of it. He stroked the animal's neck. "How much do you want for him?"

"He was Mr. Montague's horse, so he's yours now. His livery fees are paid by the bank, so you might as well use him. He's not doing anyone any good just sitting in the stall all day. Climb up on him and try him out for today. I think you two will get along just fine."

Trammel slid his Henry into the saddle scabbard and climbed up on the horse. The animal did not even budge.

He may not have been much of a horseman, but even he could appreciate a good animal when he saw one. He felt like he had been born to ride this horse.

Elias seemed just as happy as Trammel. "You look good on him, Son. You two were made for each other."

Trammel liked the view from the saddle and felt comfortable. "Thanks, Elias. I'll let you know how we do."

He tapped his heels into Starr's flanks and sent him walking along Main Street. He saw Ben watching him from the doorway of the Pot of Gold. He took a chance and nodded at the big man and was glad to see he nodded back. He had not approved of why he was in town or what he had done since coming to Blackstone, but he was glad he would be at this end of town in case trouble broke out during the march.

Trammel continued to let Starr walk along Main Street. The people who had pitched tents were beginning to wake up. He could smell cook fires starting and the aroma of coffee in the air.

The town and its visitors were also awakening and he knew Blackstone was in for a long day. Perhaps the longest day it had ever known.

He looked up when a flurry of activity at the opposite end of Main Street caught his eye. Eight men had rounded the corner and drew their mounts to a halt in front of the Clifford Hotel. One of them hung back to hold on to the horses as the men dropped from their saddles, grabbed their rifles, and ran into the hotel.

The long day had begun.

Trammel dug his heels into Starr's sides and set the horse into a full gallop. The gelding responded immediately, and he raced toward the hotel. From the corner of his eye, he thought he saw Ben running along the boardwalk.

Trammel drew his Peacemaker from under his left arm as he sped toward the hotel. The man who was struggling to hold on to the horses saw him and pulled his own pistol, but was blocked by the animals shifting around him. Screams and gunshots came from inside the hotel, and Trammel knew the trouble had already begun.

The man pushed through the animals and aimed up at Trammel.

The sheriff shot the man as he sped by on Starr, hitting him in the middle of the chest. The impact sent him flat on the ground, where the panicked horses trampled him.

Trammel brought Starr up short and jumped down from the saddle. Forgetting about the rifle, he ran toward the front door of the hotel, but stopped just short of going in. He listened from the side of the doorway first and saw the desk clerk running outside, followed by several guests.

Trammel grabbed the clerk and pulled him out of the doorway. "Where are they?"

The panicked clerk said, "They ran upstairs to Mr. Hagen's room. The Chinamen are holding them off, but I don't know how long they can last!"

Trammel let him go and saw Ben had reached the other side of the doorway. He had brought his rifle with him.

Another round of shots rang out from somewhere inside the hotel, and Trammel knew they could not wait any longer.

He moved into the hotel, his Peacemaker leading the way. Ben followed close behind.

Trammel spotted two dead Celestials at the base of the stairs and looked up to see if any of the gunmen were still in the lobby. The first one he saw was at the top of the landing, looking up at where the others had gone.

He spotted Trammel and Ben below and fired a quick shot from his rifle. Neither man had time to dodge the blast, returning fire instead.

Both bullets struck the man in the belly and he cried out before tumbling down the stairs in a heap.

Trammel did the math. He had seen eight men. Two were down. Six left.

Trammel broke to the right and Ben broke to the left as they expected more gunfire from above, but nothing came.

This time Ben led the charge up the stairs and Trammel followed. Both men took the stairs two at a time and paused on the landing before they went up to the second floor.

Trammel snuck a look around the newel post and saw two more dead Celestials slumped at the top of the stairs, but no gunmen. A new round of screams sounded as the air above filled with gunfire.

Trammel and Ben moved up the stairs at a crouch, stopping as they reached the top step. Hagen's room was around the corner and to the right.

Ben moved into the hallway and moved in that direction. Trammel looked around the corner and cursed to himself. All he saw were open doors. Hagen's room only had one door and was in the center of the next hallway.

He caught up to Ben at the end of the corridor and listened.

"Damned thing won't budge!" one of the men exclaimed.

"Must be made of —"

But Ben did not wait for the man to finish

his thought.

He rounded the corner at a crouch, aimed his Winchester, and fired.

Trammel stood behind him and saw six men bunched together in front of Hagen's door. The wood around it was peppered with bullet holes, but the door remained shut.

One man spun like a top when Ben's shot caught him high in the chest.

The remaining five turned to fire as they tried to scatter in the narrow corridor.

Trammel flinched as a bullet slammed into the wall above his head as he drew down and shot the man closest to Hagen's door. The bullet hit him in the top of the head and stopped him flat.

The remaining four tried to back down the corridor, one of them leaning flat against a doorway, returning fire.

Ben levered in a fresh round and shot the man in the side. It made the gunman flinch, but not enough to fall. He got off another shot that buried itself in the floor at Ben's feet while Trammel's bullet hit him in the chest. He bounced off the door and fell across the hallway.

The three fired wildly as they retreated down the hallway. One took cover at the corner, while the remaining two took off.

Ben and the gunman traded shots while Trammel ran back toward the stairs to cut off the retreat of the other two.

He reached the stairs just as the fleeing gunmen were halfway down the opposite staircase.

They saw Trammel and fired up at him blindly as they ran down the stairs. Their bullets hit the ceiling, but not the sheriff.

Trammel tracked the remaining two men and fired into the middle of them. The bullet struck the man in the side, causing him to bounce off the banister and tumble down the stairs.

Trammel reached the landing, aimed down at the fleeing man and fired. The bullet hit the floor well behind the gunman, missing him entirely.

His pistol empty, Trammel ran down the remaining steps and scooped up a rifle from one of the dead Celestials at the base of the stairs as a loud scream from the dining room caught his attention. He'd thought the fleeing man had run out the front door but knew now he was wrong.

Trammel worked the lever of the rifle, ejecting a round, and saw he still had at least one more to work with.

He moved toward the dining room and saw the man he had missed had grabbed hold of a maid. He had his pistol pressed against the woman's head as he held her in front of him as cover.

"Don't do anything stupid, big man," Clay's man Sully said as he moved his face behind the frightened woman's head. "You wouldn't want to do anything that might get this nice lady killed, now would you?"

Trammel slowly walked into the dining room, keeping his rifle trained on the gunman. "She dies, you die. Drop the gun and throw up your hands. Nobody else needs to die here today."

The maid squealed again as he dragged her backward toward the kitchen and the back door of the hotel.

"The only one who's going to drop his gun is you, Trammel," Sully yelled. "Unless you want to see this woman die. Just let me go and that'll be the end of it."

Trammel knew the woman would die the second he moved his rifle from him.

A series of shots from upstairs echoed through the hotel, followed by a single rifle shot he imagined was from Ben.

The gunman had heard it, too, and looked in that direction.

Trammel slowly closed the distance between them. "That was your last man. You're all alone now. The street's filling up with men right now, armed to the teeth. All that shooting brought them out. When they see you holding her like that, they're all liable to start shooting. I don't want that and neither do you."

As they crossed into the kitchen, the maid let her shoes snag on the threshold, and she allowed herself to go limp. She slid down from the gunman's grip, exposing him from the chest up.

Trammel took the shot, and two more. All three hit the gunman, who fell back into a counter before dropping to the floor.

Trammel ran into the kitchen and kicked the pistol out of the dead man's hand. A cook ran over and picked it up with a dish towel.

He ran back into the lobby and yelled up the stairs, "Hagen! You alive?"

"Of course," Hagen yelled back. "Come on up."

Trammel took the steps two at a time, mindful that there might be other gunmen around, until he reached Hagen's room. The corridor was pockmarked with even more bullet holes than when he had left, but seeing the boots of the dead man at the far end of the hall told him Ben had finished off the last gunman.

The door to Hagen's suite was open and Trammel went inside.

Ben London was out on the balcony. Hagen was in the middle of getting dressed.

"Good morning," Hagen greeted him. "What have you been up to today?"

Trammel could not believe the man's calm. "Don't tell me you didn't hear everything that was going on outside."

"Oh, I heard it," Hagen said as he showed him the door to his room. "I even planned for it, too." He pointed to the bullet-riddled wood on the front of the door.

And to the iron plate behind it. "I prepared for this eventuality. Had it brought all the way from Detroit when I turned these rooms into my suite during my convalescence. I figured if someone had tried to kill me once, they would no doubt try again. Seems to have come in handy, don't you think?"

He grinned as he knocked on the iron before shutting the door. "It was an extravagance at the time, I know, but a wise investment."

Trammel watched Hagen go back to his mirror and finish tying his black Ascot. "Why do you look so glum, Buck? Don't tell me you were hoping these ruffians would succeed in killing me. I know we've had our share of misunderstandings, but I'd like to think we haven't sunk to the level of despising each other."

Trammel did not know what to think or say, so he just said what was on his mind. "The four Celestials you had guarding you are dead. One of the gunmen took a maid hostage. She fainted, but she'll be fine."

Hagen finished the knot and seemed quite pleased with his reflection. "Which is more than I hope I can say for the man who took her."

"All of the gunmen are dead," Trammel told him. "There were eight of them."

Hagen's sharp laugh pierced the air. "That means two of them backed out. Lucien's lucky number is ten. They probably refused him when they realized Albertson wouldn't be able to pay them when they were done with me." He pulled on his black coat. "Thank heavens for the predictability of the criminal mind, not that two more would have made any difference. Thank you, by the way, for capturing them the way you did. I have to find some way of repaying you for that. Ben, too."

Trammel followed Hagen out onto the balcony. The sun had risen higher now, and thin bands of purple and orange spread across the sky in all directions.

Hagen looked over the railing and waved at the people who had crowded the thoroughfare and boardwalks of Main Street. Trammel saw Emily hurry into the hotel carrying her medical bag.

"No cause for alarm, everyone," Hagen told them. "Just a minor scrape, is all. A guest was displeased with his toast. Said we'd burned it. Just goes to show you the level of perfection the people who stay here have come to expect. You may all go about your business now. I'm quite safe, and Sheriff Trammel has things well in hand."

The townspeople muttered amongst themselves as they slowly broke away and went back to wherever they had come from.

Hagen waved down at them as they dispersed. "They love me, you know. In their own fashion anyway. They don't like to admit it, but everyone loves a man like me. And they'll love me even more after this week. Mark my words, Buck. I'll go from being hated to being beloved before you know it."

Ben broke his lofty speech by tapping Hagen on the shoulder and pointing at the end of Main Street.

Trammel looked, too.

Instead of seeing six ranch hands keeping vigil outside the barn where Mr. Hagen's remains were kept, he saw a line of twenty men. All of them holding rifles. All of them staring up at the balcony.

"Well, hell's bells," Hagen said. "That's disappointing."

A flare of movement from across the street caught Trammel's attention. It was Lonnie.

He was holding a whiskey bottle with a rag tucked into the top of it. And the rag was burning.

"Long live King Charles Hagen!" Lonnie yelled as he threw the flaming bottle up at them.

Trammel and Ben tackled Hagen, knocking him back inside as the bottle crashed against the banister and spread fire like it was water.

CHAPTER 34

Trammel kicked the balcony doors closed as bullets began to shatter the panes of glass. Ben got to his feet and slid home the dead bolt on the room door.

Hagen coughed as smoke from the burning balcony began to blow in through the ruined door.

Trammel had been in fires before and knew the smoke would kill them before the flames ever could.

The men stayed low as round after round pelted the balcony door, each shot knocking another large chunk of wood away. A few more volleys and there would not be anything left of the door.

Hagen cried out as he tried to crawl toward his bed, but his right arm gave way and he collapsed on his side. "Under the bed," he gasped through the thickening smoke.

Trammel ran at a crouch to the bed and

found a large chest with a handle beneath it. He pulled it out, undid the latches, and opened it. The case was full of ammunition and handguns.

"They're loaded," Hagen gasped as he choked on the smoke.

Trammel slid one toward him before drawing his Peacemaker, dumping the spent shells and reloading it with fresh bullets.

Ben went to the case and began feeding fresh rounds into his Winchester. Trammel did the same with the Winchester he had found on the dead guard. Both of them took a handful of cartridges and dumped them in the pockets of their shirts.

Trammel crawled over to Hagen as the gunfire began to calm down. "We can't stay here. The smoke is getting too thick."

"They're probably already in the hall, waiting for us to come out," Hagen yelled back. "The only way out is over that balcony."

Another flaming whiskey bottle sailed through the open door and crashed into the middle of the room. Ben grabbed a blanket from Hagen's bed and immediately began stomping out the flames just as another one exploded just inside the room.

Trammel and Hagen grabbed the rest of the bedclothes and tried their best to stamp them out, but there was too much for the fire to feed on. Smoke quickly filled the room, making it impossible to see more than a foot in front of their faces. Their eyes were watering too much for them to see much of anything anyway.

"Follow me," Hagen said as he moved toward the balcony.

Before Trammel could object, he felt Ben move past him toward daylight. Trammel had no choice but to follow, staying as low as he possibly could.

Rifle fire erupted from the balcony as Trammel crawled outside. The morning wind was blowing the smoke into the room, giving them a clearer view outside. He wiped his eyes on his sleeve and cleared his vision.

He saw Ben firing down at Lonnie, who had taken cover behind a horse trough across the street. Hagen was firing at the ranch hands who were running toward the building. They had scattered some, but he had brought down a fair amount.

Trammel stood and took aim at the approaching ranchers. Two more fell before Trammel got in on the action and took down a man at the back of the group. He levered in a new round just as a bullet struck him in the left shoulder, knocking him flat, but he managed to hold on to his rifle as he fell.

The banister was completely aflame and the wood was beginning to crack. Trammel kicked the burning wood until it broke off and fell out onto the thoroughfare below. Ben took a knee as he began to reload.

Trammel fought the pain in his left side as he inched toward the end of the balcony. He brought up his rifle from a seated position and aimed at where he had last seen Lonnie.

Lonnie no longer under fire, stood up and lit the rag in another bottle of whiskey. He froze when he caught sight of Trammel aiming down at him.

As he brought the bottle back to throw, Trammel shot him in the neck.

Lonnie fell backward. The bottle broke on the ground, and flames soon consumed him.

The smoke from inside the room had begun to billow out onto the balcony, and Trammel knew they had to get out of there fast. He kicked away the burning side banister until it, too, fell to the street.

He knew a jump from two stories wasn't enough to kill him, but it was more than enough to bust a leg. It was worth the risk.

With the dead Celestial's rifle in his left hand, Trammel slid over the side and held on to the last remnant of the railing still nailed to the balcony before allowing himself to drop.

He had only dropped a couple of feet before he landed on the saddle of a tethered horse and gently fell to the ground. Bullets peppered around him as soon as he landed, but died away as rifle fire opened up above him. Two sets of hands pulled him into the alley between the jail and the hotel.

He was glad to see it was Hawkeye and Dr. Moore.

His deputy looked at Trammel's left shoulder. "Boss, you're hit."

Trammel pushed him away. "Keep firing. Where are they?"

"On the other side of the hotel," Moore told him. "They tried to get in through the front, but we stopped them. Whoever was shooting up there picked off several. I don't know if they've gotten around the back."

"You two stay here," Trammel ordered. "I'll take a look."

He stifled a cough as he moved as quickly and quietly as he could down the alley. He stopped at the corner and peered around the side.

Five of the men were on the ground outside, coughing heavily as Emily ministered to them. She looked up when she saw

Trammel and said, "They're out of it, Buck. Don't shoot."

He walked over to the nearest one in the circle and shoved him with the toe of his boot. "How many left?"

Two shots rang out from behind him. One caught him in the left side and knocked him flat on his stomach.

"Guess you and your friends missed one, Sheriff," came a voice from behind him.

Trammel did not recognize the voice. He doubted he would recognize the man it belonged to either, not that it mattered.

He reached for the Peacemaker under his arm and pulled it as he flipped over onto his back and fired.

The bullet caught the man just below the rib cage. He stumbled backward for a few steps before he finally fell to the ground.

The last thing Trammel saw before he blacked out was Emily's concerned face looking down at him.

Chapter 35

Trammel sat up with a start. For a moment he thought it had all just been a dream. The burning hotel. The smoke. The gunshots. All of it just a rotten dream that disappeared the moment he woke.

But the pain that quickly swept through his body reminded him that it had been all too real.

He moaned as he slowly laid his head back on the pillow.

"Thank God," a familiar voice said. "You're alive!"

Trammel recognized that voice. "Adam? Is that you?"

But he could hear Hagen somewhere in the near distance talking to others. He heard shouts of joy and excitement as they came closer to him.

Emily was the first person he saw. She caressed his head with the back of her hand and kissed his forehead. "Thank God, Buck.

The fever is gone. We thought we had lost you." She hugged him tightly, which made every part of him ache again. "Thank God."

He felt a tug on his left side. "Welcome back to the land of the living, Sheriff," Dr. Moore said. "It was touch and go there for a while, but you made it. You are quite a specimen of resilience."

Trammel weakly patted Emily's hand. His mouth was so dry, he could barely get out the words. "What happened?"

"You've been asleep for a week, you lazy fool," Hagen told him. "We thought we'd lost you several times, especially after the fever started up."

Dr. Moore added, "I pulled four slugs out of your left side. One of them bit pretty deep. But it looks like you've pulled through the worst of it. No organs hit, no tissue damaged. You'll be back to normal in no time."

But Trammel did not care about any of that just then. "The hotel. The ranchers. What happened?"

"Burned to the ground, I'm afraid," Hagen said. "But no harm done. Best thing that happened to the place, really. Everyone got out alive — well, except for the low-down scums we killed. Twenty-one came at us and only ten survived. They were in your jail until yesterday, when Sheriff Moran came up to get them. They're all awaiting trial now down in Laramie. Including Pete Stride. We've decided he was the ringleader of the whole thing, and the men of the ranch agreed. It's not the truth, but it's neater that way, and I like neat."

Trammel was having a hard time keeping up with all the details. "And the march?"

"Never happened," Hagen told him. "Can you believe that? Everyone was in an awful hurry to get out of here after the Clifford burned down. They practically cleared that roadblock your boys set up with their bare hands. All that trouble and preparation and it never even took place. Life's got a funny way of working out."

As out of it as he might have been, Trammel could sense something had shifted in the mood of the room. "Hawkeye?" he croaked.

"He's fine," Emily said as she helped him raise his head to drink some water. It burned going down at first, but felt good. He asked for more when he was finished, and she gave it to him. "You should've seen him handling those prisoners, Buck. He was like a smaller version of you. Handled them just like you would've done. Hawkeye's becoming his own man."

Trammel was glad to hear it but was not surprised. As she lowered his head to the pillow, he lightly grabbed her hand. "What's wrong, Emily? What aren't you telling me? Something's wrong. I know it."

She traded looks with Dr. Moore and said, "Maybe we should let Adam tell you in his own way."

"Adam?" he asked as she slid her hand away from his. "Why can't you tell me?"

He struggled to lift his neck as he watched Dr. Moore and Emily leave the room. He recognized it now as Emily's bedroom, but kept that fact to himself.

Hagen sat on the edge of the bed, beaming. "I'm so glad you're back with us, Buck. Especially now that everything is wonderful."

Trammel would decide what was wonderful and what was not. "How?"

"We read Charles's will once my family finally got here. And, lo and behold, you'll never guess what happened. The old goat left everything to me." He gave Trammel's right arm a good pat. "Isn't that something? Life is funny, isn't it?"

"You?" Trammel rasped. He thought he had not heard him right. "He left everything to you?"

"Yes, sir. They thought it was a lie at first,

but the copy they found in Montague's safe and among the papers up at the ranch house confirmed it. I am the sole owner of Blackstone-Hagen."

Hagen slapped his knee and laughed. "Oh, you should have seen their smug faces when the lawyers read the will. I thought Caleb's head would explode. Oh, I'll keep them at their posts, of course. I'm not going to cast them into the street penniless, though that's what they were planning to do to me." He crossed his arms and looked up at the ceiling. "No, Buck. This is a brand-new Adam Hagen you're witnessing. Not the vengeful young man you knew last week, but a generous man who seeks to use his good fortune for nothing but peace and profit for his fellow man."

The words seeped through his weary mind until they finally reached his understanding.

And suddenly it all made terrible sense.

He grabbed hold of Hagen's wrist with all the strength he had and pulled him across the bed. "You forged that will and made Montague kill himself. You killed Charles and planted that copy in his office. You threw in with Clay to help you do it and you damned near got us all killed. *I* killed men because of you. Those ranch hands never would've attacked us if you hadn't killed Charles."

He squeezed Hagen's wrist with all his strength, hoping to break the arm. "I'm here because of you."

But for the first time in his adult life, Steven "Buck" Trammel's strength was not enough to carry the day, for Adam Hagen took hold of Trammel's wrist and easily pulled his right arm free.

"That's a narrow way of looking at things, my friend. After all, I wouldn't even have made it out of Wichita alive if it hadn't been for you. And all of your efforts to keep me alive have resulted in my wildest dreams coming true. Sure, we may have bent a few rules along the way, but we've made it here together, haven't we? And I do mean *we,* old friend, because we are in this together. You're the only man I can really trust."

Trammel's rising temper competed with the rising pain coursing through his body. "You used me."

"Nonsense." Hagen smiled. "You're getting your reward for this, too, you know. The laudanum den you hated so much? Gone. They're plying their trade in Laramie now. And now that I control my family's fortune, I'll be able to rebuild the Clifford into my version of what a hotel should be. A new mill will make this town a wholesome place to live again. Why, I plan on having the railroad run up this way to cut down on the travel time between Blackstone and Laramie. We'll make it in an hour instead of half a day. We'll need it now that everything we've wanted is at hand."

Trammel gripped the bedsheet until he thought it would rip. "The only thing I want is to see you swing for the murder of Charles Hagen."

"Not too much chance of that happening." He laughed as he stood up. "Everyone and everything my father used to control is now under my control, including the judges. Besides, we already have our pigeon for all of this, remember? Pete Stride will fit the bill nicely."

Trammel glared at Hagen as he went to leave. "I'll kill you for this, Hagen. If I have to put you down myself, I'll see to it you answer for this."

Hagen smiled down at him from the doorway. "No, you won't, Buck. You're not the type. Get better, my friend. And get better soon. We have a lot of good to do. Both of us."

And with a final wave of his hand, Adam Hagen was out the door and gone.

And Buck Trammel was left alone with the terrible knowledge that he had played a role in all Adam Hagen's evil.

The pain that burned through his body was replaced by a still greater fire.

The need to bring Adam Hagen to justice once and for all.

ABOUT THE AUTHORS

William W. Johnstone has written nearly three hundred novels of western adventure, military action, chilling suspense, and survival. His bestselling books include *The Family Jensen; The Mountain Man; Flintlock; MacCallister; Savage Texas; Luke Jensen, Bounty Hunter;* and the thrillers *Black Friday, The Doomsday Bunker,* and *Trigger Warning.*

J. A. Johnstone learned to write from the master himself, Uncle William W. Johnstone, with whom J. A. has co-written numerous bestselling series including The Mountain Man; Those Jensen Boys; and Preacher, The First Mountain Man.

The employees of Thorndike Press hope you have enjoyed this Large Print book. All our Thorndike, Wheeler, and Kennebec Large Print titles are designed for easy reading, and all our books are made to last. Other Thorndike Press Large Print books are available at your library, through selected bookstores, or directly from us.

For information about titles, please call:
(800) 223-1244

or visit our website at:
gale.com/thorndike

To share your comments, please write:
Publisher
Thorndike Press
10 Water St., Suite 310
Waterville, ME 04901